# The Tower

## FLORA CARR

HUTCHINSON
HEINEMANN

1 3 5 7 9 10 8 6 4 2

Hutchinson Heinemann
20 Vauxhall Bridge Road
London SW1V 2SA

Hutchinson Heinemann is part of the Penguin Random House group of companies
whose addresses can be found at global.penguinrandomhouse.com

 Penguin
Random House
UK

First published by Hutchinson Heinemann in 2024

www.penguin.co.uk

A CIP catalogue record for this book is available from the British Library.

ISBN (Hardback): 9781529153729
ISBN (Trade paperback): 9781529153736

Typeset in 12/16.5 pt Bembo Book MT Pro by Jouve (UK), Milton Keynes
Printed and bound in Great Britain by Clays Ltd, Elcograf S.p.A.

The authorised representative in the EEA is Penguin Random House Ireland,
Morrison Chambers, 32 Nassau Street, Dublin D02 YH68

Penguin Random House is committed to a sustainable future
for our business, our readers and our planet. This book is made
from Forest Stewardship Council® certified paper.

# Cast of characters

## The women

- Mary, Queen of Scots
- Jane – a Scottish chambermaid
- Marie de Courcelles; 'Cuckoo' – a French chambermaid
- Lady Mary Seton – a noblewoman and companion to Mary
- Margaret Erskine – a former mistress of Mary's father, James V of Scotland, and mother to William Douglas, George Douglas and Moray
- Agnes Leslie – wife of William Douglas
- Agnes 'Anna' Keith – wife of Moray

## The men

- Lindsay – a rebel lord and son-in-law of Margaret Erskine
- Moray – a Scottish nobleman and bastard half-brother of Mary
- Ruthven – a rebel lord
- William Douglas – Laird of Lochleven and son of Margaret Erskine
- George Douglas – younger brother of William Douglas
- Robert Melville – a Scottish diplomat
- Andrew Melville – younger brother of Robert Melville
- Will – a boy living at Lochleven Castle

## *The ghosts*

- Lord Darnley – an English nobleman and Mary's second husband
- David Rizzio – a musician and courtier
- Marie de Guise – Mary's mother
- Francis II of France – Mary's first husband
- Saint Margaret of Scotland
- Anne Boleyn – former Queen of England and mother to Elizabeth Tudor
- Leonardo da Vinci

## *The absent*

- Lord Bothwell – a Scottish nobleman and Mary's third husband
- Elizabeth Tudor – Queen of England and Mary's cousin
- Catherine de' Medici – Mary's first mother-in-law
- Prince James – Mary's infant son

*Summer*

From far away, she looks like a roosting bird. She squats, her cloak spread out over the grass on either side. The hem of her nightdress is lifted out of the way, and her hands – large, white – clutch at the folds of linen smock beneath, her elbows aloft, forming triangular wings. Her neck is bent towards the ground, like a waterbird peering beneath a wave. Dawn is breaking as Mary empties her bladder onto the damp grass.

When she is done, she wipes her hands on her front, like a butcher smearing away the day's blood. Her women, who have been shielding her from the men, now run to her side. In normal times, there would be a gaggle of jewelled noblewomen to accompany her, women who have known Mary since she first sailed to France as a child. But these two women are professional companions, *chamberers* of mean parentage, conveniently obscure; Mary's skeleton staff for the days ahead. For what lies beyond the water.

The three women stand at the edge of the loch, its surface burnished gold with the reflected sunrise. The first chamberer is Marie de Courcelles, or *Coucou*. Cuckoo. Cuckoo is a scowling Frenchwoman who traded the warmth and elegance of her homeland for the Scottish court five years ago. She is in her mid-twenties, blonde, and pink-faced as though she has been leaning over a steaming pot; there are stray broken veins on her nose, from a sunburnt adolescence and an adult fondness for drink. The second woman is Jane, or Jean, or Janet, depending on the name she gives you. She is young, and Scottish, and has only been with Mary for a short time. Her face seems at once familiar and forgettable – unless you meet her eyes. She is like a wren: small, quick, dark. While Cuckoo is known for her frankness, her hot passions, Jane's thoughts belong only to herself and her God.

Mary is shivering. She wraps her cloak tight around her body, and turns. Her belly protrudes, a swollen pillow of flesh, bigger than expected for a woman claiming to be only a month into her pregnancy. This will be her second child, and already she's afflicted with the same morning sickness that plagued her previously. There's a sour reek of piss, mingled with Mary's breath: hours-old vomit. She begins to cry – she cries easily, especially now – and tells her women she cannot stand it. She cannot speak or breathe without regurgitating the stench of her last meal. Her throat is still burning. Jane reaches into her bodice and pulls out a sprig of lavender, warm from her skin, and waves it in front of Mary's nose.

Cuckoo trumps her with an orange studded with cloves, a gift from Mary herself in better times.

The men are there. Cuckoo, who still speaks little of the Scots language, has both the innocent boldness of a child and the protective hostility of a foreigner; she stares them down with contempt. Jane, eyes lowered, wants to caution her.

She says nothing.

In her palaces, Mary moved like a courtesan, or an artist's model: arching her back, supple-boned, tilting her head, pouting her mouth. Playing with loose strands of hair. Biting her bottom lip as she read. Touching herself: her neck, her chest, her wrists, trailing fingers across bare skin as though lost in thought. Aware, always, of the eyes on her. Now she coughs up bile on the grass. Now she sniffs under her armpits. Now she walks away from a puddle of her own piss, her cloak trailing. Her nightgown is ripped, and she does not care.

In two days, Mary's son James will turn one. A whole year has passed since the triumph of his birth. At his christening, the archbishop tried to spit into his mouth, as is the custom. Mary refused. The priest, who kept a mistress called Grizzel, was syphilitic. No *pocky priest* would share his dribble with her baby, she said. Now she looks up and over the water, eyes bile-stung, and knows her son is with her enemies.

The men are talking with the boatman; he is as haggard and gaunt as Charon, the old seaman who navigates the dark undertow of the River Styx, ferrying souls all the way to the gates of the underworld. The three men speak in low voices, huddled together by the shore of the loch. At the centre of the loch, there is a tiny island visible. A grey stone castle stands on it, a collection of buildings and towers half-hidden by trees. Old-fashioned. Square. Brutish. Haunted, too, by men and women butchered there during a siege two centuries ago. Mary has been here before. She remembers the castle, the cold interior. In some places the water is almost lapping at the walls outside, like a jealous beast, hungry and covetous. Cuckoo accompanied her here once, three or four years ago.

'*God's blood*. Not this place,' Cuckoo says; but only Jane hears.

The boat is ready.

Mary goes first. Of course she does. Her women stand behind her in the mud and hold out their arms, palms up like peasant women herding geese, as she steps into the bobbing boat. The morning sky is still reflected on the water's surface and has changed colour to pink, as though someone has rolled out a bolt of Turkey satin over the loch.

'She goes next,' the first man says. Jane picks up her skirt. She stumbles forward, and for a moment she reaches out, as if to catch a waiting hand. But Mary looks ahead across the water, her back turned, and Jane rights herself and sits behind her. Cuckoo follows. The boat is narrow, made narrower still by the women's skirts.

The men, at the other end of the boat and out of Mary's earshot, whisper and jostle and crack jokes about her women. They wonder which of the two has the sweeter cunny. Which has been had before. Jane wants to slap them. She has a hard backhand, a solid punch; she knows this because she once broke a man's nose. In the boat, the first man is dark-haired like herself, and old – old enough to be her father. His sneering expression taunts her. Makes her hands itch. Here is a man who rapes his female servants at home, Jane is sure of it. He leers at Cuckoo, who cannot understand his words, who is still staring him down with suspicion and anger; she knows Mary hates him and that is enough for her. Jane looks at the man and knows a woman's protests excite him. He likes it when they scream, and bite, and twist their legs together.

His name is Lindsay.

The second man is younger, in his early twenties – another nobleman, his power a recent inheritance. He is the son of a dead madman. His father stormed Mary's palace apartments last winter, a full suit of armour clanking under his billowing nightgown, like a ghost in a play. His skin was grey, he was dying even then. Now his son escorts Mary to her imprisonment, eyeing her with a young man's lust for flesh and power.

His name is Ruthven.

Both men in the boat were also among that party who stormed Mary's apartments. Led by Ruthven's grey-faced father, they murdered Mary's favourite servant, the curly-haired Italian David Rizzio. He was stabbed close to sixty times; it was the next best thing to stabbing the queen.

The heavy oars slide in and out of the water, slicing through the still surface like long knives. Mary sits motionless, her face and tall straight-backed body turned towards their destination, as though she is the ship's carved masthead. Jane looks at the back of Mary's neck. Her hair was pinned up a day, two days ago, but she's slept since, and the style is mussed, unravelling. Jane can see the fine soft hair at her nape, similar to when a newborn is first bathed and dried, the thin strands puffed up like a halo around fragile scalp. She hears whispered words in Latin, and realises Mary is praying under her breath. Catholic prayers for the Catholic queen. Jane catches the odd word or phrase. *Pater Noster . . . Dominus tecum . . . Deus meus.*

Jane thinks praying in Latin must be like caressing a loved one's face with gloved hands.

Mary's elbow rests on the side of the boat, and Jane reaches out and touches the cloth of her dress to comfort her. Jane is brisk, nervous, unsure. To touch a queen – even through nightgown and smock beneath – is no small thing.

'Almost there,' Mary says, and her voice is bright and shining as a pearl, as though she is the one offering solace, her accent buttery through pursed lips. Kissable. French is by far the most kissable of all the European tongues, and teasing; there is a constant lilt at the end of her sentences. *Oui*, she says, and you are left in agony: is she doubting, or incredulous? Innocent, or cunning? It drives men and women to madness. Mary is that potent combination: both a beautiful woman and a royal. The two conditions that draw the gaze of men and women alike. Such a person is elevated, fortified by the dual allure of youthfulness and the ancient. We are compelled to look at such a person, their beauty somehow confirming all the promises of monarchy.

The boat plunges to one side, and Mary's elbow slips. Her arm is underwater, all the way up to her armpit, her shoulder, and she squeals from the shock of it, from the icy cold of the morning water. The boat rights itself, and she falls back.

'*Arrête!*'

Jane turns in her seat and sees Lindsay has been rocking the boat, a grin on his face like a child. Cuckoo has cried out in protest and he likes it, he likes to hear the word 'stop' in a woman's mouth, and he looks to Mary, too, to see her reaction. Jane raises her arms, lifting her cloak like a curtain so he cannot see the queen's easy tears.

'Perhaps I should keep going,' he says. 'It would not matter if we capsized. Ruthven and I are strong swimmers.' He looks at the women, as if to say: *And you three are not.*

The women – one Scot, one French, the last neither one nor the other – stay silent. Eyes down. Drowning is one of the worst ways to die. That, and fire: being burned alive. If they are to be killed, better something quick, like a knife between the ribs in some quiet corner of the castle.

Mary's husband once beat a man to death, right in front of her. They were walking arm in arm in a castle garden, and an old man, a servant out of work, came begging for coin. He bent to clutch at her hem with shaking hands, kissing the cloth. He struggled to stand. Mary's future husband – because they had not yet married – punched and kicked the old man until he coughed up blood and crawled through the dust and out of reach. He died two hours later. Mary still married him, her third husband: Bothwell. She wore a black velvet dress in the Italian style: her widow's weeds for her late second husband. After the ceremony, she changed into jubilant yellow silk, the colour of egg yolk. The following day, courtiers heard her shouting for a knife to stab herself with. She knew what her husband was. She remembered the old man lying in the dust, chewing his own blood clots, dying his slow death. Now, in the boat, she prays for both men. She prays for their souls. She prays for her own.

They are reaching the edge of the castle island. Jane thinks she can see faces at windows. *They are going to kill Mary.* Will they kill her and Cuckoo, too, or first offer coin for their silence? Jane does not think there is enough gold in Scotland to buy Cuckoo's loose tongue. In any case, Lindsay will not allow witnesses to leave the island. *How will they do it?* How will they kill the queen? They might try to jog the baby out of her, praying she bleeds away with it. Drowning seems like the obvious answer: why else bring her to a castle in the middle of a loch? But an assassination must be quiet, and drowning is not. She will get a blade or a pillow, Jane thinks. But for herself and Cuckoo, she knows the men will dispose of them like unwanted kittens. Sealed in a water barrel, or thrown over a wall. Skulls bashed in, their bodies discarded like waste, like vermin. They will be raped first. For men, death and desire go hand in hand. Jane knows this. She has had the knowledge pushed into her.

Lindsay whispers in the boatman's ear, and the prow turns away from the jetty and towards the shore of the castle island. Ruthven says, loudly, something about tides, and currents, and Jane looks back at him, her face like a mask. *Does he think we are fools?* They want only to humiliate her – Mary.

The boat is at the water's edge, and there are people standing in front of the castle walls. Waiting for them, for Mary. The boat's passengers are forced to climb out, wading through the shallows, splashing, each of the women's skirts floating up in a circle. A young man, about Ruthven's age, steps forward. He is hunched and wheezing in the summer air, which is lively with pollen. He bows low as Mary squelches through mud and silt towards him. She holds out her hand for him to help her out of the water, but he, confused, drops a clumsy kiss on her knuckles.

The room is sparse and cramped, with all the signs of hurried preparations: a small table with a jug, ale slopped over the sides. Two pallets with straw mattresses for Jane and Cuckoo, shoved into a corner. Rushes and herbs strewn, unevenly, over the wooden floorboards. A four-poster bed, crudely made. The bedsheets are creased on the side furthest from the door, as though a servant, in their haste, gambled on the occupant only viewing the nearest half. Jane notices (for it is her job to notice these things) that there is only one piss pot for three women.

Mary falls backwards onto the bed, eyes shut, and spreads out her arms. Cuckoo, who kneels to unlace Mary's boots, cannot see her face over the mound of her belly. The door stands ajar behind its heavy curtain. A lingering servant – or is he a guard? – grasps the handle and peers into the room, his eyes on Mary's face. Jane realises she is swaying where she stands; she plants her feet wide, like an English king.

'I need white wine for the queen, the best you have,' she tells the man.

'There is already refreshment for the lady.' He does not look at her.

'Not for drinking. The queen washes her face with wine. A small jug will do for today.'

The man laughs and disappears backwards behind the curtain, unwilling – or perhaps unable – to turn his back on a royal person: the last breach of etiquette.

'Where is my own bed?' Mary says, addressing the ceiling. Then: 'I will have his head, Lindsay will lose his head, I swear.'

The room smells of dank river water; the scent is stronger than it was when they rowed across the loch, as though the castle is submerged. Jane looks down at the rushes on the floor and imagines them standing upright, with water pooling around her and Cuckoo's legs and the wooden bedposts, rising up to lap at Mary's dangling feet. The boots are unlaced and removed; she wears knitted stockings worn down at the toes.

Mary wants to rest, to sleep. She wants the torn nightgown off, she'll sleep in her smock; she sits up, arms above her head, and Cuckoo gathers up the material in her hands and peels it off, handing the crumpled dress to Jane. They will need to ask for sewing equipment for the rips, and for the stockings.

'I'll take the right,' Jane says, and she and Cuckoo kneel at

Mary's feet to pull off a stocking each. Mary jerks a leg, impatient, and the tips of Jane's fingers brush bare skin. She holds her breath. To lay hands on Mary's clothed body is one thing, but her skin is another. A queen's touch is not like the touch of other women. With it comes a frisson: of the anointed, the sacred. It is like touching a living, breathing effigy; the cool shock of marble. Of the blessed, and forbidden, and the dead. These are the hands that held the orb and sceptre. Queen of Scotland at just six days old and raised to become Queen Consort of France. These are the hands of a queen who has touched other queens, past kings and future kings: her son, James, her blessing and her death. Their touches and caresses are imbued in Mary's skin like holy oil, and she in theirs. Generations will pass, and a royal child will be placed, new-born, into its parents' arms, and pressed against their skin the child will feel the echo of Mary and her prized white fingertips.

They put Mary to bed. It is still only morning, the two women are hungry. They sit at the small table and eat bread sliced hours earlier. Cuckoo's stomach growls; she is thinking of marchpane flavoured with rose water, of candied violets and stiff Italian biskets dipped in sweet wine and softened into white mulch tasting of anise seed. Mary's favourite is frittered pears. An assassin at the French court once tried to poison the dish when she was a child; the plot was discovered in the spring and the culprit executed. By late summer the fruit trees had ripened and the child-queen feasted safely on pear, thinly sliced and battered in sugared ale with cloves and saffron. The warm spiced scent heralded the change in seasons.

Mary has turned onto her side, and her left hand dangles over the side of the bed, her fourth finger ringless; Bothwell insisted on a Protestant ceremony, with no popish wedding rings for either bride or groom.

'How long will they hold us?' Cuckoo whispers, in French; always in French.

Jane shakes her head, she doesn't know. Cuckoo is her senior—in experience, in access to Mary—but royal etiquette is less important here than wit and a steady hand; prettiness is no longer God's blessing but a disadvantage, as is Cuckoo's native tongue. An invisible Scot is far more likely to escape this, to survive this.

A knock on the door. The guard, bearing a jug of white wine. He is smirking. Jane thanks him in a whisper, angling her body to hide the bed from his view. When he is gone, she sniffs: a sour green reek, pungent and familiar. It fills the room. The same scent from the edge of the loch: Mary's cloak trailing behind her in the wet grass as she cried over her body's stench, the lingering smell of its waste. The futile orange, studded with cloves and wafted beneath her nose.

Jane sets the jug down. 'Don't touch it,' she says to Cuckoo. She fetches the piss pot and empties out the jug's contents into the bowl.

The wine is a dark yellow.

When Mary wakes, her women will tell her there was no white wine in the castle cellar.

Jane thought that danger would come in the form of men: the men who seek Mary, who want to burn away the oil that anoints, to destroy the body that bears history, bore history.

But the danger is no longer confined to outside the prison walls.

Mary is starving herself. Days have passed and she will not eat. She will not drink. She will not leave her bed except to piss and shit and to vomit first thing. Yet her body continues to swell and swell, the dome of her belly rising too fast, unnatural; as though there is an animal crouching inside, arching its spine. Her body is bloated and tender and translucent as a gooseberry; the veins green-grey, with dirty pond water swilling about inside instead of blood. Jane and Cuckoo coax and cajole her; she has a child to feed, they tell her. But Mary screws her eyes shut and turns her face away. When she speaks, the sentences are disjointed, her thoughts back to front as though she were drunk. In the dark corners of the room, the walls are egg-freckled with mould. Behind the curtain at the door, guards slide plates of stale food across the floorboards before slamming the door shut again, as though the room is marked for plague. The women are surrounded, always, by the sounds of unseen others: the slosh of water from the cellar below; footsteps from above. At night, shadows rush across the ceiling, knives in hand. Jane raps on the door and demands more firewood, more blankets; for more tapestries to mount on the walls, and better food to tempt Mary.

No one answers.

It is evening. A fire is lit, but there are still draughts, and the stone room feels chilled as an underground vault. Outside, they hear an owl calling in triumph, some tiny scrap of fur caught in its claws. It is too dark to see the water surrounding them, but they can hear its whisper, the words muffled: secrets just out of reach. *Come closer*, it says. *Closer.* Jane sits on the bed beside Mary and feels her forehead and neck. She is feverish. Her face is puffy and shadowed in the low light, the skin almost waxy in texture. Jane looks down at her and wonders if this is still *la plus parfaite*, the same woman the poet Ronsard once called the most divine creature on earth. She recalls a rumour: a palace cook, ruminating too long over the shape of Mary's lips, overcooked a batch of oranges and accidentally invented marmalade. Other versions of the tale exist: in one, the cook stirred his spoon round and round and round, tracing the curve of Mary's adolescent breasts. The child-queen, peering up from the bottom of a cooking pot, strips of orange rind for hair and mouth. Jane imagines the simmering outline, bubbling and spitting hot liquid straight into the cook's eye. His shouts of pain.

The real Mary does not spit, she dribbles; the ale brought to her mouth leaks out, trickles back over her lips. She does not want it — *take it away*, she says, with more energy than her women thought possible. She sinks back under the sheets — she is theatrical, even now — but when Jane begins to stand, Mary grabs hold of her wrist, her eyes still shut. She clasps her hand.

'They want me dead, don't they?'

Jane says nothing. She, too, has been afraid to eat the dishes brought to their room, but she has eaten them anyway. There have been no more jugs of piss (she checks each time), and a quick end from poisoning is better than dying hungry.

Cuckoo, on the other side of the bed, looks down at the two women's hands, their fingers intertwined.

'How can she stand it?' Mary says, and she is whispering, her eyes rolling beneath their lids. 'How can she hear what they have done, and not wage war on them?'

'Perhaps she will,' Jane says.

Cuckoo tries to catch her eye. *Qui?* she mouths, and her lips stretch and form a smile on the word, as though it tastes sweet. *Who?*

'You know she wanted to marry me,' Mary says. Her lips are cracked; her women notice at the same moment. Jane thumbs the blood away with her free hand.

'Who wouldn't want to marry you, your grace,' Cuckoo says, distracted.

Mary finally opens her eyes. They are amber brown; the fire reflects off them, as though she is a fox, a night animal. The whites of her eyes are bloodshot, and her gaze roams about the room, unfocused. She looks up at Jane in confusion and releases her hand.

'I thought I was somewhere else. With someone else.'

Cuckoo ducks her head. Jane thinks she sees her smile; she ignores her.

'I thought I was with my dear Seton.'

Lady Seton. She is Mary's favourite friend, a lady-in-waiting who travelled with her to France as a child and attended her there and in Scotland. It is no surprise to Jane that Mary should mention her name. *Mary would surely prefer Seton's presence over Cuckoo's or my own,* Jane thinks with bitterness. But there is a reason why they are here and Seton is not. Jane and Cuckoo are not ladies-in-waiting, aristocratic companions. Nor are they maids of honour, the step below in rank. Jane and Cuckoo are not noblewomen. They are chambermaids. They are equipped to care for Mary's basic bodily needs. But their presence serves another purpose. Mary has been stripped of her illustrious retinue. The men who denied Mary the presence of her ladies-in-waiting, permitting only her chambermaids, meant to strip her of her rank, the signifiers of her royalty: her clothes, her jewels, and her high-born women.

'I thought I was somewhere else,' Mary repeats.

'We are at Lochleven,' Jane says, gentle.

'I know, I know.' Mary is irritated. 'I know,' she says again. 'I know, I know, I know,' and now tears well in her eyes, her mood changing so quickly that Jane forgets to arrange her face – to look at once sympathetic but hopeful, never pitying – and it is Cuckoo who produces the handkerchief with practised hand, who dabs at fallen tears, who Mary turns to now, her arms raised at the elbow. Jane cannot decide if she looks like a priest bestowing God's blessing, or a sickly child grasping for their mother's neck.

'You remember this place, Cuckoo?' Mary says. She does not wait for a response before she adds, her face turned away once more: 'The home of my father's mistress.'

There is a cough from outside the door.

The women stare at each other. They do not move; their breathing seems too heavy, too loud. The fire crackles. Mary still holds her arms up; they are frozen in place. The tableau is like a painting: the dark panes of the women's faces, and the fire the only light in the room.

There is the sound of footsteps. More people are outside the door. A stew of voices and muffled words. There is a *crack*.

Jane thinks she hears the clink of metal, of swords.

She thinks she hears the rustle of a travelling cloak.

She thinks she hears the whispers of drunken men, looking for warmth.

She offers a silent prayer that is neither repentant nor in Latin.

Standing, she strides to the end of the bed and fumbles for something underneath. Cuckoo stares at her in confusion; Jane straightens, and moves to stand behind the door. In her hands are the discarded stockings, untouched for days, now twisted and stretched out like a rope.

In a moment, she will convince herself that it is for Mary; but as she first steps behind the door, she is thinking only of herself, and of how much she would like to leave this cold, tomb-scented castle alive.

Cuckoo gapes at her in horror; Jane catches her eye and nods towards the empty jug. *Aim for the head*, she mouths. Mary is blank-eyed; she cannot seem to see the dark figure of Jane standing behind the door, fists clenched around Mary's own stockings.

The voices subside, as though moving away, up or down a staircase.

There is silence.

The women wait.

When there are no more sounds, Cuckoo begins to stroke Mary's hair. Jane has not moved since she took up position by the door. She looks over at the bed. She has heard of Mary's bravery, of her daring. All of Scotland knows she once faked a miscarriage to escape capture. Her servant David Rizzio was stabbed to death at her feet and the rebel lords sought to overthrow her, imprisoning her in her own rooms. At six months pregnant she spent an entire day screaming and writhing and convulsing, convincing all around her that she and the unborn child were dying. She persuaded her worthless husband, Darnley, to switch sides and help her escape. Everyone knows that, in battle, Mary – born under Sagittarius – rides her horse astride, dressed in Florentine serge breeches and polished armour, like a second, shining Joan of Arc. When her own half-brother the Earl of Moray rebelled against Mary's marriage to Darnley, there was a stand-off between their respective troops; Mary led her own men, straight-backed and armed with a pistol.

Jane cannot reconcile that warrior queen with the woman lying in Cuckoo's arms.

She drops the stockings and goes to her.


'Who did she mean?' Cuckoo asks, when Mary is asleep. 'When she talked of the woman who would not go to war.'

'Elizabeth.'

Cuckoo snorts. 'There'll be no army from her; the English do not give, they take. They think only of themselves. You know why we laughed at their clothes, when I was at the court in France? Because every item an Englishman wears is a different style, from a different country: a sleeve from there, a cloak from there. They are magpies; they have no identity of their own, everything is stolen: from France, from Italy, Spain, Germany. Every Englishman is a thief, a butcher and a drunk.'

Cuckoo would go on, she can talk for France, but Jane raises a hand. 'Elizabeth is not a man.'

Cuckoo shakes her head. 'She'd have better luck going to France, to her first husband's family, God rest him. She'd be foolish to put her faith in that greensick lady.'

Neither of the women discuss the stockings held like rope between Jane's hands. Though it seems impossible, the intention is clear: Jane is prepared to strangle any assassin who bursts into their rooms. In peacetime, Cuckoo would have said something, to Mary, to others; but there is a war, and they are all prisoners now.

'Did Elizabeth really propose marriage to her?'

'What do you think?' Jane says. She rubs her eyes; they itch from fatigue. 'They just joke about it. How much easier it would be if one of them was a man and they could marry, and marry their countries together.'

'How do you know all this?' Cuckoo is frowning, and Jane sees that her real question is: *How do you know this when I don't?*

Jane shrugs. 'What's written by queens rarely stays on the page.'

Cuckoo wrinkles her nose at the word *reines*, scrunching up her mouth; despite all her efforts, Jane still speaks French with a Scottish twang.

There is a noise from the bed. Mary is calling for Jane, over and over, bleating like a baby goat. When Jane crouches beside her, Mary tugs at the collar of her smock, dragging her down, close, closer.

'I cannot spend tonight alone,' Mary says. Her voice is pleading, but Jane knows it is not a request.

Across the room, Cuckoo looks away, into the fire, hiding her face.

Jane undresses; she needs no one's help, she has done so always. She knows how to unlace herself, twisting her arms to tug herself free. She clenches her fists afterwards, to hide their trembling. Mary has shared her bed before in this way, but only with her most trusted women: the *jewelled ladies*, her noblewomen, their arrival always announced by the jingling of their expensive chains and bracelets. These chosen bedfellows keep her company and guard her secrets. Jane has imagined this for herself – the intimacy, the warm weight of a royal body next to her – but never considered it a possibility until this day. Nor has she ever reckoned with the danger this might place her in. In this castle, she is not only a bedfellow, but a human shield.

'I saw you,' Mary whispers, when Jane climbs into bed beside her. Their faces are very close. 'I saw you, behind the door. An avenging angel.' Mary looks feverish, her eyes glassy; but she is smiling, beautified, like a woman on her deathbed remembering an old flame. 'How much you must love me,' she says.

Mary cannot sleep. All night she twists and turns like a fish caught in a net, always shifting, and so too does Jane, turning this way and that to accommodate Mary's long body, tall as a man's, and her protruding belly. Jane makes the mistake of listening to Mary's breathing; suddenly she is conscious of her own, and it is like she has forgotten how to breathe, forgotten the mechanics: each inhalation is ragged, she labours to slow them down, to match her bedfellow breath for breath.

The night is cold for June, the sky outside cloudless and pricked with stars. Inside the room, there is total darkness. The women, if they wake, cannot see their own hands. They might be buried alive in some pit, if it weren't for the water's whispering outside: the voice in the maw of the loch. It is like being blind. A warning for the long winter months, when Scotland is grey even at noon, and every night is an eclipse. When there is snow, it is even more suffocating; stifling every sense, the whole world muffled.

Mary is cold; she reaches behind to clasp Jane's arm and pull it across her own stomach. They fall asleep in this position, both facing the same way, their bodies curved into and around each other's—Mary soft in her companion's arms, a mollusc nestled in its spiralled shell. Her sleeve rides up, and Jane's last waking thought is of the ridged scar she feels, near the crook of Mary's elbow: that softest part of her sliced open by doctors, attempting to ease her migraines with bloodletting.

Jane hears the sound of the slap before registering the pain of it, her cheek and mouth burning. She can see nothing, but she feels the weight of Mary crouching over her: astride her, straddling her, now clutching her wrists to pin her down, pregnant belly pressed against Jane's ribs. Jane has an urge to spit upwards into her face.

'How could you?' Mary says, but her own words seem to wake her, and she fumbles, putting a hand to Jane's face; feeling her smooth face, her long hair. 'Jane?' she says. Or does she say another name?

'My lady.' Cuckoo is calling out from across the room. She sounds frightened. 'My lady,' she says again, loudly, more insistent, and Jane can easily picture the Frenchwoman's imaginings: an unconscious Mary, and a man, interrupted, frozen in his position, his hands circling her throat, or else a cushion pressed over her face. Jane waits for Mary to supply a response, but none comes. In the end, it is she who speaks.

'All is well. The queen had a nightmare, but all is well,' she says. Under the cover of Jane's voice, Mary clambers off her, returning to her side of the bed, trying not to rustle the sheets.

Jane feels her turn away.

In the silence, she imagines again a man, a cushion pressed over Mary's face. But in the vivid, unmoving picture that forms, Jane cannot decide if the cushion is intended to stifle breath, or groans of desire.

The women are losing track of time. When Mary is finally allowed to receive letters, it may have been a few days since their arrival, or six, or it could be closer to a fortnight. Jane offers to read the letters aloud, but Mary declines, sitting up in bed, thumbing through pages densely covered in inked messages: some of friendship and pity, others of warning, even anger. Jane and Cuckoo can only watch her face – expressive, perhaps too expressive for a monarch – as she reacts to certain phrases, frowning, sometimes mouthing the words, as though memorising poetry in a palace classroom. Jane makes a mental note to sift through the papers later, before remembering how the letters are 'locked' in elaborate folds; Mary would know if they were opened.

On occasion, Mary shakes back her sleeves. This is a habit of hers, the better to show off her pale hands. The sight of them seems to comfort her. They are whiter than Elizabeth's, who (Mary has heard) must smear Venetian ceruse – creamy lead mixed with vinegar – to achieve the same shade. Elizabeth, a fellow female prince, is Mary's equal, and so her only real point of comparison. Jane knows that it is her voice Mary now seeks, hidden somewhere in the letters before her; she is searching for the guiding hand behind a word, a phrase, or in the intricate folds of the paper itself.

Elizabeth uses a swan feather for her quill. Mary knows much about the Other Queen; her handwriting a close italic scrawl so unlike her own, round hand. Before her imprisonment, she waited on descriptions of Elizabeth's clothes (expensive), her height (shorter than herself), and hair (red in colour, and thinning). Elizabeth is older than Mary (by nine years). She has pale translucent skin, so fine you can see the blue veins at her temples. She has the odd pockmark, but not as many as her friend Lady Mary Sidney, who nursed Elizabeth through smallpox and was rewarded for her compassion with disfigurement and subsequent mockery from her former patient.

Across the room, Jane grows bored. She sinks into herself, into her own thoughts—a trick she has learnt from so many hours standing to one side while great ladies embroider and exchange dull pleasantries between themselves. She squints at an empty patch of floor. Elizabeth Tudor appears, her legs outstretched, her skirts fanned across the rushes. While Elizabeth is sat down there can be no comparison of height between herself and Mary, and that is how she prefers it. She wears a stiff gold dress, but above the ruff her face is a gelatinous mass, pulsating, unformed. The faceless figure turns to Jane, and she appraises it. Red curls appear. A thin, plain face takes shape. Jane adds blue eyes, then changes to brown. She imagines the infected scent of Elizabeth's father, Henry, that monarch so reviled in Scotland, with his pus-filled wound of a leg, weeping and rotting. They say that servants gagged whenever they were in his presence. The smell fills the room at Lochleven, and Elizabeth wrinkles her newly imagined nose: long, painted white.

'What are you thinking of, Jane?' Cuckoo says, interrupting her thoughts.

Elizabeth vanishes.

Jane shrugs. When she sees that Mary is occupied, she goes to the window. The loch is always closer than she remembers; barely a strip of damp soil dividing wall from water. The sky above is suffocated by vast clouds shaped like lions, muscle and sinew balled up and streaked black with shadow. Jane remembers the roars that reverberated from the lion pit in the grounds of Holyrood Palace, the wide flat faces staring up at you out of the gloom.

Beyond the water, there are huge hills rising and falling in curves, as though a giant has curled up on its side and fallen asleep.

Jane moves about, the better to see the rest of the landscape – and steps back at once.

A young man is standing outside, just to the side of the window. He is facing the wall, his palm pressed against it, bracing himself. Jane thinks for a moment that he is pissing up the side of the wall. But his face is contorted; he is frigging his member, his eyes open as though he could see through stone and into the room beyond.

The man is Ruthven.

As Jane watches, he relaxes in relief, adjusting his codpiece as he steps back, away from the wall. He meets Jane's gaze. Her mouth is dry; she wants to look away, but does not. She stares at him, and he winks.

At the same moment, there is a knock on the door.

★

Margaret Erskine is in her fifties now, but Jane can still see why the
late king wanted her for a mistress. She moves like those older
women you see at court: former feted beauties, still convinced of
their sensuality, of their power over men. There is a sway in her
hips. No matter that she is a laird's widow, a guest now in her own
home. She once had a king between her thighs, his bastard son in
her belly, and she will not let anyone forget—least of all that same
king's daughter.

Mary is sat up in bed; Jane and Cuckoo stand to one side. They
have brushed Mary's hair, arranging the nightgown about her
shoulders so the rips won't show.

Margaret drops into a curtsy before the bed: she is not low
enough, for a moment she seems insolent, but she glances down to
her knees and up again, and makes a small face, as if to say, *God's
death, these knees of mine*, and Mary makes a gesture with her hand:
*It is nothing, stand up. Speak.*

Margaret's eyes are very large and bright; in a young woman's
face, they would make her the most beautiful woman in the room.
Perhaps she still would be, even now, if Mary were not here. She is
dressed far more richly than her queen: in taffeta and lace, with
gossamer-fine ruffles of lawn at her throat. A gold and enamel girdle book peeps out at her waist. As she steps forward, there is an
overpowering scent: Jane half expects to hear the clink of a thuri-
ble chain, great clouds of burnt incense wafting in the older
woman's wake. But of course, Margaret is now a Protestant. There
will be no incense.

'We are honoured to house you, your grace,' says Margaret.
'My daughter Agnes and I welcome you.' She gestures behind her:
a squat, plump woman with a slack, doughy face. Not plump, Jane
realises; she, like Mary, is pregnant. Agnes is not Margaret's

daughter by blood, but by marriage: wedded to the current Laird of Lochleven. She is the lady of the house, their hostess; but beside Margaret she appears as a lady-in-waiting, paying court to her mother-in-law as though to a second, rival queen. At the Scottish court, everyone is connected to everyone; Lindsay is married to one of Margaret Erskine's daughters. Jane wonders if he is Margaret's favourite son-in-law.

'How was your journey here, your grace?' Agnes says, her voice simpering. She speaks without Mary's permission.

There is a pause; Jane cannot decide if Agnes is sly or stupid. She thinks of the ride here, of Lindsay and Ruthven whipping Mary's horse, on and on through the night, over bulging tree roots and hidden dips in the ground, so that the creature stumbled, and Mary clutched at her pregnant belly and screamed.

'I do love to ride, Lady Agnes,' Mary says.

Another pause. The older woman's fragrance has already filled the room; Jane can taste it. It coats her back teeth like sugar.

'Agnes shares your happy condition,' Margaret says, gesturing to her daughter-in-law's belly. 'I am only sorry that your own' – she takes in the swell beneath Mary's sheets – 'is so clearly causing you distress. We will fetch you ginger confits, sage; anything to bring you relief.' She speaks in Scots; out of the corner of her eye, Jane sees a crease between Cuckoo's brows as she struggles to comprehend.

'A woman in the same position can only provide comfort for you,' Margaret

continues. 'She will make a sympathetic companion, I promise.'

Mary looks up. 'I have my own women,' she says.

Margaret splays her hands before her, like large spotted white lilies.

'My son thinks it best if someone from the family serves as

your . . . *intimate*, during your stay. You understand we think only of your comfort,' she adds. Her voice is like silk.

'Which son is that?' Mary raises herself up on her elbows. 'Which son of yours? My host here on this island, or that other man I once called brother?'

Margaret folds her hands together. She smiles a self-satisfied smile, thinking of her favourite son, the old king's bastard, better loved by her than any of her legitimate children.

'The Earl of Moray is still your loyal brother, your grace. Anyone with eyes can see it; he is the image of his father.'

'My father. Mine.' Mary is almost panting. She opens her mouth to speak again, but she is interrupted by a shocking *crack*. She flinches, as do her women.

Margaret has twisted her neck, jerking it to one side so that the bones crunch. It is loud and familiar: the sound of a man's neck breaking just as the noose drops. Mary stares at the older woman.

'Old bones,' Margaret says, by way of apology, but the noise was so sudden and close, so animal-like, that Jane believes it was meant as a kind of threat; if nothing else, Margaret has interrupted a queen. She smiles and distracts with her snapping spine and cloud of fragrance.

'You look so tired, your grace. So like your poor mother did – oh, I do hope your women are taking proper care of you. No matter; Agnes will be with you now. She will keep the closest eye on you.'

Mary can never think of her mother without pain; Margaret knows this. She lowers those large, unnatural eyes. But Mary seems strangely unmoved, as though the dead are already here, in the room, at the edge of her thoughts. She raises herself up higher, straightening her neck.

'How strange it is,' she says. Her voice is quiet.

Margaret inclines her head; polite. Waiting. Indulgent, as if Mary were a confused child.

'How strange . . . Whenever I am in this castle, I am reminded of her: my mother.' Mary wets her lips. 'I am reminded of how you, my lady Margaret, might almost have served in her place. Your son, my half-brother, might have sat on my throne, his parents married before God, and you would both be content.' Mary leans forward. 'How happy this place makes me.'

Cuckoo looks back and forth between the two women, uncomprehending, pink-faced, as she strains to understand their unfamiliar words.

*Crack.*

This time, Margaret does not apologise.


Not many people remember that Margaret Erskine and the old king had known each other since they were children. Three years younger than him, Margaret had first encountered the child-king when he was ten years old, when her own father became his official guardian. He was a tall and self-possessed boy. She loved him from the first.

At twelve years old, Margaret was married off to the Laird of Lochleven. In such cases, the bride's family sometimes strikes a deal to ensure their child will not be bedded until she is much older.

This was not such a case.

A few years later, Margaret had grown into a beautiful, sensual teenager, supple-hipped and silky-haired with deep blue eyes that drew men in. She became the king's mistress. For the first time, sex was pleasurable for her. At around sixteen, she gave birth to the king's bastard son, the future Earl of Moray. The king was not yet twenty. He had not yet married the Frenchwoman Marie de Guise, who would eventually give birth to their daughter, Mary. The king and Margaret were happy for five more years. In bed one night, he told her he would arrange for her divorce. He was going to write to the Pope. Once he had permission, he would marry her and make her his queen. He would legitimise their bastard son and make him his heir. She need never return to that crude watery castle in the middle of a loch, in the middle of nowhere. Margaret Erskine rested her head on the king's bare chest and slept the contented, dreamless sleep of those in love.

The Pope refused.

Now, decades later, Margaret cannot bear to look at Mary; the woman represents everything she, Margaret, lost when the old king found he could not marry her. Worst of all is Mary's resemblance to her father. Margaret cannot acknowledge this similarity, even to herself. It is too painful.

Cuckoo is not surprised when Jane tells her later that night, in whispers, about Ruthven masturbating against the outside wall. When Jane says, 'He looked at me,' she does not need to explain or elaborate for Cuckoo to understand. Cuckoo has been in Scotland for five years, and during that time she has come to believe that Scotsmen are worse than any other men on this earth; maybe even worse than the English. They feign piety, with their new religion and sombre faces, but they are devils. They have rid themselves of the Virgin Mary, and now all women are whores in their eyes. In France, they have the *maîtresse-en-titre*, a formal title for the king's mistress. The Scots think this is scandalous – giving a position and place to a woman of sin – but it is only because the Scots would rather not name what is done in the dark, and so they rape their wives's maidservants, and fuck in secret. They are hypocrites, Cuckoo thinks, and all the more dangerous for it.

She thinks of Lindsay, the way he looked at her in the boat, the burble of his foreign tongue, words she knew were about her, about the other women. For years now she has got by without speaking Scots, staying among the other French servants and ladies-in-waiting who travelled with Mary across the sea: a court within a court. Now, Cuckoo does not know whether she would have preferred to understand the insults the men traded in the boat, or let them wash over her like slate-grey waters. But what transcended language was how he, Lindsay, looked at her and smirked, and Cuckoo flushed and could not escape the certainty that *he knew*. He knew about her. He knew she was not a virgin.

Cuckoo had tried to keep herself intact for her future husband. But it is not an easy feat, at two royal courts – first France, then Scotland – full of angry, hard men who cannot go to bed with Mary Stuart. Nor is it an easy feat for a woman in her twenties who feels desire, who knows pleasure. To always be the one to say *No, no*, when your own body is clenched and taut and all you want to say is *Yes, yes*.

If Jane were her friend, Cuckoo would comfort her; she would tell her bawdy anecdotes, and trade insults about the men at court. Some part of Cuckoo knows that the enemies are outside this room, and not within. But she has always been lazy, and it is easier now for her to resent Jane, to feel jealous: Jane is too competent, too clever; she is calculating, better at holding her tongue, and anticipating Mary's needs. She is not pretty, in the way Cuckoo is; she is almost mouse-like when you first meet her. However, if

Cuckoo were honest with herself, she would admit that there is something of the Anne Boleyn effect about Jane – in those dark eyes, which seem to hold secrets, and that amused, wry smile. She wonders whether Jane would have stories to tell, too, if she asked her. But Cuckoo worries that if Jane proves she can be as bawdy as herself, as talkative when talk is needed, then Mary will look from one chamberer to the other, and wonder what purpose she, Cuckoo, serves by her side. And so Cuckoo says nothing: she offers no comfort, and she asks no questions.

Night-time. By candlelight, Mary's prison seems to quiver and move. The walls are uneven in parts, covered in dips and lumps that appear almost organic, the room animated by breath, as though Mary is squatting inside the belly of some huge creature, and the wooden beams above are its ribs. Mary's women are asleep as she reads –

A letter from Elizabeth.

*To be plain with you our grief has not been small*, it states. Mary scans over lines she has read before, her mind clouded by the inexplicable sorrow that descends on her with each pregnancy, a thick suffocating quilt thrown over the depression she has worn as a second shift since her teenage years, ever closer to the skin. Elizabeth Tudor writes to chastise Mary for her hasty third marriage, to Bothwell. Mary reads again those lines she has memorised, stray words and phrases rising up from the page: *Such haste to marry . . . Murder of your late husband . . . Peril . . . Another lawful wife alive.* She cannot continue; her hands are shaking too much for her to make out anything more. She respects her cousin. But in these lines, Elizabeth speaks as though Mary were a child, and not a fellow prince with purpose. She seems to have forgotten that Mary has escaped her enemies before. She can do it again.

Agnes spends her days with the three women, their every hour accounted for until night-time. She brings her own sewing, and materials for the other women – although there is not enough to share, and the quality of the thread is poor compared to what Mary is accustomed to. Agnes likes to talk; she speaks in a high, simpering voice. On the rare occasions she is quiet, she slaps a furtive smile on her face, as though hoping others will think she's in possession of a secret joke. She applies herself to spywork with assiduous attention, finding ways to work Bothwell into every conversation. It was Mary's marriage to Bothwell that led to her downfall. He is the same man accused of murdering her second husband, Darnley. Some of the Scottish lords sought to avenge Darnley, a man none of them respected while he still breathed. Mary has not seen Bothwell since the Battle of Carberry Hill; his whereabouts are unknown, and he appears to have abandoned his royal wife to her fate. Mary was captured after the battle, but Bothwell fled the country. He will never return to Scottish soil; he will die in a squalid prison cell in Denmark, chained to a pillar and unable to stand. Before he dies he will descend into madness. But now, here at Lochleven Castle, no one could guess at Bothwell's fate. They only know he has gone, and without his wife.

'We heard, of course, what happened after Carberry Hill,' Agnes says. 'The banners the mob carried, painting you as a mermaid.' This last word is whispered; 'mermaid' can also mean 'whore', although to Jane, a mermaid is nothing except inaccessible, even virginal: the promise of bared breasts and slender torso giving way to impenetrable scales. Agnes looks at Mary – she never bothers to look at Jane or Cuckoo. 'We heard such horrible rumours about your husband; it's hard to believe them.'

No one is sure which rumour Agnes is talking about; there are so many whispers surrounding Bothwell. They say he killed Mary's second husband Darnley for her, and that is why she married him. They say he rapes every woman he meets. They say he raped Mary, and that is why she married him. They say she is a whore. They say that, on their wedding night, Mary called for a knife: she said she would cut herself, she said she would drown herself. They say that he was unfaithful to Mary with his first wife, who he divorced a fortnight before his second marriage. They say he bedded Mary while she was still married to Darnley. They say she is a whore. They say she loves Bothwell. They say she bequeathed him a jewel in the shape of a mermaid, made of diamonds and rubies. They say Bothwell killed an old servant right in front of her, and she said nothing. They say they killed the old servant together, and that Mary laughed. They say she is a whore.

When Mary does not answer Agnes, but lowers her head over her needlework, Agnes titters.

'Of course, no husband is perfect,' she says. 'Mine, of course, you know. A fine laird, you must agree with me, but of course: that wheezing! William cannot step outside without struggling for breath; you must have seen for yourself when he greeted you off the boat, wheezing and spluttering all over your hand as he kissed it. I thought, *What must she think of him!*' She giggles again. No one joins in. 'Yes, yes, every husband has his flaws,' she says, as though someone has disagreed with her. 'I am sure' – here she looks at Mary – 'your own husband has his own fair share?'

Mary forces a smile, as she has been taught to do ever since she was a child. She ignores both false and true gossip. As they stitch, she observes how eagerly Agnes seems to offer up her own confidences, even as she desperately attempts to glean information from Mary. *She is friendless here*, Mary thinks, and she tucks this information away like a hidden seam.

On and on Agnes goes, and after only a few hours in her company, Jane realises that her initial assumption – that Agnes is either sly or stupid – was incorrect.

She is both.

Unlike Jane, Cuckoo laid eyes on all three of Mary's husbands. A proud Frenchwoman, she is embarrassed by what her own country offered Mary: the stunted dauphin, Francis, who died of an ear infection. French royals have made embarrassing deaths a habit; she thinks of Philip, the heir apparent, whose horse tripped over a stray pig. Or Louis III, who was chasing after a would-be lover and smacked his head on a low door frame. But perhaps it was better that Francis died early; all the servants knew he had deformed testicles and could never give Mary a child. How ugly he had looked beside her. So unlike her second husband, Darnley, the handsome, smooth-faced Englishman she called her *long lad* because he was so tall, taller even than her – and also, Cuckoo suspects, because of what she discovered later, in the bedroom. During those first few nights after they married, Mary's chamberers would stand outside the door and listen to the moans of pleasure. They would whisper and swap gossip while they waited: the rumours that Darnley bedded men as well as women, and was poxy from brothel visits. There were rumours he bedded David Rizzio, the Italian musician and Mary's favourite servant. Cuckoo would later remember those rumours when Rizzio was stabbed to death in Mary's palace apartments, by a group of noblemen including Darnley himself. Rizzio had hidden behind Mary's skirts, kneeling, clutching her waist, her hands knotted in his curly hair. Mary, so prone to tears, did not cry that day; instead she faked a miscarriage to escape from right under the lords' noses.

He, Darnley, once caught Cuckoo draining the dregs of Mary's wine cup as she cleared a table in those same royal apartments, thinking she was alone. The next night, he waited for Cuckoo to arrive before he slowly poured the contents of his and Mary's cups out onto the floor, and watched as Cuckoo bent to scrub the wine stains with a sodden rag, the other servants looking on in silence. Afterwards, Cuckoo's brother Toussaint, a valet at court, found her and helped wash her hands, cleaning out the red grime beneath her nails. 'That poxy English son-of-a-whore will be dead long before you,' he assured her, and she forced a chuckle. The people of Scotland had never liked Darnley. Twenty years ago his father, the Earl of Lennox, took eleven children hostage and later slaughtered them. All were the children of Scottish lairds who had defected from Lennox's army. Those children were the future of their houses. Their murders were both savage and pointless; they sent a wave of grief and fury barrelling across the country and the ripples are still felt two decades later. The son of a man like Lennox could never be trusted.

Bothwell is not handsome and slippery as Darnley was. He is coarse in his manners, his build short and muscled like a bull's. He terrified the female servants. He once slapped Cuckoo across the mouth. She cannot remember why; perhaps there was no reason. She was not the first nor the last. At their handfasting, Mary appeared beautiful and miserable, her new husband ruddy-faced and already jealous of her attention, suspicious of all other men. On their wedding night, a placard was nailed to the gates of the palace. It quoted Ovid.

*As the common people say,*
*Only harlots marry in May.*

Mary's appetite has returned; she can walk about the rooms unassisted. It is now the height of summer, a rare flash of Scottish heat. The women are allowed out into the grounds, accompanied by Agnes and sometimes Margaret Erskine. The first time they stepped outside, Mary gulped in fresh air like water and bent to kiss the ground. She walks quickly, with long-legged strides; Jane wonders if the only reason Mary has begun to eat again is so that she has the strength to outpace Agnes on their walks. She has almost forgotten how tall Mary is: taller than any other woman she has met. In the open air she is larger than life; it is like she has stepped out of one of the vast tapestries that hang in palace halls, depicting the huge golden forms of Greek gods and nymphs, their woven hands the size of spades.

The sun beats down as they follow the water's edge, around the back of the castle to the kitchen garden. The world tastes fresh and ripe like an apple. Servants hunch over square plots, their hands buried amongst fragrant mint leaves and rosemary, basil and thyme. A woman with sunburn on her chest and forearms reaches down to pluck white camomile flowers. The clean air seems like holy water, purifying the women's lungs. The only annoyance are the flies: swarming clouds of tiny midges, they drift before Mary's face like a loose veil, and she flaps her hands and wonders aloud why they won't leave her alone.

To avoid Agnes's constant questioning, the women play games. *Who is the most handsome man of your acquaintance? The most fuckable?* Or: *Who is the best-dressed woman you know?* (The correct answer is

Mary.) Sometimes they are more philosophical. *What bird quality would you most like for your own?*

'It cannot be flight,' Mary says. 'Too easy.' She is still weak, but it is a mark of her charisma that she remains so engaging, even while recovering from illness.

It is very hard not to love her.

Jane chooses the ability to never lose one's way; to always know where one is going.

Cuckoo chooses the ability to speak and be understood around the world.

Mary chooses the ability to lay eggs. The other women laugh at this.

'It's true!' she says. 'By God, wouldn't it be easier?' She cups her belly. 'How easy, to simply watch them hatch. The work of birth is their own, not their mother's.'

But, Jane tells her, then the royal nest would be open and vulnerable to cuckoos.

'That I can never understand,' Mary says. 'How can those little birds mistake that ugly creature for their own child? I find it grotesque, how it pushes the mother's real children out of the nest, and then tricks her into raising it instead.'

Jane does not think the cuckoo ugly. It is a soft dove grey, with yellow eyes and beak; when it sings, the inside of its mouth is a violent, rich red, like strawberry juice. She says, 'Perhaps by the time the mother realises, the mistake is too great to undo. Or perhaps they know, but by the end of it all, they love it anyway.'

What is worse than Agnes's constant questions, much worse, is that her presence emboldens Ruthven. He now visits Mary daily, under the pretence of paying respects to the lady of the house. The young man kisses the noblewomen's hands, paying Agnes soft, courtly compliments that are meant for Mary.

'See that cat, lying in the patch of sun?' he says one morning, pointing outside the window. He is exuberant, his manners easy, as though Jane never saw him standing in that same place, leaning against the wall with his hand beneath his codpiece.

'The cat warms itself in that tiny patch of sunlight, even though the sun itself is so many miles away. Just as, even with a smile, you warm your servant here,' he says, bowing his head and smirking.

Mary looks nauseous and puts a hand to her stomach. Jane smiles to herself. She imagines that Mary is tired of Ruthven's flattery; that she is feigning the look of pain on her face. Jane is reminded of a woodpecker she once saw. She remembers the blur of movement as it beat out the rhythm of its desires against the bark. *WantWantWantWant*. It had such strange eyes, white around the edges: almost human. Its movements stilted, a stop-start, as though it were a wooden puppet, head and body attached to strings jerked up and down. Woodpeckers have obscenely long tongues: a long pink worm that burrows into freshly drilled holes. Now, Jane imagines Ruthven as a woodpecker, his tongue flopping out, worming towards Mary. The *rap-rap-rap* on the door, a din like a battle drum. *WantWantWantWant*.

Knocking to be let in.

When the light has faded, and the fire is lit and Agnes has left, Mary produces a letter, showing it to Jane and Cuckoo.

'It's from Ruthven,' she says, although there's no need: both her women saw him slip the note into Mary's hand, and have been waiting for her to tell them. 'He says he needs to speak with me. Tonight. He asks me to ensure you are both elsewhere.'

Jane thinks of the woodpecker. She is sick of men masking their wants as needs. Cuckoo offers to call Agnes back, but Mary tells her no.

'I want him to speak. I want him to show his hand. To make a fool of himself.'

'My lady.' Jane tries not to raise her voice; she tries to sound calm. 'If you are left with him alone, he may press his advantage. He may force himself on you.'

'I won't be alone,' Mary says. 'You will both be with me, here. He just won't know it.'


Ruthven returns just before dawn. The women hear his voice outside the door, loud and slurred, arguing with whoever is standing guard. Jane hears Cuckoo catch her breath beside her; she reaches for her hand in the dark and squeezes it. Cuckoo is surprised, but she squeezes back, any contest between them forgotten at this moment. Their backs are pressed against the stone wall; they breathe in the musty scent of damp wool. Mary has hidden them in the space behind a tapestry. They cannot move, cannot see anything. Can only listen.

Jane hears the door bang open, the curtain dragged aside. Even behind the thick tapestry, she thinks she can smell the wine on the man's breath.

'My queen,' Ruthven says. There is movement: quick steps. A heavy thud. Cuckoo's hand tightens around Jane's. But when he next speaks, Ruthven's voice seems to be coming from the ground, as though he is kneeling or even sitting down on the floor.

'My Mary.'

'I see you found your courage at the bottom of your glass, Lord Ruthven,' Mary says. Her voice is steady, but Jane can picture her, one hand clutching the back of a chair, holding herself upright.

'Your women – you sent them away as I asked?'

'Yes. They are –'

'I cannot be your captor,' he says, speaking over her; interrupting a sovereign queen. (*How dare he?* Jane thinks. *Would he dare if she were a man?*) 'If I am to capture you, better to capture your heart. If I hold you, it is better to hold you in my arms as your dutiful husband. By my side, you will escape, we will take back –'

'A ready speech. Did you memorise it?' Mary says over him, her voice rising.

'– and England, a country for us to conquer, to ravage –'

'Do not speak like that; like those poets who talk of islands as bodies to invade. Like lovers who come to bed with bloody hands.'

'You cannot know my love, my passion, my desire,' he says, still slurring, and he is rambling now; he has no more rehearsed lines to deliver.

'I do know you. I saw you on the day David Rizzio died. Each one of you: you, your father, Lindsay; all of you put a knife in him and imagined me in his place as he bled. I do not forget; I remember it, my lord. I can see David now; feel him clutching at my skirts as he hides behind me like a child. I can feel the pistol pressing into my pregnant belly, and I can hear his screams as you drag him away. I would not divorce Lord Bothwell; but if I did, I would not seek a husband among those who were there that day.'

There are more quick footsteps, and a sudden spattering of something liquid. Jane thinks Ruthven has vomited on the floor, but she hears him yell out as though in shock; he is spitting and sputtering.

Mary calls her women by name, this is their cue; they emerge from behind the tapestry, and Jane sees she has an empty jug in her hand – Jane thinks of that first jug of piss – and Ruthven is sprawled on the floor, drenched, wiping his eyes with his cuffs. It is a shock to see him here, in this room: the first man to cross its threshold since their arrival, an intruder in their small, closed space, their own corner of the castle. It is like a tiger has been let loose among them.

At the sight of the women, Ruthven staggers to his feet.

'You,' he says, his eyes on Jane. He turns back around to face Mary, his arms swinging about him as though he were a cloth doll, his joints loosely knotted. 'This one, she likes to watch,' he says, sneering. He tries to grab at Mary's waist, lunging, but she steps back behind the chair.

'Leave us,' Mary says, and for a moment he looks as though he will refuse, but then he staggers back towards the doorway.

'You will regret your answer tonight, you will regret this soon,' he says, stumbling, one hand on the curtain, and Jane sees his teeth are bared. 'You will regret this very soon.'

Then he is gone, disappeared behind the door; but the smell of the wine lingers, as though he is still standing before them, breathing through his mouth. Mary grips the back of the chair before her, her other hand feeling her belly, sweat glistening at her brow like a circle of diamonds. There is no sense of victory for her. Instead she is remembering the day Bothwell abducted her. His ruddy face above her own, a grim smile on his face. He, too, spoke of his plans for Scotland. His plans for *her*.

The next day, grey mist envelops the island like a haar. Robert Melville is about forty years old, a diplomat, and Mary's first permitted visitor. He comes from a family of statesmen and courtiers, and spent years at the English court earlier in his career. He is pale, with a forgettable face that he has found in fact benefits his chosen profession rather than hinders it. He dresses in plain but expensive fabrics, with a large sword strapped to his side.

Lindsay and Ruthven accompany Mary on her walk with him, her women forced to follow some distance behind, with Agnes. They walk by the waterside; any hope they have of hearing the diplomat's words is quashed by Agnes, who keeps up a one-sided conversation. The party ahead reaches the short jetty, where several small boats are tied up. Mary holds the diplomat's arm and walks slowly, carefully, as though concealing a limp. Lindsay strides forward, sneering, making a show of checking how securely the boats are fastened – *See how Mary cannot escape us?* – and not to be outdone, Ruthven follows after him.

In their momentary absence, the diplomat whirls around and speaks quickly and earnestly to Mary. Through the mist Jane squints and watches his mouth move, watches as he puts a hand on his sword and begins to fiddle with the scabbard – he begins to draw the sword, *Christ's nails, no,* and Jane is about to charge forwards, to knock the man down, when she sees him reach his fingers inside the scabbard as though searching for something.

'Lady Agnes,' Jane says, grabbing the woman's elbow and turning her so that she faces away from Mary and the diplomat, and back towards the castle walls, 'remind me again when this castle was built?'

Alone, Mary opens the scrap of paper. It is from the English ambassador. Elizabeth Tudor's ambassador.

*Should you be forced to abdicate, know that a signature obtained under duress cannot be binding.*

Mary complains of cramps, of pains in her side, in her belly; but while the doughy-faced Agnes would normally salivate in eagerness to hear Mary's confidences, to press her advantage, she is instead silent. She changes the subject. Everyone in Scotland has heard what happened after David Rizzio was murdered: how the gore-spattered lords threatened Mary, wanting her to cede power, to sign papers stripping her of her rights, and of how she faked a miscarriage, groaning and screaming for hours, fooling them all, until she took her chance and slipped away, escaping them before Rizzio's blood had even dried. Agnes remembers this tale. She does not believe Mary. She thinks she plans a repeat of the trick— to make a fool of her, Agnes.

A setting sun bleeds red and orange over the sky, across the mirrored surface of the loch. Agnes leaves, returning to her husband and, no doubt, a feast of meat pies and cakes. Mary is put to bed, clutching her belly. Jane begins to feel frightened for her. She thinks of Ruthven, of his parting words, *You will regret this*, spat out like a curse. She watches Mary toss her dark head from side to side, as though the hurt is a buzzing wasp she is trying to dodge.

'Was she like this with her first child?'

'No,' Cuckoo whispers. 'But it might not be – it might only – well, she has never coped well with pain. She was afraid – she gathered all these . . . relics around her.' Cuckoo looks almost nauseous at the memory. 'During her son's birth, she screamed so much that the Countess of Atholl offered to make a charm, to transfer the pains to another woman.'

'And Mary agreed to it? To witchcraft?'

Cuckoo nods.

By dawn, neither woman will have any doubts about Mary's pain.

When the blood comes, it comes in a rush over the sheets. Mary gasps, wriggling backwards up the bed, away from the great dark red stain and the clots of flesh, staring at them as though they did not come from her own body. Her pale face is dotted with burst blood vessels and her eyes are bulging so much that Jane feels an urge to clap a hand over them, to keep them in their sockets.

The blood keeps coming.

Cuckoo runs to the locked door and begins pounding on it, screaming in French for a midwife, a physician.

'Where is Lady Seton?' Mary is babbling, her eyes wide and staring like a hare's. Her inner thighs are striped red. 'Where are my women?'

Jane wants to say, *We are here*, but she knows that Mary means her ladies-in-waiting, her *jewelled ladies*. Lady Seton is the courtier who as a child accompanied Mary to France. The two of them are great friends, confidantes. They wear diamonds and dance in masques together. Or they did, once.

'They are coming,' Jane lies, her hands moving from the sheets to the hem of Mary's shift. 'Lady Seton is riding here now, she is coming.' False words to bring false comfort. Jane hopes Mary will understand and forgive them, if she remembers. If she lives.

'Midwife?' Mary is panting from pain, she can barely get the word out.

Cuckoo begins, *There is none*, but Jane cuts her off: 'They have sent for her, but we must go on without –'

'They must believe me, why won't they believe me? I am sincere, I am sincere, I swear it.' Mary writhes, as though from a sudden stab of pain. She is clutching the small of her back. *Mother,* she shouts, *mother.*

The dead are invisible, but they are not absent: this is what Saint Augustine writes. They make their presence felt. Already there are ghosts in the room, Jane is sure of it. No men – this is not their domain, in life or death – but there are other women, watching. She is sure that Mary's mother is here; that the late queen answered her call and now holds court at her daughter's bedside, her wraith-hands upon her, sinking through Mary's skin, through flesh and muscle to bone, the cool of the tomb robbing her of heat.

More blood. The stench of browning blood clots. Of excrement. Jane and Cuckoo look at each other. They are imagining the impossible. Will they be the ones to bind Mary's jaw? Will they be forced to light candles and place them at her head and feet? To wrap her body in a winding sheet? They will have to pray for her in Latin, and Jane will stumble over the words.

Mary is pointing up at the ceiling, as though she can see her dead mother moving about between the rafters.

'What did she do?' Jane says, desperate. 'What did the countess do to transfer pain?'

Cuckoo's mouth works, tears welling in her eyes. 'I can't remember it all. There was thread, embroidery thread, tying my lady to the other woman. I think there was blood – a small dish of blood under the bed. It was witchcraft, I do not know.'

'*You will remember,*' Jane says. She does not care, she is not afraid; she climbs into bed beside Mary. She is barely aware of Cuckoo moving about the room, searching; of the thread she now ties around Jane's wrist, then around Mary's, looping it back under the bed.

'Do not let them take me,' Mary is saying, 'do not let me be like Huntly,' and Jane knows she is thinking of the outlaw George Gordon, Earl of Huntly, posthumously tried for treason, his dis-embowelled cadaver propped up in an upright coffin throughout the trial in some macabre show of justice. Jane imagines, without meaning to, Mary's body placed in a chair before a room of courti-ers, flies crawling about her, her flesh green and sunken and rotting away. *No*, she thinks. On the blood-soaked bed she strokes Mary's hair, as she has seen Cuckoo do. She listens to her breathing. Mary is quieter now, but her stomach is still cramping and seizing as though with birth pains. She presses her cheek to Jane's, and it seems as though the pain is sloshing beneath the skin like wine in a cup, and soon it will spill over and into Jane, through her own skin, through her cheek and into her mouth and down her throat.

All at once, Jane feels cold. She looks up.

Ghosts are gliding above her head: they swim about the room in the form of great silvery fish with human faces. Their eyes are unblinking as they stare down at the bed. These are not creatures of bedside comfort, of old love; they are monstrous. They turn their stiff corpse faces towards her, their scaled bodies and tails twisting and turning in invisible, spectral currents. Mary is still staring at the ceiling, pointing, and Jane knows that she can see them too, that the countess's charm has gone awry: she is not shar-ing Mary's pain, but her dreams, her nightmares.

'Jane.'

Cuckoo is kneeling on the bed at their feet, her hands covered in blood, and she is holding something wrapped in cloth. Jane sees that Mary's eyes have shut. She notices for the first time that her own hands are also covered in blood; that Mary's temple is smeared rust-red where she has stroked her hair. She remembers with a jolt how she was half-afraid to touch Mary's skin when they first arrived at Lochleven Castle.

'Open the window, Cuckoo, open it,' Jane is saying. She thinks, *Let the ghosts out. Let them swim away into the night.*

'They're dead,' Cuckoo says, and Jane does not understand her at first; she is thinking of the ghosts, she almost says, *Of course they are, they are already dead.* But she sees again the bloodied cloth.

'They?' she says, but Cuckoo is unfolding the cloth, and Jane sees, and she understands. *They.*

It is Jane who carries the twins outside, wrapped in dirty linen, accompanied by the guard who smirked when he brought the jug of piss. The pale sky is milky and cloudless. Close to the water's edge, he digs a shallow hole in the dirt – it does not take long – and she places the tiny bodies in the ground, their souls unbaptised, and watches the man cover them up, slapping the back of his spade onto the soft earth when he is done, flattening the grave so that even Jane doubts she will be able to find it again. There is no question of a gravestone or marker. She speaks words of prayer; locked away beside Mary and Cuckoo, she has learnt the starts and ends of prayers in foreign tongues. The guard bows his head, but he shifts from one foot to another, impatient to get on. Jane lingers, a part of her longing to stay outside in the fresh air, to never again enter that cloistered space, or breathe in her own, days-old breath.

Jane turns, and it is only now that she sees it. In the damp muck by the edge of the water there is a single shoe. A woman's shoe, crudely made and stitched. The leather is worn and creased from wear. There are deep lines, suggesting the owner once spent much of her time standing on tiptoe. A kitchen girl perhaps, reaching for the highest shelf where the precious spices are kept? Or maybe she liked to dance. It is the left shoe, the side half-sunk into the wet ground as though the wearer twisted her ankle before it came loose. Jane stares at this shoe, scuffed and bruised, wondering where its owner is now. Is she inside the castle? Is she on the mainland, having fled this wretched place? Or perhaps she is long dead, lying at the bottom of the loch, her shoe washed up and sinking into soil, returning to earth as her body cannot.

Mary is lying in a bathtub as her twins are buried. When it became clear to the guard outside that her cries of pain were sincere, that she was not repeating the scenes at Holyrood – and then, later, that she was refusing to die immediately after her miscarriage – the servants were called. When Jane returns from outside, escorted by the same silent, smirking guard, the bedsheets have already been stripped, the piss pot taken away to be emptied, and a bathtub and warm water carried in. There is even a jug of red wine.

In the bath, Mary wears her long linen smock. Strips of cloth line the interior of the tub, and herbs and rose petals float on the surface of the water. The sweet-scented bath cannot fully mask the underlying odour: a miasma of the body and the blood. Both Jane and Cuckoo worry about the corrupting vapours that must linger even now: the stench of death and the loss of blood and fluids have surely disrupted the balance of Mary's humours.

Mary's own thoughts are elsewhere. She feels numb. A fog is descending on her, as it did before and after her first pregnancy. But even in this state, she is trying to calculate, to take stock. Now she is no longer pregnant by Bothwell, the lords might be easier on her. They might consider how valuable she is, young and fertile and alive, having survived the dangers of miscarriage when many other women do not. Perhaps the babies were boys; more proof of her eligibility. The moment she thinks this, she feels nauseous. *Perhaps they were boys.*

*My sons.*

Cuckoo leans forward to dab at Mary's eyes with her sleeve. Mary did not realise until this moment that she is crying. Cuckoo's touch is too rough and perfunctory, and she does not know what to say to Mary. Mary misses her ladies-in-waiting. Lady Seton – dear, devoted – would know how to comfort her. Seton would hold her and let her weep the first few days. She would be kind but she would not let Mary wallow and risk her health; she would not allow her to brick herself in, dead to the world, like an anchoress. Instead she would eventually find some means of tempting her out of bed. A diversion – a game, a dance, an outing of some kind; a way of reminding Mary how much she is admired. How well she is loved.

Of course, for every one person who adores Mary, there is another who hates her, and with just as great a passion.

For her part, Mary believes she knows why so many of the Scottish noblemen despise her – and it is not only that she is a Catholic, raised across the sea in a Catholic country. Nor is it only because she is a woman, although that is part of it. Mary is sensual; it is a part of her just as much as her innate royalty. This sensuality did not change after James's birth, when she became a mother. The world has grown used to royal women who are in some way unsexed, either on their own terms or by others. They are the long-suffering, the mothers of nations. They are unavailable. They are not lovers. They are the spouse who bore the king's children but does not possess his love, instead tolerating his mistresses, as Catherine de' Medici did for so many years, right up until the moment when she knew her husband was dying, and realised she did not have to see the beautiful Diane de Poitiers ever again. Even Elizabeth, who bares her breasts at court and prefers all men to be in love with her, seems to have closed the door on sex, on marriage. In her mid-thirties, she prefers to be loved as a brave knight loves the inaccessible lady of the house. As though she were a character in a song or play. The problem the Scottish lords have with Mary is that she is flesh and blood, still accessible, still fertile: all that power, all those royal bloodlines in one body, all to be taken by men other than themselves. The rightful heir to Scotland and England. But above all, worse than another man taking, is the idea of Mary herself taking, of her desiring and choosing someone, as she did with the unsuitable Darnley.

Cuckoo kneels behind the head of the tub, her hands wrapped in linen, scrubbing the back of Mary's neck and behind her ears. It's early, but Cuckoo is already thinking about the wine she will drink this afternoon. She hums a song that Jane does not know, but Mary listens, her eyes closed. The burst blood vessels are purple against her skin. The night seems to have aged her: there are lines around her eyes that Jane does not remember seeing before, and she knows Mary's face better than her own.

The water sloshes over the edge of the tub as Mary makes to stand, gripping Cuckoo's hand for support, the wet linen clinging to her body, to her still-distended belly. Her legs shake with the effort, wobbling like a newborn fawn's. She wants the piss pot, she needs it now; but the servants have taken it away, there has only ever been one piss pot for the three of them. Jane runs to the door, ensuring the curtain is drawn behind her. She shouts to the guard standing on the other side of the door, and she hears him rap his knuckles against wood once, twice, as though signalling that he has heard her request, that someone will be on their way. Jane wants to cry out in frustration, *Say something. Why won't you speak to us?*

*Would they reply*, she thinks, *if I were Lady Seton?*

When she steps back into the room, Cuckoo is facing her, her eyes wide, motioning for her to turn away, to turn her back; but behind her Jane sees, too late, that Mary is already squatting over the blackened fireplace, her skirt pulled up around her waist, her face twisted in relief and shame.

By the following morning all of Edinburgh has heard about Mary's miscarriage. The men smell the blood, and they lick their lips. They are wolves. The castle room becomes an animal trap. Mary lies snared – weakened, an open wound – in the same bed where she miscarried, and the men prowl outside.

They come for her only days later; the women hear the tramp of feet, and Jane knows there are too many, and the door is open before she can run to it, the curtain ripped aside. All of these men – those standing in the room, and those, too, who are absent shadows – they are all connected to each other: by the threads of birth, of marriage. If you strummed on these threads, followed them into the maze, you would find these men were all kin: great inbred minotaurs. They all look alike, and they are forced to seek dispensations to marry their kinswomen, as Lindsay did: he is married to his kinswoman Euphemia, one of Margaret Erskine's daughters, which makes him the brother-in-law to Moray.

What also connects all these men is fear: they are afraid of Mary, afraid of what will happen if she is still queen come December, when she turns twenty-five. It is the age when the sovereign can claim back properties and wardships from the Scottish nobles: an old custom that would allow her to impoverish her enemies – and many of them are standing here, in this damp stone room.

Not one man asks permission to enter, not one man bows at the sight of Mary, still in bed, exhausted, spent, her eyes on Lindsay. He has papers under his arm, he is grinning in triumph; on the ride to Lochleven she threatened to have him beheaded, and ever since he has been uneasy, more anxious than the others to destroy her, more anxious for this very moment. He wants her dead, to be safe, but this formality comes first: this, her forced abdication. He spreads the papers out over the bed, and tells her that she can read them first before signing, if she likes; his tone makes it clear that he does not care.

'I will not sign,' Mary says.

'Yes, you will,' Lindsay sneers. He is in no mood to argue, to enter into debate; he has never excelled in verbal sparring, in court manners and witty asides. He has eczema in his ears, and his idea of a joke is to flick pieces of dead skin at those around him, laughing at their revulsion. With his enemies, he has always preferred action over words. When Mary first arrived in Scotland off the boat from France, announcing she would continue to attend Catholic mass at her private chapel, Lindsay was at the head of a mob that vandalised the sacred place and called for the priest's murder. Only weeks ago, it was Lindsay who challenged Bothwell to a fight to the death at the battle at Carberry Hill, baying like a bull and swinging an ancient rusty sword over his head. Mary intervened; the men did not fight, but she did not forget.

Jane and Cuckoo are standing at Mary's bedside; they can only watch, reading over her shoulder the documents spread out before her, on the same bed where her babies died. The documents would see her abdicate in favour of her toddler son, and promote Moray – Margaret Erskine's son, Mary's own bastard half-brother – to regent. Three pieces of paper to unmake a queen, to undo her sovereignty, to blot out the holy oil. *It's absurd*, Jane thinks. She sees Ruthven, by the door behind the other men. She raises her head. He seems to sense her gaze and turns to look at her. He smiles, showing his teeth, and she can almost read his thoughts: *There you are. The one who likes to watch.*

'I will not sign,' Mary repeats. She holds her palms up, as though someone is trying to force the papers into her hands. 'Call Parliament, let me answer for my supposed crimes in person.'

'Take her to the table there, she can't sign here,' Lindsay directs Cuckoo, as though Mary has not spoken; he has read *The Schole House of Women*, that seminal text, and agrees with its author that woman was not made from the rib of Adam, but that of a dog. He stares at Cuckoo, impatient, but she doesn't move, although not out of defiance; she hasn't understood the order. She does nothing. His eyes widen at this supposed act of disobedience; she is out of arm's reach on the other side of the bed, so instead of shoving or slapping her as he wants, he shouts his next words, spraying spit: '*Bitch, take her to the table.*'

There is a pause.

'*Qu'est-ce qu'il a dit?*' Cuckoo whispers, finally, out of the corner of her mouth. *What did he say?*

But Lindsay does not wait for anyone to answer her; he slaps a hand down on the bed, a thumb's width from Mary's ankle beneath the sheets. He is going to drag her out of bed, the women think. '*Get up,*' he shouts, 'get up now, we are leaving; by the blood of

Christ, if you don't sign, I will row you to the middle of the loch
and push you over the side myself.' Mary yells in fright – he is
about to lay hands on her, it is unthinkable – as he shouts, '*Damn
you, whore*,' and Jane and Cuckoo both throw themselves forward,
to knock his hand away, to wrench her free, but he has already
turned; he walks to the table and slams his fist down onto its surface, *bang*, and he watches Mary as he does so, watches her flinch,
as though to tell her that he wishes it was not the table he has
struck, but her: her oval face – so like her mother's – and that tall
body, taller than his own. There is a knife in his other hand – Jane
did not see where it came from; perhaps it was always there – and
he plunges this down, too, stabbing the table, burying the tip of
the blade into the wood, and Mary is crying – she cannot help it,
she has always cried easily – and he says, '*I will cut your throat. By
God's nails, I will.*'

And Jane believes him.

The women half carry Mary to the table, where the knife stands
upright. Some of the men by the door look uncomfortable; no one
agreed in advance that Lindsay should threaten her in such unam-
biguous terms. But they will all stay silent until she has signed the
papers. There is one handsome young man who looks almost nauseous. This, the women will later learn, is George Douglas,
younger brother of the laird of the house. Another one of Margaret Erskine's sons, and the one who most resembles her. Already he
is thinking, *How beautiful the queen is. How I wish I were not here. How
I wish she would look at me.*

Mary has stopped crying – by God, she will not smudge her
signature with tears, she will not let them have her despair for
posterity – and takes the quill Lindsay presses into her hand, and

begins to write. She does not know that Lindsay's threats will prove empty. The lords will not kill her now. England's Elizabeth has threatened to go to war if the Scottish nobles touch Mary, their *anointed queen*. The head should not be subject to the foot, she says. Mary does not know that when Elizabeth eventually hears of the abdication, she will call for her chief advisor, William Cecil, and it will be the angriest he has seen her. She will not acknowledge Mary's son as king.

Mary, the quill in her hand, looks up at Lindsay. 'When God shall set me at liberty again' – Jane thinks she will say, *When I am at liberty, I will have revenge* – 'I shall not abide by these.' Mary gestures down at her signatures, scratched out in her round, cursive hand. 'It is done against my will.'

There is something in her voice: she is too confident; she is like a card player hiding her hand. *What was in those letters?* Jane thinks. *What did the diplomat tell her, when he produced that hidden scrap of paper from his scabbard? Surely her crown is her greatest card of all?* Jane glances at Cuckoo, but she is blank-faced, uncomprehending.

Lindsay wears a vicious smile. He has what he needs. He slides his pinky into his ear, searching, scratching with his nail. He removes it and – very carefully – flicks a grey flake onto the table. He turns his back on the queen-that-was, and the other men follow his example. Their backs to their queen. The last piece of etiquette broken.

There is a picture Jane saw once: a woodcut of the moment when the snake tempted Eve in the Garden of Eden. But instead of a snake, it is a woman, a mirror image of Eve herself. The same pert breasts, the same rounded stomach, the same long, blonde hair. Only, the snake-woman has no arms, and where her legs should be, her torso tapers off into serpentine coils. In the picture, the snake-woman shuts her eyes as, over her shoulder, Eve hands Adam the apple.

Jane remembers the picture, and is certain that Lindsay has seen it too.

Lindsay and Ruthven are gone; they have left for the Tolbooth of Edinburgh, the city jail and the place where important men gather for official business. Lindsay will deliver the abdication papers with a flourish, a smirk on his face. He will hear them read aloud with smug satisfaction. The men's continued absence brings a rush of relief for Mary and her companions, although it does not last long.

The women are moved to another part of the castle, into the high, medieval tower. They are housed in the top rooms. Mary is too tall for the doorway; she is forced to crouch down, dipping her chin down to her chest. The furnishings of their new prison cell are an improvement: now, she is better kept than days ago, before her abdication. There are lush, bright tapestries; a finely carved bed; and by the east window there is a small space for a private chapel, with a piscina, a stone basin for cleaning sacred altar vessels after mass. Protestants do not use altars, yet here they have constructed one for the Catholic queen-that-was. But the women are also deprived of paper and ink, and are better guarded, high up away from the island grounds, from the loch, with their new, obstructed view intended to prevent them from signalling to any supporters on the mainland. Where they were once isolated, accompanied only by shadows and the sounds of footsteps, the women are now never alone; servants carrying dishes flavoured with tarragon rush in and out of the new rooms, their faces frank, their eyes never lowered. The laird, William Douglas, now comes to their rooms personally with the evening meal. He is not like his handsome younger brother, George; he is hunchbacked with wheezing, and inspects the doors and locks them behind him when he leaves, as silent and surly as his wife, Agnes, is sly and simpering, clutching at her own belly more frequently since Mary's loss. All of this does not matter, however. There is a more pressing issue.

Mary's health has worsened since her miscarriage. Her skin has turned yellow, as have the whites of her eyes; it is as though she has been painted with gold – she, who was once named the Golden Fleece when she was a young dauphiness, a gilded prize won by France, her new husband Jason of the Argonauts. Now, almost a decade on, the people call her Medea: that witch, that jilted murderess, butchering her own sons by Jason when he took a second wife.

There are other symptoms. Mary's body seems to have swollen in size, her face and limbs puffy. There are pustules, and her urine is a dark, unnatural colour; she is feverish once more, and complains her bones feel heavy, very heavy, weighing her down deep into the mattress. Jane calls for rosemary flowers boiled in water, to sweeten Mary's breath. She lifts her head for her to drink, cupping her scalp. Her breath is sour, almost metallic; Jane holds her breath, and thinks, but does not speak, what they all fear: *poison*.

'We need a surgeon for the queen,' she tells Cuckoo; but Agnes – who has re-joined them, who sits on the other side of the room away from the bed, a handkerchief soaked in rose water pressed to her nose – begins to hum tunelessly, as she always does whenever the other women dare lapse into French, which she barely understands.

Jane repeats herself in Scots, speaking loudly over Cuckoo, who hisses that her voice will soon fade away from lack of use, and Jane – who cannot understand how Cuckoo managed for so long in Scotland with only a smattering of Scottish words – thinks, but does not voice, the solution.

Agnes, whose free hand strokes her still-pregnant belly, does not comment on the need for a surgeon; instead, she slowly wags a finger when Jane speaks the word 'queen', a smile on her slack face.

'Why does she do that?' Cuckoo says, pacing back and forth, speaking rapidly. ' "Queen", that is *La Reine*? How dare she,' she says, when Jane nods in assent, not looking at her, 'how dare she. Tell her that a piece of paper means nothing; that Mary is still queen in this miserable country, and that she reigned over France as queen consort; she is a widow of France, she is still a queen.' She stamps her foot in agitation, all her anxiety now directed at the squat woman humming from behind her kerchief.

'My lady,' Jane says, addressing Agnes, 'if we cannot use "queen", what title do you suppose we use in its stead?'

Agnes inhales deeply into her scented handkerchief, as if giving herself time to think, smiling that simpering, secret smile of hers. She is saved from making any proclamation by Cuckoo, who begins to repeat loudly, in Scots: '*Surgeon*.'

In the bed, tears run down Mary's bloated cheeks and into her mouth, but her face does not move at all. She cannot hear her women. She feels broken; she has felt this way on and off ever since she was a girl. Like a broken necklace, restrung but incomplete, the pearls scattered into darkness. It is as though she is choking on something invisible, and those around her can't understand what is wrong; they flap their hands and lift her eyelids and open her veins, and all the while she is hocking and gasping and unable to breathe. This feeling is crushing, cyclical. It is to be an animal trapped, thumping the ground in pain; it is large and rough-edged. It is to be chewed apart by grief, and you don't know who has died. It is emptiness. It is to drown, over and over again.

Some women know from birth how to speak to other women. They make friends easily, and can elicit a laugh with only a raised eyebrow. Agnes envies them all. Ever since she was a child, she seemed to lack that indefinable quality: the ability to read someone's face, to know when to talk and when to stay silent. She could not judge which women liked to gossip about others or preferred to trade stories about their marital beds. She could not keep secrets. Other girls would whisper behind their hands – knowing, as she did, that there was something not quite right.

As an interrogator, she was poorly chosen. When Mary first arrived at Lochleven, Agnes's family asked her to mention certain subjects, to slip the names of certain men into conversation with the Scottish queen. But she lacked the subtlety required: that ability to ask a question without speaking. Nor can she speak any French; every night she leaves Mary's rooms and feels as though she is emerging from underwater, once again able to hear clearly, to distinguish sound. She sits exhausted on her bed and speaks to her unborn child, which she imagines to be as red and wrinkled as a peach stone. She bends her head over her belly and whispers and complains about the other women, and the baby inside her listens, its feet pressing against her sides. She has other young children already, but with each of them she has found that once they are out of the womb she cannot speak to them in the same way. And so she begins trying for another.

Agnes is a poor interrogator. But she is also a woman who has spent her life watching other people, studying their behaviour as carefully and curiously as an ambassador at a foreign court. Eventually, she will prove herself a spy – and only then will the other women know just how closely she has been watching.

A surgeon is brought to Mary by boat the following morning, to tend to her fever. He is an older man, stooped and bald-headed and laden with instruments: saws, scalpels, tiny glass cups, and worst of all, a jar of black leeches, sucking and sliding up the sides. He asks if Mary has been bled before, and in the silence Jane answers for her, peeling back Mary's sleeve: the ridged bloodletting scar in the crook of her elbow is held up and presented to him for inspection; he leans in close and shakes his head.

'The leg would have been a better choice, given the lady's star chart,' he says.

He produces a crude ink sketch of a man, with twelve lines pointing to different parts of the body, each with a corresponding star sign. Surgeons believe a person's zodiac governs specific body parts: Aries the head, Pisces the feet, Cancer the breast, and so on. It is an old theory, open to interpretation, but it is still popular. Cuckoo traces her finger across the drawing from *Taurus* to the man's neck. Jane does not look for her own sign. Instead she scans down the page. A line connects *Sagittarius* to the man's upper leg.

Blood will need to be purged to combat Mary's fever, and the surgeon proposes a place on her thigh, above the knee; the use of leeches, he says, will allow for little mess, and only a small, triangular mark compared to a blade's incision. Any excess blood he will collect in a vial. Jane is pleased by his confidence, but she is also repulsed by the contents of the jar: a black, squirming mass, the leeches like huge slugs, wet and writhing.

The women burn herbs to stave off contagion, and the air seems to shimmer with their bright scent.

Mary lies back, her yellowed eyes half-open, looking at the leeches with indifference as the surgeon opens the jar and lifts one out: it twists and coils its body up towards his fingers. He motions to Jane to pull back Mary's nightgown and smock, which she does, arranging the fabric in such a way as to show the barest minimum of flesh. She wishes that Mary had been born at a different time, on a different day and under a different constellation, so that some other, less intimate part of herself might be used and bled instead.

The leech settles on skin. Jane can see the lined markings of its body, the green stripe around its belly. It has no face. As she watches, it begins to pulse and bloat, and she realises the creature has begun to gorge on Mary's blood.

Hand on her mouth, Jane turns away, retching. There are tears of nausea pricking her eyes.

'*Out*, out you go.' The surgeon glares at her. 'The room is too crowded as it is; out, out,' he says to Jane and Cuckoo, before turning to Agnes and asking her, in more deferential tones, if she will take up the place by Mary's bedside, intimating that it should have been hers from the start.

Agnes – a new, embroidered handkerchief covering both her mouth and her nose – glances at the leech jar; but both surgeon and patient are staring at her now, expectant, and Agnes rises, still breathing through the scented cloth.

The sky is heavy with clouds, wide and billowing, like linen smocks hung out to dry. In the courtyard, crowded with chickens and ducks and stinking of animal dung, Cuckoo is striding back and forth, stamping, aiming kicks at the ground.

'Did you see what was embroidered on that handkerchief Agnes was holding? Did you see? A lion and a dragon; because you know – the queen has told me, or someone else did – you know that Margaret Erskine boasted about dreaming of a lion and a dragon when she was made pregnant by the old king; when she was pregnant with Moray? Now Agnes will be sister-in-law to the country's regent; she sees that her family has risen, and she waves her ugly dragon in our faces.'

Jane, standing just behind her on the stone steps to the tower, breathes quick, shallow breaths. Every time she thinks of the leeches plastered to Mary's skin, her stomach lurches.

Cuckoo has stopped talking; she looks up at her companion. 'Come on,' she says, holding out her hand. 'A walk to the water; no one will mind us going. They do not care if *we* escape; they only watch the queen.'

This is not entirely true, however; after only a few paces, they hear footsteps, and look over their shoulders to see Agnes's maidservant, her skirts flapping about her ankles and a scowl on her face as she follows them, keeping a short distance behind them.

'I didn't think you were afraid of blood,' Cuckoo says to Jane, ignoring the woman.

'It wasn't that. It was the sight of the leech; it was the way it swallowed.'

*Does Cuckoo relish this?*

'Yes, it looked very thirsty from where I stood. Still, it was a change; I haven't seen you like that before,' Cuckoo says.

'Don't get used to it.'

They look for cobwebs, to help Mary's fresh wounds scab over. At the water's edge, a woman is wrestling with a small sack, its contents moving. She is the same sunburnt woman who picked white camomile flowers in the kitchen garden, on the day Mary laughed and wished she could lay eggs as birds do. As Jane watches the woman, something drops from the sack she holds and scrambles to find its feet, before the woman picks it up by the scruff, shoving it back inside.

Jane calls out to the woman, who looks up, indifferent; she already knows who they are, and she does not care. At Jane's request, the woman holds out the bag, to let them see what's inside.

There are four kittens.

'You know in England, cats are buried in the walls of houses? Dried up and bricked in – an old superstition to keep the mice away,' Cuckoo says.

'You'd fare better by investing in a live cat than a dead one,' Jane replies, before she asks the woman, in Scots, whether they could have one of the four kittens for Mary.

Cuckoo, who guesses what Jane has said without need for translation, says, 'What would she want one for?'

'A plaything, until someone can fetch her dog,' Jane says.

'Cats aren't pets.'

'When the poet Thomas Wyatt was held in prison, they say it was a cat that saved him from starvation,' Jane says. 'The creature brought him a pigeon to eat each day. Perhaps our captive queen will have equal luck.'

The kittens are all different colours: ginger, tawny, tabby, black. Jane reaches inside the sack to stroke the black kitten. Beneath its velvet coat, she can feel its ribs and spine. She knows Mary will not want such a thin, unlucky creature.

'What will happen to the other three?' she asks the woman.

The woman merely points towards the deep centre of the loch.

Jane pretends to deliberate. She points to the fat, blue-eyed ginger, and to the black. 'I'll take both and let her decide.'

The woman shows her how to hold them by the scruff.

'Why two?' Cuckoo says in French behind her. 'She won't want that one.'

Jane shakes her head. When they are out of sight, she drops the black kitten by the edge of the trees. She nudges it forward with her foot.

'The Devil lurks in black cats,' Cuckoo says.

Jane does not say anything, but she smiles down at the cat.

'You never smile,' Cuckoo observes.

'Don't I?'

'Perhaps you do. But I never see it.'

Mary is in danger of drowning. Her women can see it. They understand better than the surgeon that not all Mary's ailments can be treated with leeches. In her various palaces, Mary's servants knew about her depression. It was never spoken of, but all felt it: the very air would feel greasy with her despair. In those times, her *jewelled ladies* would soothe and comfort her. Together they would gather her up – worn-out, threadbare – and gently hem her frayed edges. Now she is without them. She has lost a crown and her babies are dead. In recent days, Jane has wondered jealously if someone like Lady Seton would have a better chance than herself at healing Mary. Of helping her to resurface. But Seton is not here. And so Jane returns to her queen, armed only with a kitten. Like Mary, the creature knows how it feels when Death brushes the back of your neck, before fumbling his grip.

Mary has always liked animals: hawks, horses, caged birds, and the scampering dogs she kept about her at court, soft armfuls to be scooped up and carried about. When she first arrived in Scotland, she used to exercise every day: riding, hunting, falconry, golf, and in the evenings she and her *jewelled ladies* danced until their heels bled. Here in Lochleven Castle she has been locked up, stationary and sluggish, her heart never quickening. Mary now retreats into her past, remembering how she used to ride over rough ground and open fields without fear, passing hills of purple heather and overgrown meadows thick with cornflowers, the Scottish air cool and fresh as she searched for the perfect location to release her merlins. Merlins are smaller than most birds of prey, roughly the same size as a blackbird, but they are among the bravest. For falconry, merlins were – are – Mary's preferred choice. She remembers the exact weight and pressure her birds exerted when they returned to her gloved hand. Their soft white chins, their bright yellow talons, their huge eyes. She remembers watching her favourite merlin circling the air over a freshly ploughed field, chasing furrows and diving for some unfortunate wild creature or hopping bird. But there are no merlins and no horses at Lochleven Castle.

The ginger kitten is the perfect distraction, as Jane knew it would be. It stretches itself, padding across the satin quilt towards its new mistress. The leeches and the surgeon are gone; Jane wonders what the man has done with the vial of Mary's blood. Will he sell it? Or will he keep it, and trade on stories of today, bringing out the vial and holding it up to the light: *Look, I once touched the Scottish queen's thigh.* Either way, her blood is currency. Her touch is to anoint. When wisps of her hair come away on the brush, or stay on the pillow after she rises – this happens more often now – the bronze strands aren't swept away but are kept, gathered in handkerchiefs and tied in ribbons, ready to be enclosed in letters. Every thread is a form of payment, of favour, shed from the head that has borne two crowns (Scotland, France) and should, in all justice, bear a third: that of England. Three pieces of paper will not change that.

The kitten seems docile and content, and Mary reaches a yellowed hand towards it and whispers that she will call it Elizabeth, Liz or Lizzie for short, *named for my sweet cousin*. 'I have heard she has hair the same colour as this little cat's.'

Jane has a suspicion that Elizabeth is in fact a tomcat, but she does not say so.

It is just after dawn, and Jane is half-asleep when she finds she is alone in the bed. She looks up, and sees Mary at the window, partly concealed by the curtain, like a child playing hide-and-seek. Jane gets up, as she must, because a sovereign cannot be alone, even a sovereign who no longer has a throne, and she takes up her position behind Mary, standing a little to the side. She shivers in her underclothes, her feet bare – there is the crunch of dried herbs underfoot – and sees that Mary has wrapped the curtain around her. At least Jane knows she is warm. In the pale light, Mary's skin has reverted to its natural pallor. She stares out the window, and Jane is forced to stand on tiptoe to see over her queen's high shoulder. A murmuration of starlings swoops low over the tower. They resemble a great piece of moving cloth, forming shapes that they twist and wring out over the sky.

'I remember seeing this when I was a child,' Mary says, indicating the birds. Her voice is low. 'It was sunset. The horizon was red and pink stripes, and my governess said the starlings were dancing on the Devil's back. Dancing and clawing until he bled across the sky.'

Jane does not speak for a moment. Who can understand the

mind of a prince? Perhaps Mary is preoccupied with childhood memories: longing for that former innocence, for reassurance. An embrace. *Everything is fine. All is well.*

'The sound of their wingbeats. It's like *this*,' Jane says, and she puts her hands together as though in prayer, rubbing her fingers back and forth, and holds them close to Mary's ear, so that she can hear the dry whisper of their movement.

'Yes,' Mary says, 'like that.' She catches Jane's hand and, without turning around, puts it to her cheek. They stand there, quiet.

'I thought I knew grief; that I was better acquainted with it than most women,' Mary says.

Jane thinks of the bruised city women, wracked with poverty and abuse; she thinks of tavern-keepers' daughters rented out by the hour, bearing strangers' children and back at work by nightfall, their breasts wet with milk. She thinks of how her own father – a high-ranking servant – spent his days tending to the needs of powerful men, and his nights blackening his wife's eye. Jane thinks of Lady Huntly, forced to attend her husband's posthumous trial, his corpse propped up before Parliament; her son, John Gordon, beheaded for his father's crimes on Mary's orders; and later her daughter, Jean Gordon, abandoned and divorced by her husband, Bothwell, so that he could marry Mary a fortnight later: Mary, who had personally paid for Jean's wedding dress, made of finest cloth of silver.

But Jane does not serve Lady Huntly, or her daughter Jean.

'You know I watched my first husband die?' Mary continues. 'Francis was not what his father hoped him to be: he was stunted, and his male parts were deformed – I know this now. But I had spent my entire childhood learning how best to please him; how best to be his wife. How to make him love me. On my wedding day, I was the happiest woman in the world. I was at his bedside when he died, and at his father's only a year before him; I watched them both die in agony.'

Everyone in Christendom knows the story of how Henry II of France died. A splinter of wood pierced his eye during a joust; his wife, Catherine de' Medici, desperate to find a cure, ordered the palace surgeon to inflict the same injury on four wretched convicts, one after the other. The men all died, including the king; the stunted Francis inherited his crown, only to die shortly afterwards from an ear infection, howling like a baited dog.

As though she can hear her thoughts, Mary says, 'Jane, I feel . . . I feel like a rider thrown from her mount. Winded and blinded. I am rolling and dodging the blows of hooves I know will come.'

She looks frail; Jane is tempted to say, *Come back to bed*, and lead her by the hand, but this is the first time she has stood up since the surgeon's visit, and she worries that if Mary is forced to lie down again, she will never get up.

'I have been threatened before,' Mary says. 'If it seems that they are set on the path . . . that I am in danger . . . will you stay with me, Jane? To dance on the Devil's back?'

What can Jane say, but *yes*.


Mary's belly aches; her women do not know if this is common for women who have miscarried (and if they did know, they would not say). By early evening she is clutching her stomach, and her women look at each other and pray that her womb is empty, expunged. Lizzie The Cat is coaxed out from under the bed, and to distract herself from her bellyache Mary lifts each paw to inspect, pressing the pink pads to see the claws revealed, like tiny needles. The ginger fur seems to have darkened overnight to fox colour.

Cuckoo is subdued, inattentive in her work, her face drawn; Jane tries to get her alone, although it is difficult with Agnes, who surveys them in her swollen glory, still apt to shush them if they break into hurried French. By the entrance to the tiny chapel, Jane pulls Cuckoo aside.

'It's nothing, nothing, Jane,' she says. She puts her hands to her lips, as though they're already trembling with the weight of the lie. 'My brother, Toussaint; he was a valet at Holyrood. He came across the Channel with me when Mary returned. He is my only family in this miserable country, and I don't know what has happened to him. He might be dead, or he might be on a boat to Calais, leaving me behind.'

Jane assures her that they will soon get word; that she is sure that Cuckoo's brother will be prospering in Edinburgh. Even as she speaks words of comfort, Jane feels secretly relieved; she had thought Cuckoo was in possession of some secret knowledge about Mary's health, or of her son, James. *Am I so hard-hearted?* Jane isn't sure. *Have I learnt to care less, or more?*

'Could you send a letter to him? Smuggle it out somehow?'

Cuckoo glares at her, and Jane remembers, too late, that Cuckoo is illiterate. After all, why would a chambermaid need to read or write? Hers is a visual language, formed of embroidered symbols, of sigils and coats of arms and colours. White for purity, black silk for mourning. Why can Jane read the written word, and Cuckoo cannot? Perhaps it is the difference in their upbringings: in Scotland, the new church has brought with it an emphasis on education, mostly for boys but for girls, too. And Jane was an only child, with a mother who quietly encouraged her, while Cuckoo was raised alongside an older brother, who shouldered the burden of self-improvement and penning letters home to their parents. But both women were raised to be chambermaids. The real difference between the two can be seen in Cuckoo's dogged avoidance of speaking Scots, and Jane's absolute determination to learn French. Jane arrived at court not long after the birth of Prince James. In this febrile atmosphere she kept her head down. When she heard that both her parents had died of a fever, she did not do or say anything which might attract attention. Instead of weeping for her mother, she immersed herself in the queen's language. Abandoned the speech of her childhood. At night she lay awake, mouthing new words to herself. *Le chien, le chat, jaune, vert.* Dog, cat, yellow, green. It was a kind of second infancy. A reinvention of self. By day she would sneak glances at the books and scraps of poetry lying scattered across Mary's rooms. Sometimes she would steal away to the kitchens, just to listen to the French cooks barking out instructions.

'We will have to work on your accent,' one of them joked, sometime after she began to converse with them. She showed no embarrassment at their teasing. She was young and ambitious and had a purpose. Her parents' death opened a pit inside her, and she filled it whole with Mary.

A few months later, Jane was standing for the first time on the shore of Lochleven Castle.

At dusk, the women hear the beginnings of a party down in the courtyard. Someone plays a fiddle, someone else a whistle. A drum rolls, and there is singing, and the sounds of squeals and raucous laughter, as though someone has just told a dirty joke. The party spills out into the gardens, and the scene is lit by great bonfires, and the smell of roasting meat wafts across the tiny island. The singing grows louder, and the music faster, and as the sky darkens the women can only see the black outlines of dancing bodies moving before the flames, like shadows.

Agnes slips from the room and does not return, leaving behind her maidservant: the girl who followed Jane and Cuckoo down to the water's edge. She looks sulky.

Cannons are wheeled out and fired into the night, the sounds reverberating through the castle walls and scattering the swans and geese on the water. There are cheers and whoops after each cannon is fired. The music swells and swells. The atmosphere seems frenzied. Among the crowd are servants dancing with abandon, leaping over the smaller fires. All are convinced of the importance of this moment, believing – as so many have before, and will again – that *this* day, *this* time is uniquely momentous. In dark corners of the kitchen garden and down by the water's edge there are couples rutting as though the world has ended and another is dawning. In a sense, it is.

Mary has not said anything since those first words of song sounded at the bottom of the tower. Now she looks at the maidservant, and she says, 'What are they celebrating?'

'Don't you know? Really?' the girl says, and in her corner, Cuckoo hisses softly at the insolence. The girl wags her finger. 'The laird and Lady Agnes are celebrating because King James has been crowned in Stirling, and all of Scotland is making merry. We have a king and your power is abolished; you can't avenge yourself now on the laird, or my ladies, or the Earl of Moray, or Lord Lindsay, my lady's brother-in-law. You cannot touch them.'

Mary has dropped to her knees, her head in her hands.

'We are rejoicing, and you cannot prevent it,' the girl says, and she lifts her chin and goes to the door; she is eager to join the party, anyone can see, and she scowls as if it is Mary, and not Agnes, who has ordered her to stay put.

'Jesus, Jesus . . . What, am I dead already?' Mary wails, dragging her fingers down her face. 'He will avenge me on them, you will see,' she shouts, and the girl shakes her head, as though pitying, and turns away.

Mary is clawing at her face and hair; she begins to shriek, rocking from side to side, and Cuckoo sinks to the ground beside her. Cuckoo is hysterical in the face of Mary's misery, weeping and shouting, and Jane goes to their side, but Mary is already standing. She runs to the window and throws it open, leaning forward, looking down at the flickering light of the bonfires, half-hidden by trees. The singing goes on; they have not heard the sounds of misery yet.

Mary breathes in the night air, she throws back her head, and out of her mouth comes a sound she has never made before. It is unearthly— – it is another woman's voice, it is many women's voices; a cry of pain, betrayal, a shout of anger. Behind her, Cuckoo is screaming, wailing, and Jane, too, has begun to scream: for their freedom, for their vanished countries. Mary's voice grows louder, one long note that trembles and rises; she is burning, she is a woman on the rack, she is a woman in labour, she is a queen who has lost her crown, she is a witch. She is a faceless woman silhouetted in a castle window, far above the flames.

The note dies; the three women fall silent. The singing outside has stopped, and when Mary looks down, she thinks she sees a crowd of pale faces all lit by flames and staring up at her, as though the tower is her pyre.

Days later. Mary's sister-in-law visits. Her name is also Agnes, although everyone calls her Anna. She is close to thirty years old, elegant and sleek, carefully dressed. Each item of clothing is sober in colour but beautifully made; Jane is sure the hems alone would betray their expense. A thick rope of pearls is knotted about Anna's neck, looping down to her breastbone; a flash of white, like a pine marten's bib. She is a staunch Protestant, like her husband the Earl of Moray, but she still wears a wedding band. Their union was reportedly a love match, and the wedding celebrations were lavish, the Edinburgh skies lit up with fireworks funded by Mary's royal coffers.

In the cold month of February this year, Anna miscarried a child. She cries when she sees Mary in her tower rooms, kneeling before her and pressing Mary's hands to her own heart, until the two women are clutching at each other. They speak of their pain, and of their children: both the living and the dead.

'They are buried by the water's edge,' Mary says. 'My two boys.'

Jane looks up.

Anna is shaking her head, twisting the pearls in her hands, *click click*. 'You remember my boy, my little boy who died.' She and her husband lost their first and only son during childbirth, three or four years ago. 'I call him William in my mind, for my father,' she says.

'William.' Mary squeezes her friend's hand. 'And you have your little Elizabeth. I am sure she is already as clever and lovely as her mother.' She pauses. Anna waits for her to speak, patient, her head tilted to one side. Mary swallows. 'My dear, I . . . Have you heard any news of Lady Seton?'

Jane looks up just in time to catch Cuckoo's eye. For once they are united in thought: *Why are we not enough?*

Anna seems to be thinking along the same lines because she says, her voice mild, 'Would you rather Lady Seton had come here instead of me?'

'No. No, of course not,' Mary says smoothly. She leans forward to kiss Anna on the cheek. 'I am so happy you have come.'

Anna is also here to see Margaret Erskine; Jane doubts there is a woman in Scotland with a less enviable mother-in-law.

In the evening a formal dinner is held, and Mary is allowed to attend. She leaves her tower rooms arm in arm with Anna, leaning on her for support, and for a show of good faith. The older woman is her jailor tonight, but a sympathetic one. Agnes trails in their wake, hands on stomach, waddling bow-legged, her feet wide apart as though to emphasise how great her belly is becoming.

'What do you think of her?' Cuckoo says the moment they are gone.

'Nice necklace,' Jane says.

'It's not nearly as fine as Mary's. She has a string of black pearls the size and colour of Muscat grapes.'

'I think she's here to spy,' Jane says, pouring herself a cup of wine. 'I think Moray sent his wife here to watch and report back on his sister's mood.'

Cuckoo rolls onto her stomach and dangles a bit of wool above Lizzie The Cat's head, pulling it up and up until the creature is forced to bounce on its hind legs. Jane smiles to herself, remembering Cuckoo peering into the sack of kittens by the edge of the loch, her nose wrinkled. *Cats aren't pets.*

'If that's true, what you say about Anna spying on us, then I'm sure Mary has guessed the same.'

'Has she? I fear she's too trusting,' Jane says. 'It's because she had such a happy childhood. They say Elizabeth doesn't trust anyone, because her childhood was so wretched. Could you ever trust anyone again, if your father ordered your mother's head chopped off?'

'I saw her ghost,' Cuckoo says. 'Anne Boleyn's. At the Château de Blois. Before Anne was queen she was raised at the French court, an attendant to the queen. She was there at the same time as Leonardo da Vinci, you know. I turned a corner and saw them both together, examining a painting on the wall.'

Jane smiles. 'Two ghosts for the price of one. Tell me: if they were staring up at a painting, does that mean you only saw the backs of their heads?'

Cuckoo will not be discouraged. 'She had long dark hair, worn loose to her waist and shining like a crow's wing. Nothing like her daughter's. Then she seemed to turn her head as though she heard me, and they both vanished.'

Anna came bearing gifts: sweet nuts, and dried plums and pears. The choice is thoughtful, personal; it was Mary's mother, Marie de Guise, who first introduced both fruits to Scotland, importing them from her estate in France. The women now crunch on the almonds; Cuckoo grinds them into a grainy pulp in her mouth, imagining them to be marchpane. She is annoyed that Jane made fun of her ghost story. *She believes she is better than me*, Cuckoo thinks. *As though she has never exaggerated before.*

When she has drained her wine, Jane laces her fingers together. She remembers clapping games from her childhood: the easy patterns of movement lulling you into complacency – hands together hands across hands together – before a sudden change in direction.

'Were they really boys?' she says, lightly, not raising her head. 'The babies, I mean. Because I didn't see – when Mary said it, before . . . I didn't know. Were they?'

'Does it matter now?' Cuckoo says. She is almost defiant.

'No,' Jane says. 'No, I suppose it does not.'

*Crack.*

In her apartments, Margaret Erskine cracks her fifty-year-old bones and watches Anna, her daughter-in-law, flinch at the sound. Anna is the wife of Margaret's bastard son, the Earl of Moray. Anna is both attractive and pious, and Moray is fond of his wife; Margaret knows this. She has read some of their love letters. The pages fell into her lap by way of gold coins and a loyal servant. In fact, it is precisely Moray's fondness for his wife that makes it so very difficult for his mother to like Anna at all.

'I suppose you have already prepared a report of Mary Stuart's health? To give to my son?'

Margaret always refers to Moray as 'my son' when she is with Anna, and never 'your husband'. A less intelligent woman than Anna would have risen to this by now. But Anna only smiles mildly and puts a hand to the heavy rope of pearls around her neck. She does not answer Margaret's question. Instead she says, 'You know that my lady Mary was with me, when my sweet son – your grandson – was born, may he rest in peace. In her present sorrow, I am only too happy now to repay the many kindnesses she has shown me.'

'Come on, girl, this isn't some hearing before Parliament. You and I are on the same side,' Margaret says – and she means it. She does not like Moray's wife, but she likes his royal half-sister even less. Anna only shifts in her chair, relaxing her posture and smiling that mild smile. She has large, almost bulbous eyes. They are a similar colour, Margaret realises with a start, to her own. She does not know how she never saw it before. And Anna's hair: a faded chestnut. Perhaps – surely that is the same colour Moray remembers when he thinks of the Margaret of his childhood? Her hair began to fade and grey almost the moment the king cast her out of his bed and married that Frenchwoman who bore him nothing but a daughter: *Mary*.

Margaret's suspicion that her favourite son chose a wife who resembles his mother does not disgust or disconcert her. It pleases her.

There is a knock on the door. It is Margaret's youngest son, George Douglas; she looks at him now and swells with the sight of her own beauty reflected at her in the face of her tall, handsome child, now a young man. In his presence she herself feels young again. He bows, and the two women look up and smile at him.

'I'll be there shortly, George,' Margaret Erskine says, and watches him bow again and shut the door behind him. She turns back to her daughter-in-law. 'What lovely eyes you have, Anna,' she says. 'I never noticed them before now.' She takes a sip of wine and swallows – she has been having difficulty swallowing recently. She resembles a vulture gulping down a lump of flesh, her eyes bright and wet and staring as she feels the liquid finally slide down her gullet. She does not know that hidden somewhere under her layers of satin and lawn, beneath the skin and the fat, lies the seed of the cancer in her stomach, no bigger now than an apple pip. When she dies in five years' time, the tumour will have blossomed and bulged to the size of a balled-up winding sheet.

★

It is mid-August, the sky a turquoise blue and cloudless, and Jane is proved right about the elegant Anna and her spywork. The Earl of Moray arrives at Lochleven, armed with his wife's gossip about his half-sister; he knows about how frail her miscarriage has left her, about her easy tears and ill-health. He is dressed sumptuously in lace and dark velvets with a blue-black sheen, like the wings of a magpie. His chest is puffed up; he has all the appearance of a man very well pleased with himself. His eyes – Jane, standing to one side in the tower rooms, hasn't decided if they are too close together or too far apart – are separated by the long Stuart nose, his father's nose, and he wears this inheritance with pride.

His person is tall, like his sister Mary; their heads brush the ceiling, and the room seems too small for them both. It is as though they are of another species: those Greek heroes, half mortal and half god; dazzling, and belonging nowhere. Food is brought to the rooms, and Jane notices the cook's skills seem to have improved miraculously in time for Moray's visit. There is fresh lemon salad dressed with rose vinegar and served with imported olives and capers. There is pink Scottish salmon fried in butter and claret, topped with battered parsley, and followed by cheesecakes, fresh blackberries, sugared flowers, and prunes soaked in red wine and spices and encased in decorated pastry.

Moray examines the little chapel built for Mary, and he tells her how fortunate she is, how indulged. As though she is not a sovereign queen. Then again, in his eyes, and in the eyes of the other lords, she is not. She is diminished. A former queen only.

'I will speak plain with you,' he says.

'Must you?' she says, in that teasing, buttery voice, her accent stronger than usual; she is trying to charm him, soothe him. Her half-brother ignores it.

'This state you find yourself in, it is your own making,' he says.

'I thought it was Lindsay's.'

*She gives Lindsay too much credit*, Jane thinks. He has all the rage of a baited bear – but who owns the dogs? Who holds the whip?

'Your match with Darnley . . . you'll remember I was against him from the start? A worse match could not have been found; Queen Elizabeth agrees. You were bewitched by him, it is the only explanation. By God, he had the loosest morals at court. That cock. That weak-hearted man. But even he appears saint-like compared to your third choice. The very man accused of murdering Darnley. Your stupidity staggers me, sister.' Moray's tongue is stained with blackberry juice.

Mary's eyes have not left her brother's; a simple trick she often uses, to make you feel like you are the only person in the room. It's a skill she learnt as a child, watching Diane de Poitiers, the golden-haired *maîtresse-en-titre,* the royal mistress to King Henry II.

'Bothwell used me ill, I'll admit, brother. I have been unlucky in marriage. Perhaps if I had been permitted to marry a foreign prince . . . But Elizabeth blocked me at every turn; there was never a suitor to her liking except for her own favourite, that horsekeeper. You remember when she offered him up to me, like a tray of sweetmeats? As though she had not already taken a bite. What a trio we might have made. I am told they call each other Bess and Robin but he can never have her; she has sworn to remain unmarried.'

'Perhaps that would have been a better course for you, sister, given the circumstances,' Moray says, looking anywhere but at his sister.

'You forget I bore Scotland a son.'

He, impatient, aware she has led him away from his point, says, 'We were talking of your own defects, not of Elizabeth's.'

'I am sure in your eyes I have many defects, my lord.'

'In all of Scotland's eyes. In their eyes my own sister is branded an accomplice in the murder of Darnley, and is a whore for Bothwell.' He leans in. 'You know what they say, don't you? That you are a liar. That you cannot be trusted. That your conduct is as insincere as if you were treading the boards in some play; as though Scotland were your own personal theatre.'

Jane watches him wet his lips, as though for the briefest moment he allows himself to imagine Mary dressed in a man's clothes, her long legs in hose.

'You have done no good for your country,' he says. 'You have brought shame and embarrassment on us. How can we hold up our heads? *You* have done this to us.' He jabs a finger at Mary. 'The moment you chose Darnley –'

'You disliked him for usurping you; for your diminished power. A woman cannot marry her own brother, even if he is only half.'

They glare at one another. Jane thinks they both know the other's weaknesses: they are truly siblings in this way. He knows she craves approval, that she desires above everything to appear sincere; she is always posing, but to be thought of as posing is mortifying to her. She is like an actor who cannot bear an audience to perceive his craft: she would prefer it to seem natural, unforced. Unstudied. And Mary knows her brother is bitter, that he craves the power of which his illegitimacy robbed him. Jane has heard women's whispers: when Moray met his sister as an adult – dressed in white silks and diamonds, a widow of France – he felt a lurch of lust. What person did not – does not? She is like nothing they have ever seen.

'Why do you keep her from me?' Mary says suddenly.

'Who?'

'You know who. Lady Seton.'

'Ah.'

'I know she wants to join me. I know she will have petitioned you. Do you deny her just to spite me?'

Moray shifts in his chair and sighs loudly, peevish. 'You have greater problems than an absent lady-in-waiting. I heard Lindsay threatened to have your throat cut.'

'To drown me, too, don't forget,' Mary says; she is wary now.

'I hear he has much planned. I hear he has his heart set on burning you. He wants you destroyed—either your body or your wits. You feel trapped here, I know. But Lindsay and his supporters would rob you of every comfort befitting your rank. There would be no indulgences; no altar for you to kneel at. Your clothes, your jewels, he would ensure they went to the highest bidder. Half the court would be wearing your silks and furs on their backs. I could act on your behalf, my lady. As regent, I would protect your interests as family alone can. Only give me your blessing. Send your servants away. I would discuss the matters of kings and queens.'

'You are not a king, brother; my son is.'

'Of course. But as regent, would it not be my role to think as kings do, to carry out those tasks that James would desire were he yet a man? To guard and protect his kingdom?'

Mary leans forward and grasps both her brother's hands with her own, her eyes still on his. 'I think of my son every day. It is to be in purgatory, with no news of him; unable to hear from him, to speak to him. I am in darkness. It is like we are dead to one another.'

Jane glances at Moray, and wonders if he is thinking: *What purgatory is that? Which Bible verse speaks of purgatory?*

He extricates his hands from his sister's hold; he does so delicately, finger by finger. 'When I am regent, you will see him. You will see your son.'

Mary nods, and gestures to her women. *Leave us.*

Moray is still talking after midnight, still berating his half-sister for her many failings; it seems he has waited for this moment for years. The next day is the same. One moment he is a kindly older brother, their father's son, the next he tells her that she has shamed her country, she has brought a plague on Scotland; she is its cancer, and he, Moray, is the only cure. He berates her until she weeps, and then he switches tack again, telling her she should smile. *I am here now*, he says. When he finally leaves her side, she is exhausted, and he is exhausted, although he would not admit it. But he is also grimly satisfied; he has her blessing. He will be Scotland's new regent.

Parliament convenes and confirms Moray's appointment as regent. The rustling of paper, the scuff of boots. The rebel lords declare Mary's abdication 'lawful and perfect' and vindicate themselves in a single stroke, stressing that Mary was 'privy and part of' her husband Darnley's murder. The men shake hands afterwards and are well pleased with themselves.

This is not all. A new proposal is drafted.

*In no time coming should any woman be admitted to the public authority of the realm.*

Never again do these men want to scrape and bow to a female ruler. They try to enshrine this into law, but it is left as a draft proposal only. Not because of any lingering respect for their own queen-that-was. Moray is too desperate to please England's Elizabeth Tudor to ever legalise such misogyny.

There are bay leaves, strewn across the rushes and crushed underfoot. There are herbs and dried flowers, and a sprig of lavender nestled in the soft gully between Mary's breasts. There are dried orange slices and cloves, pomanders made of silver. There are handkerchiefs soaked in borrowed perfume, and parcels of dried rose petals wrapped in cloth. The room is a perfumery, yet all these scents cannot mask the reek beneath: all three women have their monthly blood, all at the same time. All are irritable, from the squeezing pains in their bellies and the fish-stench of the room, of each other, of themselves. The stink of clotted blood between thighs is in addition to the other, usual smells: the sour whiff of the piss pot, bad breath, oily unwashed hair, and the close stale fug of a shared prison cell. Each night they stew in yesterday's breath and soiled sheets. Dark globules of flesh like pomegranate seeds. When Mary wakes, Jane must see to washing her, to wiping away the night's stains, before tending to herself, scraps of fabric rolled up and stuffed inside her. But – and perhaps she is imagining things – Jane feels something close to kinship with her now, knowing that they bleed and ache together; she cannot help thinking that her courses now match those of a queen's. Mary is a Stuart, but she is also a woman, and more so now, to Jane, than she ever was when she was pregnant, her stomach that perfect round curve. There is no finest cloth and satin girdle for her courses now. In the uneasy days and weeks after Mary's abdication, Margaret Erskine digs in her heels, determined to humiliate her still.

For Mary, the return of her courses – the first since her miscarriage – is a sharp pain. She longs to disappear, to burrow away into darkness like a small, trembling animal; a rabbit with quivering body and flitting heartbeat, fleeing from the hunt. Perhaps her women know this, perhaps they don't, but they insist on a walk about the gardens; they placate Agnes, they agree to additional guards. Anything to leave these fetid rooms and breathe fresh air.

In the gardens, Jane walks just behind Mary, to her left. A breeze lifts and flirts with the warm summer air, teasing the women's loose wisps of hair and kissing their skin. Mary's scent is blown about; Jane believes she would know it anywhere. She could be blind, and she would still be able to identify the smell of Mary's body, the bitter taste of her illness, the scent of her sweat and her hair.

There are insects buzzing everywhere, the swarming clouds of midges; they, too, seem to know Mary's scent, because they trail her like a cloak.

Jane looks out across the water, to Kinross, to the faint outlines of the laird's stables, the horses he keeps inland. To the right of Kinross are the Orwell Standing Stones, great ancient monuments, each of the stones standing erect at over three yards tall. No one knows what they are for; perhaps for witchcraft, perhaps to mark a god's grave. In the trees you can see glimpses of russet-red squirrels. By the water's edge are frogs and brown otters trying to warm themselves. The clouds are low and grey today, and below the sky the loch is silvery, with a filmy, pale sheen on its surface, like seafoam. When Jane was a child, she was told she had the eyes of a selkie: dark, shining brown. Selkies are shapeshifters. They feel the pull of the sea so strongly that they will don their sealskin coats and leave behind forever their husbands and lovers and children, just to answer its call. Jane has never felt that pull to the water, the yank on your ribs tugging you out towards the coastline. But she can sympathise with a selkie's selfishness. The desire to leave all obligations behind; to put on a new skin and disappear from view, only to reappear, reborn.

Night, just before dawn. Jane hears whispers outside the door. A woman's voice, low and lilting and accented; it sounds like money. It is not Agnes. It is not Margaret Erskine.

Jane hears the creak of the door, and she opens her eyes.

A woman is standing before the bed, dressed in a travelling cloak, the stub of a candle illuminating her face, the light winking off the gold and enamel jewels at her throat. For a moment, Jane forgets that the real Mary is lying asleep in the bed beside her; here is her double, from her man's height to her style of dress and her auburn hair. But the woman steps closer, and Jane sees it is not Mary after all.

Lady Seton is tall, if not taller than the queen herself. On Mary, the stature is utterly natural: a body fit for a royal person. A marker of God's favour. On Seton, however, the height seems ill-fitting. Her shoulders are hunched, as though she has spent her entire life stooping. Jane imagines her as a lanky child, bending awkwardly to speak to friends, one leg bent beneath her skirts in a kind of curtsy. Perhaps this is why she has an air of lopsidedness. Surrounded by diminutive companions; how they must have teased her. And how Seton must have taken comfort in Mary, in that royal body so like her own, and one which moves through crowds with such grace. A body fit to rule. Jane has heard the two women would sometimes dress as men, binding their breasts and masquerading as gentlemen in Edinburgh's streets, just because they could.

Jane has sat in the same rooms as Seton before; but while she, Jane, was invisible, a chamberer with lowered eyes, Seton was Mary's particular friend, one of her *jewelled ladies* and a companion since they were both barely five years old. She is known to be serious in nature, pious and loyal. Her eyes are deep-set, surrounded by shadow. She looks tired; she has ridden all day from her brother's ancestral seat a few miles from Edinburgh. Both she and her brother Lord Seton are supporters of Mary, and she has been petitioning to join Mary's side ever since the latter arrived at Lochleven Castle; now, and only after Mary's abdication, has she been permitted. Here at last, Seton stares down at the bed, her gaze travelling over Mary's sleeping form, the white hands clasping Jane's waist.

The candlestick is lowered. Jane isn't sure if Seton recognises her. The women meet each other's gaze; Seton steps forward, gesturing first at the bed, and then at herself. There are jewels on her fingers, precious stones. She seems to be asking to take Jane's place.

Jane shakes her head, the smallest movement, glancing from Seton to Mary, and back. *It would wake her.*

Seton stares at her for a moment. *Move,* she mouths.

Again, Jane shakes her head. Her pulse jumps in her neck.

There are parcels under Seton's arms; they are bulky, wrapped in cloth, and seem too heavy in her arms.

She drops them.

The parcels land on the floor with thumps, clanks – God knows what is in them.

'Seton?' Mary is awake. Her voice is thin and strained. 'Seton, am I dreaming?'

Seton has dropped into a curtsy, but Mary is already standing up on the mattress, she is jumping off the bed, she is running to her, her arms around her friend's neck, and Jane is still on the bed, unsure whether to stand up, or to leave, or to roll over and face the wall.

'Seton, Seton,' Mary says, rocking where she stands; she is crying, both women are crying, they are thanking their God, and it is almost as though Mary has been alone all this while.

# *Winter*

The linen is closely woven, but through the cream-coloured fabric Mary can still see the blurred shapes of her women around her. The indistinct movements of their hands, their dark dresses silhouetted before the pale morning sunshine; she can see them all if she squints between the gaps in the weave. She is enveloped in folds of cloth, in the scent of her own night-time body. Someone is tugging at her sleeve, and obediently she raises her arms above her head, and the same someone reaches up and fiddles with the cuffs before sliding the sleeves up over her hands, and Mary thinks it must be Seton beside her; she is the only one tall enough to reach.

More fabric is pulled over her head, and now Mary can see the black embroidery thread, the undersides of the marigolds sewn into her smock. On this side of the fabric, the seamstress tidied her stitches, concealing error, tying off knots, perhaps forgetting the wearer would become so intimate with the interior, the mirrored, uneven flowers now pressed against her eyes: petals in lieu of Charon's obol. These are the only flowers Mary has seen in weeks. Winter has come to the castle. There is a pervading smell of damp. Outside, the lush greens are gone, replaced by grey skies and endless sheets of Scottish rain. In the mornings the grass and remaining leaves are laced with frost.

Mary stands naked in the middle of her prison room. A fire is already lit but she still feels the cold, her flesh goose-pimpled, the hairs on her arms and legs standing up. She ducks her head, sniffing at the dark hair at her armpit. She puts her hand to her stomach, to the silvery markings where the skin has stretched; she has gained weight in her imprisonment, which she finds strange: she has never felt emptier, like a pumpkin scooped clean of its flesh. She is hollowed out by grief. To her right, Seton tosses last night's smock to Jane, who catches it and begins to fold, eyes down. Cuckoo has the fresh smock ready, handing it to Seton, who gathers it up to drop it over Mary's neck; each movement is choreographed when dressing a queen, like a dance. The dancers themselves have changed places since Seton's arrival – in the summer months, it was Jane who rose on tiptoe and helped Mary into her smock, but now Seton leads the dance, and Jane and Cuckoo have had to learn new parts. Among them, only Agnes – standing in the corner of the room, huffing and puffing and swollen like an overripe melon – does not seem to know the steps.

Once again Mary is enveloped in fine linen, and all around her is the rustling of taffeta and satin as her outer clothes are readied. She stands in her new smock scented with dried lavender, expectant, her arms outstretched horizontally, and the women converge around her, lacing her into whalebone, pulling stockings over her bare feet (she hears the scratch cf her skin, the hard soles of her feet roughened from years of dancing at royal courts, of smiling widely through pains and blisters). She steps into her petticoat, into cambric, into the bell-shaped farthingale that holds up the weight of her dress, the black and white satin doublet: new clothes, some sent by her half-brother, Moray, two months after he was made regent. To humble her, he chose English cloth, which is not as fine as the foreign-made materials she is used to. The linens were woven locally; the loch's soft water is perfect for soaking flax. Moray still believes these packages he sends to be a grand gesture, a mark of his generosity, even as he sells off his sister's own priceless jewellery without her consent. Even as he keeps her from her firstborn child.

Mary misses her son. Since the miscarriage, she has thought more of his birth: the immediate relief of it, and the joy in his health, in his sex; she had prayed for a son, both for her country, and also as revenge – to show the lords, to show her husband Darnley. In those first moments after James was handed to her, Mary remembers looking down into his perfect, wrinkled face and thinking, *Your father will be jealous of you his entire life*. The future king Darnley could never be. How hard Darnley had worked, to kill his own son before he was even born. And how hard Mary had worked in turn to keep her son alive. She remembers how, when her husband and the other lords stormed the palace apartments to kill her servant David Rizzio, Darnley had pinioned her, her arms behind her back as another man pushed a pistol to her pregnant belly. She remembers how, when they rode to Dunbar Castle at a gallop, she had vomited, and begged her husband to slow down, but he had laughed, and forced the horses on, and told her that it didn't matter if she miscarried: *We can always make another*. She had vomited again, and wiped her mouth, and she did not give in.

Mary lifts a hand to pull at the ruff at her neck, to loosen it at the front of her throat; but Seton has already caught her hand, she is sliding gleaming rings onto her fingers: the same rings Seton had herself worn on arrival at Lochleven. Jane holds Mary's elbow to support her as she steps into shoes made of soft leather, before kneeling to lace them for her. Jane's movements are stiff; she has slept poorly since her ousting from Mary's bed. Cuckoo snores when she has too much wine, which is often now.

When she is dressed, Mary sits before the fire and Seton begins to work an ivory comb through her hair, and this, too, is a familiar dance: Seton knows, from years of experience, how Mary likes her hair dressed; she knows when to press the comb's teeth against her scalp, and when to be gentle; she knows how Mary winces if the soft hair around her ears is tugged too tightly. 'My lady,' Seton calls her in company, but every time she does Mary gives her a look, a smile, which suggests to the others that Seton is less deferential in private. In public, their communication seems almost telepathic; their looks and glances speak eloquently of shared jokes, shared grief, shared history. Seton's forename is also Mary, but she has not been called that name in years. There is no space for another Mary.

In the corner of the room, Jane watches. She watches Seton's careful touches, and the way Mary shuts her eyes. The exposed nape of her neck, her loose hair piled up on her head and pinned, piece by piece. Last night Seton caught Mary's eye and gestured silently to her across the supper table. *There's something stuck in your teeth.*

Neither Jane nor Cuckoo would have ever dared say anything.

Jane thinks with bitterness of the intimacy – friendship, even – she had begun to imagine she shared with Mary, before Seton arrived. 'Saint Seton,' as Mary affectionately calls her. Jane has no nickname. She is only ever Jane.

Mary's eyes are bruised with fatigue; she lets her head loll back in Seton's hands, as she did once when she first arrived at the castle, and Jane cupped her head as she drank.

'Jane.'

Mary holds out her hand, and Jane goes to her, kneeling by her side, a rare smile on her face; Mary calls for her by name less often now, since Seton arrived at Lochleven. Jane waits for Mary to speak, filled with anticipation.

'Would you fetch a dried pear?'

Shortly after Seton's arrival, Mary took another medicinal bath. While Seton and Cuckoo took Mary into the other room to dress, Jane was left alone, tasked with readying the bathtub for the servants to later carry away, removing the strips of linen that lined its sides. But when Seton returned to the room, searching for Mary's slippers, she found Jane had stripped to her smock and climbed in the water herself. Above the waterline, the wet fabric clung to her torso, translucent; Seton could see the pink-brown outline of her nipples.

Seton was disgusted. To take a bath, even in clean water, was to risk infection, and yet here was Jane, luxuriating in a bath milky-grey from another's body. She remembered then the presumptuous way Jane had lolled about in Mary's bed before she, Seton, had entered the room.

But a part of Seton was also jealous: of Jane, of the intimacy of lying in the still-warm water, the surface bobbing with dried rosemary leaves and skin flakes and short, stray hairs from Mary's body, dark and wiry. But worst of all, worse than any of this, is that Jane saw Seton looking at her body. Jane lay there, eyes shut, and Seton allowed herself to stare at her chest and her waist, and at the faint triangular shadow visible beneath the billowing cloth that floated over belly and thighs. When Seton's gaze returned to Jane's face, the dark eyes were open and watchful.

And so Seton stumbled out – she had always been clumsy – her heart pounding with two competing emotions: revulsion, and shame.

There was also a third sensation Seton had felt at the sight of Jane lying in the tub, an ache deep inside her – but she refused to acknowledge it. Not yet.

When Seton had left, Jane sank down beneath the water, submerging her mouth and nose and eyes. For the first time, she understood how a selkie must feel the first moment they dove beneath the waves, restored to their slippery, silver form. Jane had first climbed into the bath on a rare impulse; it was the sort of presumptuous act that Cuckoo might succumb to, not Jane; she often caught Cuckoo eating leftovers from Mary's plate, and drinking wine from her half-empty cup, and holding up Mary's dresses to her own body, for all to see. But kneeling beside Mary as she wallowed in the rose-scented water, Jane had begun to itch. Her skin prickled at the places where Mary's filth and birthing blood had stained her skin. She and Cuckoo had scrubbed themselves pink afterwards, but suddenly Jane was overwhelmed by the need to scratch, to cleanse herself. A kind of frenzy took over her. The bath would be an almost-baptism: a purification, a renewal. For a brief moment Jane had believed that bathing in used water would be more, and not less, purifying, because it was Mary who had bathed first, the holy oil of her coronation imbued into her skin; even though Jane had witnessed her defecating in a fireplace, seen her walking through a puddle of piss, seen her bloody incontinence. In Edinburgh, there had been men and women who lined the streets and rushed forward to touch Mary – her gloved hands, the hem of her dress – convinced that they would be healed, or granted good luck, just from their close proximity to the divine. Servants know better than most that royal bodies are exactly that: bodies. But there is still that part of Jane that thrills at Mary's hallowed touch.

Now, weeks later, Jane remembers and relives the moment Seton interrupted her bath. *Perhaps I was rude to stare back at her with such defiance,* Jane thinks. Perhaps that is why Seton seemed angry. But then Jane recalls how Seton looked at her: so unguarded, almost as if she hoped Jane would see her looking. The memory of it is too much for Jane to comprehend.

Mushrooms have sprung up in the untamed grass by the banks of the loch. Cuckoo presses down on one with her shoe, but it springs up again when she removes her weight, fleshy and buoyant. Mary, who would normally laugh, walks ahead, arm in arm with Seton as the others trail behind, looking out across the water to land, and shivering in the cold air. The women are allowed out once a day, and always supervised. Like the choreography of Mary's morning toilette, Seton's arrival has caused a shift: now she and Mary lead the way, followed by Agnes, and then finally by Jane and Cuckoo. These daily walks should be a relief, a chance to breathe fresh air, but Jane chafes against her place in the new order; she longs to run ahead, to slip her hand into the crook of Mary's elbow. *What was the point of my devotion to Mary, if everything returns to how it was before Lochleven?* Jane brushes this thought away. Seton's presence is still a novelty; she has news to share, fresh conversation. Soon, very soon, Mary will remember Jane.

The shadow from a tree dapples the skin at Mary's throat; shadows like the black pearls she once owned. By April, Elizabeth will have the necklace, won in a bidding war against Catherine de' Medici. If Mary knew this, she would be glad; she would rather her cousin wear it than that sour shopkeeper's daughter. She, Mary, will eventually write to Catherine, asking for her mother-in-law's help.

None will come.

Mary and Seton discuss the weeks before Mary was brought to Lochleven. They pick memories apart, dissecting the days, the weeks, the events of the past year. Seton's presence has restored some part of Mary to herself. In recent days, Mary has thought more of Bothwell, and of the first time he bedded her. He had kidnapped her. She remembers his rough hands knocking hers away, cupping her breasts, and she, like dry sand, shifting and retreating beneath his weight. She knows that many people – even her own women – do not believe what she has since said about that night, that he forced himself on her, because everyone knows she desired him for a brief time; and Bothwell knew it, too. He said, *You want this, you have wanted me for so many months*, and it was partly true. But not like this, she said, again and again. *Not like this, no, no.* When he pushed his mouth against hers – not to kiss, but to gag her – the scream was at the back of her throat, low, like the sounds made by the men and women who are burned alive. She does not know if she conceived the twins that day. Physicians preach that women must be in pleasure to conceive a child; but she, Mary, felt no pleasure, only detachment from her body. Take Mary's body, you take Scotland; that is what Bothwell knew, and Ruthven, too,    .

when he burst into her rooms drunk, here at Lochleven, as her women hid behind the damp tapestry.

Two armed guards walk behind the group of women, keeping their distance as though they are contagious. Mary pauses; she has stopped to look down at the shoreline. A dead fish is rotting there, green-grey and half-submerged in the shallow waters, flakes of its body slowly drifting loose. Flies gather on that part of the fish lying exposed to the open air. Behind, Jane thinks they are standing close to where the twins are buried, somewhere around here in the soft earth.

Mary turns her head. 'Jane, Cuckoo,' she says, and they both stand up straighter to hear her speak their names again. 'Do you remember that game we played? We asked what bird quality we would most like for ourselves. I remember I banned mention of flight; I believe I said it was too easy a choice.' Mary stares into the distance, watching pink-footed geese glide across the surface of the loch. 'I've changed my mind.'

Jane watches her: Mary's face pinched with longing, close to tears as she often is. *Have we always longed to fly?* Jane thinks. Did our ancestors stand, as we do now, and imagine soaring up over trees, sprouting feathers? Or is it a recent phenomenon, now that the world feels so uncertain, and so full of possibility? They say that Leonardo da Vinci – whose works hung on the palace walls in France where Mary grew up – drew out the plans for a flying machine before his death. *Who is to say it's impossible?*

This time feels restless, a time of plague, a time of change – they are standing on the precipice. The chinks of light have begun to show. In England, Elizabeth wears wide jewelled dresses, and the men – once broad-shouldered, with huge codpieces during her father's reign – have shrunk in size to accommodate her bulk, unmanned by a bastard redhead in her thirties. Men are smaller, and more unsure of themselves. Beyond her borders, Elizabeth keeps a string of dancing suitors jigging up and down to her own rhythm. If she can do this, if she can unman an entire country, who is to say we cannot find a means to fly? And who is to say that an unmade queen cannot be remade?

The air is oily, the clouds heavy-looking. Dark birds dart across the sky; all around the women is the chatter of starlings above their heads, and the clapping sound of swans beating their wings, poised to take flight, pulling away from the water, and the trilling of the garden birds in the trees, their tiny bodies more sound than flesh.

'So many birds. They are like the sirens of myth, calling me to the mainland. You will all have to bind me to this tree, as Odysseus's men did, when they tied him to the mast of his ship,' Mary says.

'If we didn't, would you follow them?' Jane says.

Mary glances at Agnes, who is listening closely; she turns back to Jane, and smiles at her, but does not answer. She walks on alone, red and gold lights in her hair beneath the winter sun. Flies circle about her, a floating black crown, and she waves one hand in the air, swatting at them.

When the others are ahead, Seton catches at Jane's wrist. Her voice is low and insistent. 'What did you mean by that? Are you trying to catch Mary out, in front of Agnes? Trying to suggest she'd like to escape, so that the Douglases might use her words against her?'

'Why would I do that?' Jane is wary; she already knows that this is not truly about her comment to Mary, made a moment ago, but instead about the unspoken tension that has existed between herself and Seton for weeks, ever since Jane bathed herself in Mary's used water.

'I don't know,' Seton says quickly. 'You have cared for her, you have kept her alive, and you have grown in her esteem, I see it; but in Scotland's eyes, she is no longer queen.' She raises her chin and looks down at Jane. 'Perhaps you have ambitions, and her abdication thwarted them; you would rather serve the Douglases, or curry favour now that the Earl of Moray is regent.'

Jane tries to pull away, but Seton twists her arm back and pulls her in close, the warmth of her breath between them.

'Perhaps, because you are not of our faith, you would rather serve Scotland than a French queen-that-was,' Seton says.

'This is a Protestant country. The queen does not hold my faith against me. Why should you? All my lady's court was Protestant except herself and those who'd travelled to Scotland with her. And you are wrong, she is not a French queen. She left France when she was a teenager. She is not French. She is a Scot.' Jane wriggles out of Seton's grip and walks backward; she realises she is panting, and puts her hands to her breast. 'I ask no thanks. A sick queen is a sick Scotland; I nurse her, and I nurse this country.'

Seton grasps at Jane's words and twists them, like a skinned rabbit turning in front of a fire. 'You nurse her only to return her to power, to raise yourself up; you think nothing of the woman, as I do. To escape now, as she is, would kill her.'

'Imprisonment will do the same.'

They stare at each other. Jane feels a wrenching sensation in her belly; she is overcome with heat, with what can only be hatred. Nothing else.

A swallow dives between them, a whirr of movement and red and black; it flies so close to their faces that they stop to look at it, turning their heads in unison to watch it land and bounce from branch to branch, flirting its tail.

Then Mary's voice, calling them both to her side, and instantly the women wheel about and walk towards it, their feet unbidden, as though it is the only voice in the world.

A Sunday. Mary kneels in the tiny chapel William Douglas created for her: a sop, a precaution in case she escapes and reclaims her throne, and seeks revenge on her captors. It is hardly a chapel, Mary thinks. Only a secluded corner of a room, just an altar where she may kneel. She can still smell the fish she and the other women ate last night. Mary rocks from side to side, trying to find a comfortable position, and dried stalks of lavender crunch beneath the weight of her knees, releasing their perfume. From the other room, she can hear the quiet conversation of her women. They know to leave her to her worship. She prays for them, and for her son. But she no longer prays to survive each night. Elizabeth Tudor promised the Scottish lords that she would wage war if they laid a finger on her fellow queen. She did this soon after Mary was captured, before the abdication. Only now does Mary know how she has been played by her bastard brother. How she has been cheated. No, she does not fear death, at least not today. Now the threat is a life spent in a jail; of time wasted. Her son, James, will have grown since she last saw him. She does not blame the child for the treachery of full-grown men. She misses him – and she misses her throne. She closes her eyes and imagines she is in her own oratory at Holyrood Palace. The room is full of light, and contains a large statue of the Madonna. The wooden ceiling is decorated with panels depicting saints, and a window looks down onto the west entrance of Holyrood Abbey – already more like a crumbling ruin in appearance, damaged during the English raids some twenty years ago. But the foundations stand, built in 1128 in the shadow of a volcanic mound. *Holyrood*. Named for the holy relic Saint Margaret brought to Scotland: a splintered fragment of the True Cross; the cross that bore Jesus's dying body. Mary has long admired Saint Margaret, the 'Pearl of Scotland'. Like Mary, she was a woman of two countries: a beautiful noblewoman born in Hungary to an exiled English prince. Like a princess in a fairy tale, Saint Margaret was shipwrecked on the shores of Scotland and married its king. When he was killed, she died days later of a broken heart. She was famous for her piety, for her loyalty to the Catholic Church. Under her influence, the mass was changed; it was no longer spoken in Scotland's many Gaelic dialects, but in Latin. Saint Margaret sought to unify Scotland this way, and she also wanted to heal the rift between Scotland and its sister England.

Hundreds of years later, when Mary was first pregnant, she had the exhumed head of Saint Margaret brought to her at Edinburgh Castle: a relic, to aid her during the dangers of childbirth. Before the pain came, before the Countess of Atholl cast her spells, Mary remembers staring into the hollow skull eyes of the once-beautiful Queen of Scotland, and praying that she would accomplish what Margaret could not: that she, Mary, would unite England and Scotland. A gift for her unborn son.

But perhaps the relic had been a morbid choice: she still remembers her maidservants' squeamishness. It is one thing to hear the rattle of bone inside a box, and another to see human remains up close: a dismembered head, the yellow teeth still in their sockets. Mary remembered its sunken, teak-brown presence during her miscarriage, here at Lochleven; she remembered, and in her birthing pains she saw the ghosts of her mother and Saint Margaret floating high above her. Neither looked at her with compassion, or moved their lips as though in prayer. Their faces were still and unmoving and as unseeing as the relic itself.

Mary, her own eyes still shut, feels the weight of her knees pressed against the rushes and the cool floorboards; she feels the warm wooden beads of the rosary in her hands. Ever since her miscarriage – or perhaps even before then – she has felt disconnected from her own body, somehow separate and lacking substance: vulnerable, almost liquid, like the viscous contents of a cracked eggshell. Here, kneeling at prayer, Mary feels solid once more. Dance and prayer: those are the two exercises that tether Mary to herself. Anyone else might think they are quite separate activities, utterly divorced from each other. But, if seen from the right perspective, what is dancing, except a form of worship?

Mary prays for her women: *Jane, Cuckoo, Seton.* Especially Seton, her dear childhood friend. They are not similar in character, despite outward appearances: their tallness, their French mothers, even their handwriting. Seton is protective and sensible and honest; in her there is none of that woman's guile spoken of by poets and preachers (that *monstrous regiment of men*). She is not flirtatious, as Mary and some of her other *jewelled ladies* are; a native of Virgo, Seton embodies that sign's innocence. She takes herself very seriously, and when her face is at rest it appears anxious. She was teased as a child and then as a young woman, perhaps too much, perhaps mercilessly; Mary now believes her friend took every one of those jokes or taunts very seriously indeed, and Mary regrets those times she herself laughed at her friend's expense. Friendship among women is not always a source of comfort. There is pain and petty grievance and jealousy. There are silences and estrangement, hurts and jibes and insults veiled as advice or humour. There is thoughtlessness. In a group, there is always one who is easier to tease than the others, the hen that is pecked raw by its flock. Like an older sibling, Mary worries. Seton is sensitive; perhaps too sensitive. Mary knows from experience that people are always afraid of that which is different – and Seton, a novice nun trapped in the near-six-foot-tall body of a fine lady, is certainly different. She is hunched and clumsy, ill at ease in her body. In fact, Mary can only think of a few times where she has seen Seton hold herself with confidence – all on the streets of Edinburgh, when they were masquerading as men.

In men's clothes, Seton walked the streets tall, straight-backed, with a lolloping, easy grace, like a greyhound: lithe and long-limbed. Mary did not feel the same; she liked the protection of her wide skirts, the way they forced others to part before her, to make space. And she liked the way her body looked in dresses: the nip at her waist, the whalebone bodice supporting her breasts. While she felt exposed, even vulnerable in men's clothing, she saw that her friend felt powerful. Seton's face was luminous; there was nothing wanton or sinful in her expression, as priests might imagine there to be. She was alive and lit within herself, tethered to her body as Mary was when she danced. It was Seton's own strange act of worship. In her breeches and grey doublet, she was a cloudwalker. She was armour-clad and winking bright beneath a battle-day sun. She was the pale tossed surf lapping the coast. She was the white stallion of ancient kings.

In the cold set-in of winter, what cheers Mary are memories. Memories of her cosseted childhood in France. Of riding her horse, Madame de Reale. The triumph of her first wedding. The birth of her son. The first nights she spent with Darnley, before their marriage spoiled as quickly as unsalted meat. Playing with her beloved terrier puppy. Dancing and holding masques after her arrival in Scotland, her dresses stiff with pearls and her diamonds at her breast. Playing the virginals. Riding at the head of her troops, a pistol strapped to her side. How alive she felt then. She does not know – she cannot know – how her memories will soon be everything to her. How soon she will live each day in her past. Now, here at Lochleven Castle, she speaks often with Seton, who has been there through all. The most loyal of all Mary's *jewelled ladies*. They sit huddled in a corner of the rooms, cold hands clasped, missing their fur-lined gloves. Seton recites memories as though they are prayers, and Mary closes her eyes in religious ecstasy.

Some memories are more painful to recall than others. Alone, as Mary slips into her past to comfort herself, she also begins to remember the days running up to her imprisonment here at Lochleven Castle. Memories she has tried to suppress. She remembers Carberry Hill. She remembers her capture. And she remembers her breakdown.

Carberry Hill. The sun was in her eyes, blinding her. The day was unseasonably hot and Mary was thirsty; she and her supporters had no access to water, cut off as they were by the rebel lords who protested her rule and her marriage to Bothwell. They sought to avenge her second husband, Lord Darnley; at least, that was their excuse for all this treachery. They wanted to wrest power from her and from Bothwell. Among them were men who had known all along Bothwell's intention to rape Mary, to force her into marriage. They supported the match. But at Carberry Hill, their allegiances changed. Some grew squeamish. Others only noted that the wind had turned. The day dragged on and Mary's supporters peeled away, vanishing like vapour beneath the unbearable heat of the sun. A victory was no longer possible.

She surrendered.

Mary remembers looking over to Bothwell, the cause of this crisis, the father of her unborn second child. On horseback he looked taller than he was. His ruddy face made redder by the heat, he returned her gaze. Dark eyes, and that long moustache upturned at the corners. Rakish. A military man. He was both her rapist and her protector. Bothwell had been a supporter of Mary's mother, Marie de Guise, when she served as her daughter's regent and tried to hold Scotland for her. In her choice of wedding gift, Mary had sought to remind Bothwell of this history, gifting him furs that had once belonged to her mother. Against all reason, she still hoped for kindness from him. A new start. This same man who had once beat an elderly servant to death right in front of her. After the surrender at Carberry, he looked at his wife for a moment more.

'I'll come for you,' he said to her, and in his mouth the words sounded more like a threat.

Bothwell turned his horse away, urging it into a gallop, accompanied by more than twenty of his own horsemen. Mary's husband of just one month. She did not know – she still does not know – that she would never see him again.

The leader of the rebel lords led Mary's horse by the bridle, just as Bothwell had done in his triumph after the rape, as though she were a beast he was bringing home from market. She rode her horse astride, just as she had always done. The sun beat down and her mount tossed its head and she reached down to brush away a fly on the animal's neck. The smell of dry grass and horse dung and the leather of her saddle and, somehow, of the heat itself, the stench of it rising off the backs of men and horses alike.

Mary struck a deal with the rebel lords. A pact. She was led to believe that she was to be returned to Holyrood Palace. That she would still be Scotland's queen. And so she lifted her chin, and as her horse was led back towards Edinburgh, she tried not to look at the banner the rebel lords carried. It was sketch showing Darnley's murder, his naked body in a garden, and Prince James – the child Darnley had so resented, whose paternity he'd sulkily questioned – kneeling beside his father's corpse. A speech bubble voiced the young prince's prayer: *Judge and revenge my cause, O Lord.*

Perhaps Mary should have foreseen what would happen next.

It begins to snow, delicate flakes that fail to settle on the ground, melting into nothingness. Inside the castle at Lochleven, Mary's rooms feel like a bird's nest: cluttered, warm. Like a woman still pregnant she gathers objects to her side, she rearranges furniture (or at least commands it be done) as though forming a barricade. Today marks the start of Yule. In Protestant Scotland, the festivities are seen as superstitious extravagance, papist somehow, even the decorations of holly and ivy deemed idolatrous. All these men and women who wear pearls and silks but who refuse to light candles or bring greenery into their dark homes on Christmas Eve.

Last year, James was baptised only a few days before Yuletide, in a solid gold font gifted by the boy's godmother, England's Elizabeth Tudor. The Scottish court was at Stirling Castle; they celebrated for three days and nights, fireworks and cannon fire bursting high above the River Forth. Masques were held, and a feast was served on a mechanical stage turned by nymphs and centaurs; Mary had remembered and been inspired by the feast held on her first wedding day, when clockwork ships revolved about the Palais, the scene depicting the Argonauts' quest for the prized

Golden Fleece; and she, Mary, the rightful queen of two
kingdoms – Scotland and England – was named the fleece. Those
two days – her first wedding, and later her son's baptism – are her
favourite days, her crowning moments.

Last December, the baptism celebrations lasted twelve days: a
full twelve days of feasting and dancing. By the following June,
the baby's father, Darnley, was dead in a hole and four months
mouldering, worms chewing on his syphilitic cock, and a desperate Mary was attempting to melt down the golden christening
font, hoping to turn it into coins to fund Bothwell's army. But
Elizabeth's gift proved too large, too solid, refusing to soften.

The women work on embroidery patterns in front of the coal
fire, parcels of coloured threads open before them. For such an
active person, it is a surprise that Mary has always liked embroidery; it appeals to that same part of her that writes poetry, stanza
after stanza. Poetry is an art form made for her; she is her own
muse, she needs nothing as inspiration but her own desires, the
quick-quick knife wounds of grief and lemon-yellow happiness,
unspooling her own innards, steaming hot: desires, jealousies. She
has written some beginnings of poems here at Lochleven, but she
tosses them into the fire. She is learning, finally, to be more careful; she wants nothing that Agnes can read or show to others.
Nothing that would hurt her, haunt her. When she was a girl, she
was too careless with her words, her signature: she signed blank
documents for her mother, who was her regent, and as a teenager,
she even signed away Scotland itself. Had she died without an heir,
her first husband, Francis, would have claimed Scotland as his
own. As it was, he died first: seven years before Lindsay burst into
her prison rooms, and forced her to sign her rights away once
more.

Jane sits on a cushion on the floor next to Cuckoo. They are sorting through woollen handfuls, silken skeins of thread that fall through their fingers. There are mainly dull, earthen colours, dark greens and browns. Mary asks for damask and peach, to line the rosy interior of an elephant's ear. In the silence that follows this request, Seton looks up, stricken, her mouth open, as if she would slice her own breast like the pelican and dye her lady's threads with heart's blood, the shade of love expectant.

'No matter,' Mary says, 'another time.'

An embroidery of the ginger kitten Liz is proposed, but there is no burnt orange or gold thread either. The women try to think of animals, plants, flowers that require little to no colour. Jane watches Mary bend over embroidery, her menagerie of grey-brown creatures prowling in Jane's imagination beyond the castle walls, guarding their captive queen from those men with swords in place of needles, their cracked palms bloody with bargains. In these darkening months since Mary's abdication, she says, often, *In my end is my beginning.* So it is with Jane's stitches, the mouse-coloured cotton left to right, reaching back over itself, right to left. She marks the days, hours, in cross-stitch.

The moon rises outside, its colours numerous: blues, lilac, brown-green, mould, rot, whites, pinks. A painter could not capture them all, though Jane wishes they would try. Servants bring warmed wine and dishes of small almond cakes spiced with cinnamon. When Mary's eyes tire of needlework, she switches to cards, playing against Seton and also Agnes, who sits swaddled in a chair and wrapped in damp-smelling furs, an empty brown paw pressed to her throat. Jane and Cuckoo sit apart, sipping wine and speaking in French: since Seton's arrival, Agnes has stopped humming whenever Mary's women converse in that language; by the end of each day, she is purple from concentration. Jane finds it easiest to talk to Cuckoo when they are both merry from drink; Jane smiles more, and Cuckoo, in French, talks loudly and fluently on her favourite subject: the men she has met, and the men she has not met. She has already dreamt of her future husband. 'I see him in my mind's eye,' she says, slurring her words, her face flushed. 'I am looking up at him and his face – I can picture it, and his dark red hair. I think he is a Scotsman, though he does not have their rough manners; he is only rough when I ask him to be.' She grins.

'So any tall man with red hair is a candidate?' Jane says. 'Will it be the first you see? What if he's a poor beggar; will you say his nose is off and it can't be him?'

'Always such dry wit, Jane.'

'What about when you do find him; how will you converse if he's a Scot?'

'I've been practising,' Cuckoo says, smirking, and she sits up on her haunches, unsteady, and calls out across the room in broken Scots: 'More wine, Lady Agnes?'

The lady looks insulted, but beside her Mary shakes her head and smiles, indulgent, and on her right Seton smiles, too, her eyes on her friend Mary's face. Seton is shuffling the playing cards, and Jane notices the bitten-down fingernails, and the fluid way she deals the cards, her movements precise, so unlike the awkward way she walks and stands. Were her nails like that when she first arrived at the castle? Jane doesn't think so.

Seton is remembering France, where both she and Mary grew up, where they were both happiest: *France*, where the morning light is yellow and soft and diffused, with its promise of heat to come. The leaves of the trees there are all gilded gold by the sun. Walking in the palace gardens among banks of flowers, arm in arm with a teenage Mary who wore a red dress that tasted, to Seton, of cinnamon. Since she was a child, Seton has been able to taste colours: pink is rose water, orange is mutton, and yellow is the fresh tang of a mint leaf on her tongue. Here, in Scotland, here by the water's edge in winter, everything is misted and grey, as though they are lit not by the sun, but by the moon. There is nothing for her to taste. She wonders if Jane has ever been to France. She imagines her, standing beneath the trees that flank the swept roads leading to every chateau, the trees meeting to form long tunnels of green; Jane, standing below, bathed in the dappled yellow light of a French summer. Seton feels a jab of pain in her breast: pain, or something like hatred.

Seton had a French mother, just like Mary. From an early age it was pointed out to her that she was Mary's double, and not only in looks and height: she is known for having a round penmanship so similar to Mary's own hand that she often copies out letters as the queen dictates. When Seton first arrived in France, barely six years old, the French king disliked the idea of Mary surrounded by Scottish girls instead of his own children, and he sent Seton and the other two girls to live for a time among the nuns at the Dominican royal priory of Saint Louis, in Poissy. Seton thinks often of this place. The quiet rhythm of the nuns, like bees in a hive – each individual valued, aware of their part to play. The chimes of bells. The chanting and musical harmonies. The paintings and statues, the holy relics, the stained-glass windows and the library. Every day she felt God amongst them all. The French court was nothing like the priory, run and populated by those clever women of her childhood. The teenage reunion with Mary was bittersweet: the intense thrill tinged with the ache of homesickness, and the realisation of how beautiful Mary had become. Seton was a poor copy of Mary, an uglier version, a *first draft*, the other girls said. If the priory was where Seton learnt of women's brilliance, the court was where she learnt of their cruelty.

Mary's emblem is the marigold, a flower that always turns toward the sun; but in this grey country, it is Mary who is the sun, Seton thinks. Anguished by her own heat, by the energy needed to burn day after day. The person every face turns towards. She is drinking and eating more, Seton has noticed. She is performing *Mary*, that glittering character who never tires, whose every gesture is calculated to seduce. But the effort needed to call upon *Mary*, for her to rise up, is greater now; she is like a reluctant spectre, and sometimes Seton can see the delay before she appears behind Mary's eyes. But when she is there, Seton forgets that she could ever leave; and that is the greatest trick.

Jane and Seton have avoided each other's eyes since their argument by the water's edge; both women furiously replay the moment when Seton twisted Jane's arm back, pulling her forwards, breathing hard, their faces so close they could count the other's eyelashes.

Cuckoo drinks more wine, swilling it inside her cheeks. She looks at Jane, one eye slightly unfocused. 'How did you learn French?' she asks, adding begrudgingly: 'You speak it well, for a Scot.'

Jane shrugs. 'I listened.' She has never been to France; she has never left Scotland. Like her native sign, the Scorpion, she stays close to the ground, lurking in the same patch of earth. But some part of her already understands that if she ever escapes this castle – either with or without Mary – she may never return here, to her country of birth. She understands this.

Or perhaps she hopes.

She thinks again of Seton, standing in *her* place to dress Mary in the morning, *her* place at the table beside Mary, and lying in *her* place at night. But Jane now suspects it was Seton's place to begin with, and Mary only allowed Jane to inhabit it in Seton's absence. '*Saint* Seton,' Mary calls her. The name sets Jane's teeth on edge. She is jealous. She is threatened by Seton's unaccented French, by the casual way Mary links arms with her, their similar appearances and shared religion, and by the way they embraced when Seton first arrived at Lochleven. Seton is what Jane wants to be: one of Mary's *jewelled ladies*, the women she loves and gives pet names and presents to; her sisters, her *family*, the women she called out for during the bloody hours of her miscarriage. Women who do not disappear in a crowded room, overlooked and forgotten. Jane knows she must carve out her own place beside Mary now. One that cannot be stolen.

*Here*: a golden memory, made up of jewelled fragments like the shards of a stained-glass window. These fragments do not belong to Seton, but she and Mary know all of each other's stories; Seton finds the fragments scattered, out of order, as though the window has smashed, and carefully she begins to rearrange, to reconstruct a memory to comfort Mary, and piece by piece she rebuilds the picture of –

Château de Chenonceau in the Loire Valley, one of the most prized chateaux in all of France. It was gifted to Diane de Poitiers, the mistress to the French king, Mary's future father-in-law. Diane, who until her lover's death was the political and sexual rival of Catherine de' Medici.

The chateau is a white manor house standing on the River Cher, suspended above the water. Even then, when Mary first visited, the chateau was already nicknamed Château des Dames – the Ladies' Castle– because it was designed by and built for women. Here was a place given over to the senses, to delights, to intellectual pursuits. It was here that Mary learnt as a child how to converse, how to move with grace, to trail fingertips over her skin; here she learnt the power of pleasure and sensuality. Under candelabra and flickering candlelight, she wore gowns made of cloth of gold, silver, of sheened damask with spangles, all fabrics designed to glitter under certain lights. On the banks of the river, Diane built gardens, surrounded by stone terraces and lined with exotic flowers and plants, among which women might travel the globe. Here Mary first tasted a freshly plucked banana. She drank wine made from grapes grown in the estate's vineyard. And it was here, too, that Mary became convinced that to be loved by a man – desired by a man – was both an aspirational state and an advantageous one. She watched Diane walk through the corridors of her chateau with the surety and contentment of one who is adored. Diane, the mentor of Mary's youth, with her pale gold beauty and taste that could not be bought. Best of all, she saw the influence Diane wielded: the country's politics, culture, and even the king's marital bed were all under Diane's control. At night he would visit his wife, Catherine, but only if Diane wished it. While Seton lived amongst the nuns at the priory of Saint Louis, it was at the Château de Chenonceau that Mary witnessed a different kind of female power.

The following day there are storms. Sheets of rain and hail pass over the loch, and the tower seems to groan, swaying with the wind. Mary prays, working her rosary beads in her hands; she stays away from the windows, frightened of shattering glass. Seton kneels beside her, their prayers overlapping like children's nursery chants, Seton's words rising up to meet her missing chorus. There is lightning; Jane is the only one who sees it, like a crack in the sky. She imagines the loch whipped up into a great wave and swallowing the island. She imagines crashing beneath the water, falling, until the silvery ghosts of dead women emerge out of the silt darkness, flicking their fish tails, their eyes blank and pitiless.

To distract herself from the storm, from the sight of Seton and Mary together, Jane tries to recall the details of Holyrood. She counts the rooms, the beds, the paintings, the priceless tapestries on the walls. She remembers the nymphs, the nameless women carrying clay pots and vases; there was one depicting the Nine Muses, she is sure of it. In her mind's eye, they step out of the tapestries, disappearing and reappearing before her, here in the rooms at Lochleven. Melpomene, muse of tragedy, sits by Mary's shoulder and whispers in her ear: *There must be some way Jane can regain your favour?* Melpomene is the mother of mermaids, blessed with beauty and wealth but cursed never to be happy. She is a mermaid herself today, her chosen form for this watery castle. Her tail is long and glistening: you expect a fish to be soft and slippery but instead it is solid and sharp. *Why are mermaids so desirable to men?* They have no cunny, no sex organs; just endless scales. Perhaps the impossibility is what draws the men to them. Men always want what they cannot have.

Terpsichore, muse of dancing and good times, sits sulking in the corner of the room: she is mother of the sirens, those silver-tongued, bird-bodied women. She is picking at her nails, hunched over her task, her stomach skin visible in gentle rolls beneath a thin gown: too cold for this climate. She watches Mary out of the corner of her eye and remembers better times, when they went dancing into the morning almost every day. Masques, pageants. Where is *that* Mary, the high-spirited beauty? The one who had a glance for every man, even her own brother – she flirts as easily as she breathes – and whose feet would never tire, who could charm whole courts, whole countries? All of France was in love with her, their young dauphiness dressed in white. Melpomene looks over her shoulder, makes a rude gesture at Terpsichore.

Jane snorts.

'What?' Cuckoo says, looking up, eager for conversation.

'Nothing.'

There is a hissing noise. Jane leans over the back of her chair, and sees behind her the glowing eyes of Liz The Cat. She has become too big for the rooms; far from bringing comfort, she now scratches at their clothes and hands when they try to pet her. But Cuckoo refuses to cast her out now that winter has set in, and Jane thinks of the little black cat she freed, perhaps shivering under some archway or beneath a shrub in the gardens.

There is another roll of thunder, and Mary shivers, and claps her hands over her ears.

'We should play a game,' Seton says, her voice loud as though to block out the thunder and cracks of lightning. 'We need a game where all of us are players. Something to divert.'

After some back and forth they agree on 'Who Am I?' where each player takes it in turn to impersonate a person – usually famous, although sometimes a mutual acquaintance – and the others must guess, asking questions until they reach an answer.

Cuckoo plays first; she sticks her pinky into her ear as though scratching loose pieces of skin, a look of relish on her face, and the others guess at once: Lindsay. Mary claps her hands. 'You caught his expression so well,' she cries, showing her teeth like a cat.

Seton goes next. She lies down flat on her stomach, her head turned, one eye close to the ground, as though she were trying to see into the rooms below. There is a pause, so she glances up at Mary and pulls a face, her mouth turned down in an expression of distaste. Mary jumps up in her seat. 'I know, I know!'

It is Catherine de' Medici, Mary's first mother-in-law. There was a rumour that, while her husband was alive, she had a hole driven into her floorboards, so that she could lie down and press her face to it and watch the king and his mistress Diane de Poitiers making love in the apartments below. When Henry lay on his deathbed, the splinters of wood already lodged in his brain, Catherine took pleasure in barring Diane from the room, despite the king's pleas to see his lover. Jane has heard this last story, and while she pities the doomed king and his mistress, she does not blame Catherine. It is surely one of the cruellest rules of etiquette, to force a wife to look away and shut her eyes while her husband tups another woman.

The stone tower seems to sigh. The floor creaks, and in distant rooms below the women hear a stifled shout, as though a servant has yelled out in terror and their companion has slapped a hand over their mouth. Jane wonders how old the stonework is, how strong the walls. Her mouth feels dry. *I pray to God they hold.*

'Jane, it is your turn,' Seton says, and Jane refocuses her gaze on the women around her, huddled about the fire, looking to her, hopeful, as though all their fears might dissipate should she manage to divert them, to weave a pretty enough mystery for them.

Jane takes a moment to choose, finally selecting a woman they all have heard of, and none of them met. She sits up, her back straight, rigid, her chin lifted. 'Tonight, I feel as though my skin is dusted with mother-of-pearl, and there are rings on every finger,' she says; but the words feel almost alien on her tongue. *Where did those come from?* It's like reciting a poem or prayer she learnt as a child, listening to the verses arrive as though another is speaking. Jane's voice has changed; it has become haughtier, rasping, although she does not remember choosing it.

The women confer among themselves. *Another hint, please*, they say.

'I play the virginals,' Jane says.

'What great lady does not?' Cuckoo interrupts.

'I play the virginals *very well*. Better than you, my lady,' Jane says, and she looks up into Mary's eyes and feels at once almost stung: she cannot remember meeting her gaze like this, head on, as though they were equals. She glances away, glances down at the herb-strewn floorboards.

'Are you married?' Cuckoo asks. She speaks loudly and quickly over the sound of thunder.

'No, not married.'

'Do you want to be?'

Jane opens her hands, raising her eyebrows. 'Who can say?'

'Do you have a lover?' Mary asks, leaning forward.

'Many say I do,' Jane says, and again she listens to her new voice, its command, its strained low tones, as though she has spent many years trying to sound deeper, to sound like a man. Did she imagine this voice, or did it take possession of her instead? She looks across the room, half expecting the Elizabeth of her imaginings to be sitting on the bed, waving at her. Her skin prickles.

Mary is smiling now; *does she know already?* 'This lover, would we know him?' she says.

'I sent him to you, my lady,' Jane says, and now she is eager for this game to be over, eager for them to guess her identity.

*Ah*. Mary comprehends; she whispers with the women. 'What colour is your hair?'

'Red.'

*Oh-ho*. Cuckoo opens her mouth as though to blurt the answer, but Mary puts a hand on her arm. 'You must hold my gaze, Jane, as a queen would,' she says, quietly.

Jane looks into Mary's eyes, almost orange in the firelight, the pupils very large. Jane feels at once hot and cold; she has never stared into Mary's eyes for so long.

Mary leans forward, her neck flushed from the fireside; she speaks as though to a lover. 'Wouldn't it be easier if we could wed?' she whispers, and Jane opens her mouth to reply; but Cuckoo cries out, *Elizabeth, you're Elizabeth*, and the spell is broken, and Mary lifts her head as though emerging from a trance, and begins to clap, applauding, all three women applauding Jane, the beat of their palms matching the rain drumming against the windows.

The day of Carberry Hill. The smell of the horses, the sound of the drummers and heralds. The borrowed, ill-fitting clothes Mary wore. The lords promised her reign would continue should she surrender. They promised to reunite her with her son. The betrayal. The slow realisation of her suffering to come.

'Let me pass.'

Seton – Mary's most loyal friend, her sister in all but name – was there at Carberry Hill. She was there beside Mary as they looked out over the battleground at the start of the day. They had sought shade and sat together on a wide rock and Seton held Mary's hand, comforting her when Bothwell would not. When Mary surrendered and the enemy soldiers closed in to escort her back to Edinburgh, it was Seton who first realised something was wrong.

'Let me pass, I am Lady Seton, you know me,' Seton said, striding forward, taller than any of the men on foot, reaching out to try to grasp Mary's hand. The enemy soldiers pressed in close around Mary's horse. Their leader had his hands on the bridle.

'The queen will ride with us,' the man said.

'Seton,' Mary called out over her shoulder, but the soldiers flanking her forced her on without Seton, without the company of any of her own women. Only rough soldiers. She began to suspect then that something was wrong. Why separate her from her women? The answer was simple: a monarch is distinguished by the size of their entourage, by the magnificence of their clothes. Now Mary was alone, without her *jewelled ladies*, without women who might dress her in clothes befitting her rank. The purpose was to humiliate Mary. To strip her of all signifiers of sovereignty. The lords will continue to do this in the days ahead when she is sent to Lochleven with only two chamberers, and without her own wardrobe. Her half-brother the Earl of Moray will do this when he finally sends her new clothes, and chooses English fabric to humble her.

On the outskirts of Edinburgh, Mary wiped her handkerchief across her face and looked down to see it was covered in grime. Her face was grey with dirt and dust. It was then that she first heard the crowd, their words bubbling up like boiling water. *Whore. Burn the whore. Murderess.*

The soldiers and their royal captive processed through the grey streets of Edinburgh, and at every corner, at every turn, there were more people. They were hurling abuse. Some crowd members had been paid off by Mary's enemies; some were spoiling for a fight. And among them were men who became incensed at the sight of the young queen riding astride her horse, incensed and transfixed by the back and forth of her hips in the saddle. Mary could already feel tears pricking in her eyes, her body no longer subject to her own rule. Neither the rebel lords nor the people lining the streets seemed to believe she was a queen any longer. She listened to the voice of the crowd.

*Burn her, burn her, she is not worthy to live, kill her, drown her.*

Everywhere around her were people trying to push past the soldiers who flanked her, their faces wild as they stared up at her and screamed and spat and said those words, calling for her death. Those same people who had once welcomed her to Edinburgh, their pretty new queen, who had once reached out to touch the hem of her cloak for luck. They now seemed like wild animals to Mary, and she tried not to cry, focusing on certain sounds – the sound of her own horse whinnying, of its hooves on cobblestones – as she tried to drown out the screams of her own people baying for her blood, for her incineration. Snatching handfuls of air as they grasped at her. They seemed ready to tear her apart. She put a hand over her pregnant belly. *Help me, God. Help me.*

It is Twelfth Night, marking the day the three Magi visited the infant Jesus. The men, dressed in red and green silks and encrusted with jewels, knelt amidst the straw and animal dung and offered opulent gifts to a newborn Christ. His birth unpicked the fabric of the world, upending all order: his arrival was like a Blood Moon, when spiders destroy their own webs, and creatures call out at midnight, and bats are driven wild, spinning across the night sky. This is why the Feast of the Bean is held on Twelfth Night, to make a game of that disorder: it is no longer something for kings and queens to fear, but to celebrate; any misrule contained within one day of merriment. During one of her first winters in Scotland,

Mary held such a feast. A bean was baked into the Twelfth-night cake, and one of her *jewelled ladies* found it in her slice, pulling away the crumbs and holding the prize aloft between forefinger and thumb. Her reward was to be Queen of the Bean for the day, to wear Mary's clothes and sit on Mary's throne. The queen's skirts were too long for the girl; she spent the night kicking her legs out and laughing as jesters cried out her name and dancers twirled before her.

Seton was also there that night. Before the bean was found, she remembers praying fervently that her own slice of cake be empty; that she would not have to stand before the court, singled out in such a way. She could not bear to wear Mary's clothes, their shared similarities only throwing her defects (as she thought them) into greater relief, or for Mary herself to see her friend for what Seton knew herself to be: a poor copy. *God played a strange trick when he made Lady Seton.*

Mary has requested that such a cake be made for her here, at Lochleven. There will be no grand feast held, no masque, but she hopes to have music and games and the Twelfth-night cake in her own rooms. She makes this plan known to her women as an after-thought, with only hours' notice, and they all scramble to prepare, to bring these hopes to life: they bribe the cooks with money from Seton's purse, they make last-minute alterations and repairs to their clothes, and they speak to the Douglas family. In the court-yard, Jane finds the handsome young man who looked nauseous at Mary's abdication; he is one of the laird's younger brothers, George Douglas. He has his mother's unusual eyes but they are not cold like hers. They are wide and smiling. When Jane speaks to him, he promises on behalf of the family that there will be no trouble, no reprimand, and that he will personally provide musicians for the women. He makes these promises grandly, in such a way that Jane worries he has no authority to make them. Cuckoo, who stood back during the exchange, her eyelashes lowered prettily, now whispers to Jane about his good looks, when he is barely out of earshot: *His eyes*, she says, *his mouth, his cheekbones*. God, to have a face like that between your thighs.

'No red hair, though,' Jane says. 'So he is not your dream man. Bad luck, Cuckoo.'

The women spend the morning watching the courtyard below, keeping an eye out for George and his musicians. In his absence, they are distracted by the chickens scratching and pecking among the flagstones, their plump bodies bobbing up and down like empty barrels in water. The women remark on their brown and white colours and shapes, and the way they interact with one another. Jane puts on a voice for one fastidious hen, fussing, constantly preening itself, and Mary laughs, and smiles, and so Jane does more voices, until she is the only woman talking, describing the birds' interior thoughts as she imagines them, and the other women watch the birds and listen and laugh.

'Here he comes, with all his swagger – *Where's my dinner?* – and Mistress does not like that, oh no, this is her courtyard – *Don't you know who I am? Don't you know how hard it is to find a nice plot of land, Monseigneur?*' She puts on a voice in Scots for the cockerel. '*By the blood of Christ, out of it woman!*'

Mary laughs harder than ever, so Jane continues to curse loudly in the same voice. Cuckoo does not understand all of the jokes – but she understands the curses, and laughs where the others laugh, looking at Jane as though she is a picture she now realises she has only ever seen upside down.

'You are bawdier in Scots, Jane,' Mary says, finally. 'I suppose it is your native tongue. You are braver with your words.'

Seton says nothing, but she is grinning: at the jokes, and at the sight of Mary laughing. She catches Jane's eye, and for an instant there is a softness between them, a thawing.

They both look away.

A moment later, the women watch as a boy in his early teens gathers up the same, fastidious hen in his arms, pinning her wings to her side before snapping her neck with his free hand.

Two lute players arrive in the late afternoon; they stand in the corner of the room and sing a folk song, their voices harmonised, and Mary clasps her hands and smiles up at them until they fumble their words, confused, and play the wrong notes, and Jane sees she is practising on them: there is the familiar tilt of her head, that same gesture of old; there, she moves her fingertips over her mouth, tracing down to her throat, and Jane thinks, *Ah, here she is. Where have you been?* It is like a glimpse of sun between clouds. But Mary is still tentative; she does not have the same confidence she once did, when instead of toying with musicians, she could undo kings. At the sound of the music, Lizzie The Cat yowls and bolts under a chair.

The Twelfth-night cake is placed on the table. The cooks have outdone themselves; it is soaked in ale and butter and decorated with sugared flowers and marchpane fashioned into leaves and painted green. Around the edge of the polished silver dish there are more confections: tiny edible copies of woodland creatures, including a marchpane stag with miniature antlers. Jane remembers the open hostility of the summer. The jug of piss. Ruthven and Lindsay have not returned to the castle. Without their malevolent presence, has the household repented? Perhaps, like Jane herself, they were all sure that Mary would not survive a week within the castle walls. Yet here she is, alive, and the island inhabitants are learning to regret their spite. Mary may forgive, but she will not forget. Neither will Jane.

The musicians strike up a new song, and Mary makes a show of cutting the cake herself and serving it out slice by slice to her women. Agnes has joined them; she is trying not to enjoy herself, but the presence of the cake thwarts all her efforts. She eats quickly, swallowing great lumps, wetting her fingers in her mouth and then running them over the plate so that the last remaining crumbs stick to the skin. Cuckoo is pulling her piece apart, searching for the bean.

'Jane.' Seton has leaned forwards; she has not touched her own slice, instead staring at Jane's. Both women look down at Jane's plate: the bean, nestled beside a piece of almond. Jane is aware that Seton is looking at her; were Cuckoo sitting beside her, she would have already proclaimed the discovery, she would be shouting, *Jane has it, it's Jane, see here, look, look.* Jane stares down at the bean, not wanting to show emotion, to show how thrilled she secretly is; and Seton misunderstands, thinking she sees discomfort in her face. She opens her mouth, as though to say something. But Mary notices the two women, and she moves to look herself, staring down at Jane's plate, and when she sees the bean she laughs and kisses her on the cheek — her lips are soft — and in a whirl of skirts she has pulled Jane to her feet, she is pressing a cup of wine into her hands, she is calling to Cuckoo to help her remove her jewels, and she orders the players to bow: not to her, but to Jane. She takes her by the hands and pulls her away, into the other room, and the other women follow; it is left to a grumbling Cuckoo to heave

Agnes from her wooden stool, bracing one foot against its claw foot, clasping Agnes's hands until finally she pops out of her seat like a cork from a bottle. On the bed there are Mary's dresses and sleeves and satin bodies, and she is asking Jane which she would like, before answering herself, *the velvet*, a dark red gown embroidered with gold, and Jane is ordered to stand in the middle of the room and she is undressed; she tries to help the others but they slap her hands away. She has never worn red before. They unlace her; they remove her own dress, exchanging it for the spangled velvet with matching velvet slippers on her feet. An enamel necklace is unclasped from Mary's neck and looped around Jane's throat; the metal is already warm from a day's wear, pressed against another's skin. Seton twists the chain about, arranging it in place, and Jane's eyes are level with the pale hollow at her throat, framed with lace; the two have not stood so close together since their argument in the castle grounds, when Seton called her ambitious, implied she was secretive, calculating. *Am I those things?* Jane ponders. *Perhaps. But that does not mean I am disloyal.* Seton's neck is so close that Jane can see a pulse jumping, and small imperfections on her skin: the odd freckle, and a mole with dark hairs growing from its centre.

She has a sudden, inexplicable urge to put her lips around the mole and taste it.

Seton steps back. She slides a gold ring onto Jane's finger, and then, standing with the other women, she surveys her.

Jane cannot see herself, so she looks to Cuckoo: her expression isn't confused, or disappointed, or smirking. She is envious. Jane looks into the corner of the room, where Agnes has sat, not deigning to touch the chamberer, and sees she is disconcerted: Jane sees herself in the other woman's eyes, and knows she looks well; not like a child playing dress-up, but one of Mary's *jewelled ladies*. As dark-eyed as a selkie, she is dressed in a borrowed skin – one that allows her to slip beneath a wave and emerge as something else entirely. To be visible.

The women sashay back into the rooms where the lute players are singing, and as she walks Jane kicks out the long skirts cut for a queen, so that she should not trip over. She is led over to the best chair, where Mary usually sits, and when Jane is seated Mary arranges her own skirts and sits at her feet, smiling up at her. Jane thinks of the enchantress Circe, who sat with a lion curled on the ground before her like a common cat. When the lion put his golden head in Circe's lap, and surveyed her with amber eyes, did she ever think: *What have I done?*

The musicians take a short break, massaging their fingers in some corner of the kitchens in the floors far below, the place from where the women sometimes catch the scent of baking bread. In the men's absence, the women lounge about, and Agnes downs cups of wine, hiccuping, one hand on her pregnant belly, her lips and chin and teeth stained red, the colour seeping into her skin, spreading across her cheeks and nose. Seton sips ale; her hair is dressed beautifully, although Jane notices that she is not as kind to herself as she is to Mary: the hair by Seton's ears and temple is pulled taut, so tight the scalp can be seen beneath. *Doesn't she get headaches?* Beside her, Agnes commands Cuckoo to pass her the marchpane stag, but Cuckoo makes her face as innocent as she can and says that surely it should be Jane who has the stag, since she is Queen of the Bean?

When the musicians return, Mary calls for a dance; something informal, with simple steps. Agnes will sit out, and the women line up without her. It is agreed that Seton and Mary will dance the men's parts, since they are easily the tallest, and Cuckoo angles herself so that she stands closest to Mary, so that she will be in a pair with her.

Seton and Jane stand opposite one another. Night has come, it is dark outside, the curtains drawn, the fires stoked, and the two women stand in the flickering light and consider each other: one auburn-haired and tall as a demigod, the other dressed as a queen in velvet the colour of blood. Seton frowns for a moment; *she must be unsettled*, Jane thinks, *to see me dressed in Mary's own clothes.* In the half-light, Seton also resembles Mary, more than usual; she is standing tall, poised for the dance, no longer stooped and round-shouldered like a blacksmith bent over his anvil.

The players pluck out the first notes, and out of the corner of her eye Jane sees Mary throwing out an arm and bowing to Cuckoo as a man would, laughing, one hand at her chest as though afraid her breasts might spill out. When Seton bows, she does not laugh. She moves with studied grace, softening her arms, as though she were often reprimanded as a child for being too stiff, too wooden in her movements.

The dance includes moments of pause, hands suspended in the air, heads turned, as though time has stopped. Jane knows this tune, this dance, but she has never noticed these pauses before. Are they intended for the dancers to catch their breath, or for a moment of looking, of suspending the moment before skin meets skin, palm to palm? Building the anticipation, the desire.

It does not seem possible that a man could have designed this dance.

In her palaces, Mary was known for keeping late hours, dancing and playing cards until the early morning. Before his murder, David Rizzio was her companion in this, the only one of her friends whose energy seemed as boundless as her own. She turned a blind eye to David's preference for men in his bed, so agreeable and accommodating did he prove. In the early hours, the two of them used to watch the pink sunrise from her apartment window at the palace. The consummate courtier, David never showed his fatigue, always ready to propose a new game, to pick up an instrument or to sing on command, the whole party transfixed by his high tenor voice, his lips as soft and full as a girl's. When Mary declared she was hungry at four in the morning, it was David who rallied the servants, who laughed and called for more drink with which to wash her meal down. So it is the same now, on Twelfth Night: Mary calls for more music, more drink, for pies and cold sausage and dried apricots, and Agnes can only look on as her own servants run to obey the queen-that-was, fetching and carrying silver dishes polished to a shine. One of the musicians seems to be sleeping where he stands; he continues to play, plucking at the strings, but his hands must be moving of their own accord because his eyes are drooping, his small pink mouth open in an 'o'.

'He looks like the little cherubs you see in Italian paintings,' Mary whispers. 'If only we had an artist here, he might come and sketch this poor man and use him as a model.'

Mary has been painted several times in her life. She cannot remember every painting, cannot remember her own face as it was. But she remembers sitting for the painter, the sharp smell of linseed oil, the white paint for her skin. She does not usually wear lead make-up, but she thinks she wore some then, for one of the paintings. How it itched her skin. His gaze on her, the painter's gaze. She wore red, because her monthly blood was due, and she did not want any stain to show. Portraits never show open smiles; everything is serious, with stiff grim bodies rendered on canvas:

open-eyed corpses. Mary thinks this is a shame. She is prettier when she is animated: laughing, flushed from dancing, eyes glittered over with drink and the joy of being watched and desired. She likes to be looked at. In all her marriages, she was happiest when there were others to witness her: the throngs of onlookers who lined the streets in Paris and shouted her name on her first wedding day. When she first heard the rumour about Catherine de' Medici watching her husband and lover through a drilled hole, Mary remembers feigning horror at the rumour. But it was not horror she felt in her breast, but something else. If she had articulated it, Jane might have understood her. Jane would see that Mary has spent her whole life training to be looked at.

Cuckoo is lolling about on velvet cushions like a cat, paddling her feet to get comfortable. Seton speaks with her, their heads close together, and Jane looks away; she dips her nose into her cup and drinks. Mary stands to go to the piss pot, and Agnes, who had already half-risen to go herself, is now stuck with accompanying the queen-that-was to the other room, to hold her elbow as she squats and relieves herself.

Out of the corner of her eye, Jane watches Seton and Cuckoo. Seton turns her head and Jane notices a single frown line between her eyebrows. How old is Seton? The same age as Mary: twenty-four, twenty-five. One day Seton's face will wrinkle and sag. There will be deep creases – smile lines – around her mouth and eyes. Jane thinks she would like to see them.

Seton's voice is low. She takes Cuckoo's hand and sits beside her on plump cushions by the fire. She invites Cuckoo to put her head in her lap so that she might stroke her hair – the world has truly turned upside down tonight, Jane thinks. A part of her feels jealous; she does not like being on the outside. As she watches, she feels a phantom hand tug at her own hair the same moment Seton runs a hand across Cuckoo's scalp. Jane strains to hear their conversation; she thinks, *What does Seton want?*

'Hours; it lasted for hours,' Cuckoo says in answer to a whispered question, forgetting to lower her own voice. 'My poor lady, she was in shock, in such pain.' Another whispered question, Seton's fingers teasing a curl out of Cuckoo's loose hair. 'Oh, neither of us; we both stayed, we were locked in . . . I wrapped the string around Jane's wrist and my lady's, and then I went – Oh, that was my idea . . .'

Jane turns away, shutting her eyes; she knows how this story goes. The string, the charm meant to transfer Mary's pain to another, to her: Jane. She had thought the spell hadn't worked, that it had gone wrong: she did not feel the same pain as Mary, but instead saw her nightmares, the ghosts of dead women swimming among the rafters. In the months that have passed since that night, however, when Jane has lain awake, her throat closed and cold sweat on her skin, she has considered the possibility that the charm worked after all, in its way: perhaps she took a bite of Mary's fears, swallowing them whole, and Mary was soothed, and better able to bear the pain herself. But on different nights, the silent ones, Jane only remembers the screams and the bloody sheets, and the silver tails twisting, the spectres swimming closer and closer to the bed.

'I was surprised she did it,' Cuckoo is saying from the depths of Seton's skirts. 'She is usually so sensible. So cool. Like a mouse when you first meet her, she is so short; but she seems to grow taller the longer you spend with her.'

When Jane looks up, she finds Seton's eyes are already on her, the fire behind turning her hair gold, as though she is burning.

★

It is already well past midnight, they are closer to dawn than dusk, when Mary asks that Jane, Queen of the Bean, be her bedfellow for the night. Mary is undressed first: the misrule of Twelfth Night extends only so far, it seems. The women gather about her, Jane still in her red velvet, unlacing Mary, stifling yawns, swaying where she stands, reminded of that first day at Lochleven, when she and Cuckoo put Mary to bed, the two of them exhausted from the hard ride through the night, but unable to even sit down until Mary's own needs were taken care of. So it is tonight, but Jane feels no resentment: she fumbles with laces and cuffs, clumsy, delaying the moment until she must relinquish the red dress.

When the candles are blown out, and they are in bed – Jane has not slept here since Seton arrived at Lochleven – the clean scent of Mary's skin and hair, familiar and exotic, seems to overwhelm Jane, enveloping her, sticking to her like honey, so that tomorrow she will again know the alien pleasure of moving through the day in a body that does not smell like her own. Jane's thoughts drift to Seton lying in the other room, perhaps kept awake by Cuckoo's snores.

'You looked well tonight, in my velvet,' Mary says. 'I'm sorry there was no throne for you.'

Jane leaves a pause before speaking, to ensure she will not interrupt her bedfellow. 'I preferred it this way,' she says, and she speaks the truth: there was an intimacy between the women, a camaraderie, Mary's careful hands arranging her own sleeves on another's arms. When she celebrated Twelfth Night in her palaces, did Mary dress those other women crowned queen for a day, her own fingers positioning their hems on the ground? Jane doubts it somehow.

'It is not yet the morning; you are still a queen until we wake. Think of that, three queens on one island: myself, my cousin

Elizabeth. You.' In the darkness, Mary wets her lips. 'It was a strange comfort, when you masqueraded as her; when we played games during the storm. I have never met Elizabeth. Never heard her voice. For so many years I have wanted to speak with her; never more so than now. I would seek her counsel. I would put aside our past arguments and I would ask her advice, one prince to another . . . I would ask her what I should do next.'

The air seems to ripple, as though a window has been opened or a sheet shaken out above their heads. Jane holds her breath; she senses that Mary is peering at her, trying to make out her expression. She is expecting her to say something, or hoping for it. Jane remembers the whispered words by the fireside. *Wouldn't it be easier if we could wed?*

'Perhaps,' she says, tentatively, 'perhaps Cuckoo guessed my identity too soon that night. Perhaps you would prefer to converse a little more, to confirm who I am.' She has guessed right; beside her, Mary wriggles from side to side like a child the night before her birthday.

'Cousin,' Mary says, almost breathless. 'Cousin.'

'Cousin,' Jane repeats, in that same rasp her voice made by the fireside, the night the wind threatened to pull down the tower around them stone by stone. She feels foolish somehow. The bed quilt feels heavy, weighing her body down.

'I would thank you, first. I know now that it was your hand that guided the noblemen, your threats of war that cowed them. I am alive in part because of you,' Mary says, and Jane lies still, uncertain. 'The last time I was here, in this castle, it was with Darnley. That was two years ago; already he was a fool, but he was still the handsome fool I first met. Even then, he must have been infected with that French disease. He was taking the mercury cure before his death: his teeth were loose, and he took sulphur baths, but his pustules remained. His outside finally betrayed his inner cruelty. When he helped kill David Rizzio . . . Later, I heard you told the Spanish ambassador you would have taken your dagger and stabbed him yourself – him, Darnley – if he had been your own husband. Yet you were so horrified when he was killed.'

Mary's tone is almost accusatory, but Jane feels a tingling warmth in her belly: *These are the words of one prince to another.* Mary's private, inner thoughts. And here is Jane, Queen of the Bean, speaking with the voice of that missing third sovereign; or, at least, speaking the words Mary wants to hear.

Jane is careful in her choice, crafting her every phrase. She says, 'Perhaps I would not have been able to wield a dagger against him. I don't know; I've never had a husband to betray me.'

'No, cousin. No, you have not.'

More silence, so quiet Jane thinks she can hear the sound of the loch far below them. She wonders if Mary has fallen asleep beside her; but no, her breathing is quick, shallow.

'You once said that you would rather be an unmarried beggar-woman than a married queen. Did you mean it?'

'Yes,' Jane says, and she speaks with conviction; she herself has seen enough of men, enough of wedded couples, to believe it of Elizabeth. To believe it of any woman.

'If you were in my position – imprisoned, friendless, your husband a captive – what would you do?' Mary says.

'You are not friendless. As you say, I would not let you die at the hands of those men.'

'Seton thinks I should write to the French court, if I can. I should leave Scotland and claim my rights as a widow of France.'

Jane stumbles towards the right words. 'But you are a queen in your own right. When you were first in France, perhaps others did not consider Scotland as your own, but as your dowry. When your first husband died, you had to unlearn all you knew.' *Does she dare?* 'It is your own body and blood that contains power. Think of it: Scotland was only ever his because it was yours to give.' She swallows. 'It is yours to reclaim.'

The women are quiet. They listen to the sounds of the island waking, of the night birds trilling their final notes, and the distant stirrings of servants in the floors below, rising from their beds before light to prepare the day's meals, and to clear away the evidence of yesterday: cleaning silver dishes, throwing leftover scraps to yipping dogs. Somewhere in the room, hidden from human eyes, Lizzie The Cat is purring.

'I have my answer,' Mary whispers. 'My guess is that you are Elizabeth Tudor.'

'You are right.'

Beneath the sheets, Mary reaches out and finds Jane's hand. She squeezes it.

The night after Carberry Hill. The crowds in Edinburgh baying for her death. The banners showing Darnley's naked corpse, the infant Prince James kneeling beside him, praying for vengeance. She remembers how she was not taken to her palace as she had expected, but to the provost's house in the city centre. She was thrown into a locked room upstairs, men guarding the door outside and whispering abuse to her. It was the first time in her life that she had no female attendants to shield and comfort her, no change of clothes. No food. No water to wash herself with. She was alone.

It was a long night, and Mary could not sleep. She was

unprotected, at the mercy of men who had sought a way to dispose of her for years. Perhaps she would be raped. Perhaps she would be assassinated. It was the first night that she had ever used a piss pot without a servant hovering nearby, ready to carry it away. As she squatted, she felt sure that the guards could somehow see her through the cracks in the door. There was no privacy there. No dignity. She was utterly vulnerable. Later that night she pounded on the door, shaking it on its hinges.

'I am your anointed queen,' she shouted to the guards outside, her voice hoarse, her throat constricted from crying. 'If there are charges let them be brought, let me answer them in a hearing before Parliament. Let me prove my innocence.'

She should have known that the rebel lords had never wanted her innocence, never would give her a chance to prove it. They wanted her guilt. She could hear the crowd that had gathered outside her window, still shouting their insults, naming her a whore, a witch, an adulteress and a killer.

Mary slid down the length of the door, huddled on the ground. She felt that she was drowning. She could not breathe. She wept with abandon like a child, like the unhappy child she herself had never been, pampered and cosseted as she was at the French court, encouraged to act as a tiny adult, to move and speak and dress as a woman would, trussed up in satin and a bodice stiffened with over a hundred rubies and diamonds. She had not been taught the lesson of despair then. But she knew it before Carberry Hill, and she knew it there in that poky room in Edinburgh, listening to the screams and jeers of her people outside, a cacophony of rage. The dark fug caused by her pregnancy seeped into her like ink in water, staining her insides black. The room seemed airless. *Death would be better*, she thought.

In the morning she was still lying by the door, woken by the jolt of her morning sickness. There was nowhere to vomit but in the already-full piss pot; the stench of her hours-old urine filled her nose and made her gag again. The horrible yellow liquid bobbing with bile. She wiped away her tears and realised she could hear shouting. She had fallen asleep to the noise of the crowd and now they were still outside. She ran to the window and threw it open, leaning forward to look down into the faces of the people standing on the street below. Some were taken aback by her appearance. Others only raised their voices.

'Please,' she shouted, 'please.' She fumbled with her clothes, unlacing herself; she meant to bare her pregnant belly, to ask for mercy for her child, but in her wild confusion she bared her breasts. Tears were running down her face and a woman on the street below felt one hit her cheek like a drop of rain. Mary's hair was dishevelled, her face still smeared with dirt and battlefield dust. The crowd stared up at her, some in pity, others only to deride, to leer at the queen's nakedness, to memorise this sight as a story to tell in the city taverns that night. 'Whore,' they shouted. 'Whore.'

The lute player is crouched in the little oratory, his back to the wall. Around him, near-total darkness. He is half-hidden by the small altar erected specially for the queen-that-was. A strange thrill runs through him, hiding here in this sacred space with his unholy thoughts. But then, it is a Catholic space, he reasons. They are lucky it has not been torn apart, as the Scottish lords did to Mary's chapel in Edinburgh. He can hear the sound of slow breathing somewhere at the other end of the room, on the other side of a screen. *Has she fallen asleep?* he thinks. He has an urge to scratch his balls and tries to resist it. It cannot be much longer. Soon he will have what he came for. His lute rests somewhere by his feet. The man imagines picking it up and plucking a few stray notes into the near-silence, his fingers caressing its ebony neck, the smell of its spruce belly and the faint animal whiff of the strings, which are made from guts.

A hand comes over his mouth. The man starts; someone is standing behind him. Their breath stinks of alcohol, and they are swaying on the spot as they touch him. He does not speak, and she – the blonde-haired Frenchwoman – does not speak either. She takes his hand and tugs him into the darkness – he cannot see where – past the debris of Twelfth Night, pulling him down onto a pile of cushions. He can still hear the faint sound of a third person breathing slowly, asleep for now.

Cuckoo lies on her back, dizzy with anticipation and drink. She knows this is a risk, but the wine has blunted her thoughts, her inhibitions. She alone saw how the cherub-mouthed lute player stared at her; how he feigned sleep to make her laugh, and so that she might go to him at the end of the night and rouse him from his dreams. He took her wrist and whispered that she was beautiful and wanted, wanted by him. At court, Cuckoo was used to these kinds of overtures, possessing as she does many of the markers of some idealised beauty: blonde hair, red cheeks, pert breasts. But it has been many months since she was at court, or had by a man, and recently she has begun to feel old. Her birthday is in April, when she will find herself in her late twenties. She does not like being the eldest woman among Mary's retinue, even if only by a couple of years. And so, when the cherub-mouthed lute player whispered in her ear, she felt almost relieved. In gestures and broken Scots, she told him to wait for her, to hide himself in the rooms and wait until she finished her duties and the other women were asleep.

It is freezing cold. Cuckoo is sure that if there were light enough she would see her own breath fog the air, and his too, the lute player's breath, as he pants and fumbles with his clothes above her. Cuckoo hopes that he will be good, that he will give her pleasure, otherwise what is she risking everything for? He caresses her face, and she smells a curious animal whiff on his fingers. She opens her legs for him and he touches her, less clumsily now, which pleases her; she reaches up and grabs at him, tugging. She feels her teeth begin to chatter and she clenches her jaw just as he pushes himself inside her with such urgency that she suspects it is only part desire, and the other part the need to keep his member out of the cold. He strokes her hair, as though remembering its colour. They move together, one of his hands braced somewhere near her head, the other hand kneading at her thighs and belly, which she wishes he would stop. But he is good otherwise, a competent lover; a warmth building in her body. She shuts her eyes tight and imagines her 'dream man', the tall red-headed Scot. When she feels the musician stiffen above her, she quickly does what she has done before: she bucks, her feet on his hips, pushing him off her, out of her, wriggling backwards so that he releases himself with a gasp over the cushions.

There is silence. The lovers listen for the sound of Seton's regular breathing. They both hear it at the same moment, and relax. The lute player kisses Cuckoo on the mouth and begins to stand up, but she pulls him back to her.

Jane opens an eye. In the dawn light, another morning spilling through cracks in the curtains, she can see the nape of Mary's neck, the skin pale and gleaming like opals. She listens to her regular breaths, a catch in one nostril; perhaps she's caught a cold. (She makes a mental note to call for wine and honey paste from the kitchens.) She looks at the back of Mary's head, the shape and curve of her skull visible beneath the long hair piled on the pillows.

*What do you dream of?*

She need not ask; she already knows. Mary does not sleep, except to think of *him*. Bothwell. Jane, like many others, remains convinced that Mary loves Bothwell. Their unnatural lust for one another is so commonly spoken of among Scotland's people that even clever Jane, who has spent every waking hour alongside Mary since their arrival, cannot dismiss the thought of it. At Lochleven Castle it is Jane who sees the pale stains of desire on Mary's shift, on the bed sheets, and who comes to her own conclusions. When she shares Mary's bed she hears her quickened breathing, half waking from a dream. She does not know that Mary dreams of someone else. Or rather, something else.

But here, in the quiet, Jane closes her eyes and remembers Mary sitting astride her, still dreaming, her pregnant belly pressed into her chest and her hands around her throat. Jane has heard stories about the violence of that Other Queen. Fired by her jealousy of other women, Elizabeth Tudor will pinch and shove and smash precious items. But Jane fancies that in Mary – or at least in Mary's dreams – any violence is directed at a man: one man. Him. Bothwell. The husband who divorced his wife to have her, and later persisted in visiting that first wife of his. Lurid pictures begin to form in Jane's imagination. Perhaps Mary dreams of Bothwell and his first wife, swaddled in lambskins on a cold night. His mouth sucking at his first wife's breast; her breath a fine mist in the air. The animal-stink of their rutting. Perhaps Mary raises a hand to her husband, Jane thinks. She sits astride him, and strikes him, and in their violence –

But who can understand the mind of a prince, except for other princes? It is morning now, the red dress and the velvet slippers and fine necklace of last night are all gone; the Queen of the Bean has vanished, like mist, like a cup of wine held between careless fingers. She is undone in a stroke. As dawn fills the room, Jane drifts back into sleep.

On the other side of the bed, Mary dreams. She does not dream of Bothwell, as Jane wrongly supposes. She does not see him except in nightmares. Instead, she is lying in bed beside Elizabeth Tudor, who tells her that she need not feel guilty.

*Guilty about what?* Mary asks.

*I see it in your face. You resent his crown.*

*It is too soon. He is not ready. I am not ready. I am supposed to be dead when James is king.*

*I know how you feel. How can you ever truly love your own winding sheet?*

In the dream, Mary begins to cry – she is always crying, why is she always crying? – and Elizabeth takes her hand and does not let go, she is like iron, and they look down and neither woman can tell whose fingers are whose; they are interchangeable.

*You see?* Elizabeth says. *We are twinned.*

Mary wakes with a start. The sheets are stained with thoughts of the English throne.

Cuckoo feels a sharp kick to her leg and opens her eyes with difficulty, her temples throbbing. In the early morning light, she sees Mary standing over her. Cuckoo and the lute player are still both sprawled on cushions, dried semen staining the dark velvet. Her skirts are pulled up to her bare buttocks. On the other side of the room, she can still hear Seton's slow, even breaths.

'I heard a man's snore,' Mary whispers. She does not look down at the man, only at Cuckoo, who feels herself shrink backwards. 'The others are asleep. The guard will be here soon to unlock the door, and when he does, he cannot see a man leave. No one can.'

Cuckoo tugs down her skirts. She tries to stand, almost tripping over in her haste. Her stomach lurches. In Cuckoo's eyes, Mary looks somehow more awake, more solid than she has in weeks, months. And she looks angry. Cuckoo expects Mary to slap her across the face; she could not blame her. Instead, Mary aims a kick at the lute player's leg and he grunts, looking up and starting as he sees Mary Stuart. She raises a finger to her lips. Mary is not a stranger to escapes and disguises. In the days before Carberry Hill, she disguised herself as a man in order to evade her guards and reunite with her husband of one month, Bothwell, ready to meet the rebel lords in battle. Despite what is said about her, she is both brave and cunning. Above all, she is resilient. Her brain whirs, then: *click*. She knows what must be done.

'Cuckoo, fetch one of Seton's cloaks, and a veil.' Mary looks down at the man and then at his lute. 'A petticoat, too,' she says.

When a guard opens the door to Mary's tower rooms, he finds two of the servant women waiting for him. One is cloaked and veiled, her head bowed, her body very rotund. Behind them, he sees Mary; his eyes are drawn automatically to her, and he barely looks at the others.

'Please, sir, one of my chamberers took a turn in the night and is in desperate need of fresh air,' Mary says, her hands clasped, her eyes on his; he feels hot under her gaze. 'The other girl will accompany her, as you see,' she adds.

The man shrugs and makes way for the two women. It is Mary

he guards, not her women. The door shuts behind them. When they have gone, walking briskly to the courtyard, he puts the back of his hand against his cheek and feels it burning.

When the blonde-haired girl finally returns, she is accompanied by a gaggle of women, among them Agnes and her maidservant. The blonde pushes past him, and in his haste to move back, to allow the lady of the house room to pass, he does not see that the cloaked girl of this morning is not among them.

Cuckoo finally catches Mary alone. She kneels before her, tears in her eyes. She opens her mouth, ready with excuses – *I was drunk, I was weak, he tempted me; never again* – but it is Mary who speaks first, checking over her shoulder to ensure none of the other women will hear or see them.

'You understand, Cuckoo, that I cannot have any scandal here, nothing the lords could reproach me with,' she says quietly, in French. 'And we must be focused. I must escape this place, you see? We can have no distractions. We cannot trust anyone here but ourselves and each other. I trust you, Cuckoo. Or I did, until this morning.'

'Please,' Cuckoo whispers. 'My lady, I swear, it won't happen again.'

'No. It won't. We will forget this,' Mary says, and finally she puts a hand on Cuckoo's shoulder. She starts to walk away, and then turns back. 'You were careful? There will be no child?'

'No,' Cuckoo says. 'No child.' She speaks with total certainty, but she will still cry with relief the next time she bleeds.

'Good.'

Mary does not say *take care of it*, or offer advice on some concoction to drink. Her views on abortion are well known. Early in her reign in Scotland, one of her maids fell pregnant by the royal

apothecary. The couple sought an illegal abortion but were discovered. It was Mary who personally authorised their hanging. A
few years later, Mary herself fell pregnant after Bothwell's rape.
Abortion was not a possibility. She wept and raged, and then she
married him in that bleak Protestant ceremony, the service con-
ducted by the Bishop of Orkney, the groom's own cousin. A dark
unnatural fug had descended over her by then, a chasm opened in
her chest as it had once before, when she was pregnant with James.
She wept uncontrollably, her body no longer her own to govern.
On her wedding night she called for a knife. She threatened to
drown herself. *Let me die*, she said, *let me die*. Mary has known deep
distress many times in her short life. Her body has betrayed her
over and over and brought her to her knees. And each time she has
risen, as she does right now. The lute player has given her an idea.
An idea for her own escape.

The night after Carberry Hill. The despair of the morning, of
hanging out of a window with her breasts bared to the jeering
crowd below. Her acute desperation. That evening she was
finally escorted back to Holyrood Palace, where her *jewelled ladies*
were waiting for her, including Seton. They did not take her to
her old, once-cosy apartments, the ones in which David Rizzio
was murdered; Mary never set foot in those blood-soaked rooms
after his death. Beneath tapestries of nymphs and dancing girls,
the women bathed Mary and dressed her in informal clothes: a
fresh shift and a loose dress that was really only a nightgown.
She was fed, finally, and she ate with her mouth open, ravenous,
and Seton was forced to put a hand on her wrist to steady her, to
make her slow down.

The evening meal was interrupted. Lindsay and Ruthven were

there, curt and gleeful. They ordered Mary to get up, to ready herself to leave Edinburgh.

'Give me just a moment, please,' she said, reduced to begging. 'Give my women a chance to pack a change of clothes for me and to prepare themselves.'

'Your ladies won't be coming with you,' Lindsay sneered, cutting her off. 'A couple of chambermaids, that's all you're permitted.' None of his facial expressions reached his eyes; he was cold, reptilian.

It was Seton who ensured Mary had a cloak to wrap around herself; it was Seton who held her hand until Lindsay roughly pulled them apart; and it was Seton who wept as Ruthven lifted Mary onto a horse, his hands groping her hips and waist.

'I will come to you as soon as I am allowed. I promise,' Seton said through her tears.

'I know you will,' Mary said. 'I know it.'

The ancient Greek philosophers declared that old age begins at fifty years old. Margaret Erskine does not know if this is still truly the case for men, but she knows it is not the case for women. It is sooner than fifty. For years now, she has been striving to remain visible among those who cannot see her, who do not want to see her now that her body has undergone the change that comes to all older women's bodies. The change that is so disgusting to the world, to men. She is still experiencing it. She still burns up with hot flushes over her face and neck, her fingers fumbling to loosen her ruff. Her skin is dry and papery: an old woman's skin. In the day she is beset with stiff joints, stiff muscles, blazing headaches, a rapid, skipping heartbeat; among all these symptoms, it is easy for her to misdiagnose her stomach aches, her fretful swallowing. At night she wakes drenched in sweat and it makes her weep, to know that she is rotting from the inside out, like a plump fig that falls apart in your fingers, the insides a brown mulch only fit for wasps. Her anger rises quickly, suddenly, and she lashes out, at once dreading and craving attention. *I am still here*, she thinks. *I am still here*. Perhaps it is worse for women in other countries; as in Italy, where a woman's monthly blood is believed to contain magical properties. Ingredients for sorcery. Do the French believe the same? Margaret does not know.

Since Mary's arrival at Lochleven Castle, Margaret has had servants report to her. She knows when Mary bleeds, and when she does not. Margaret understands she should pity the woman for her miscarriage. But in reality, a part of her is envious of Mary's fertility. She is jealous, too, of her fecund daughter-in-law, Agnes, despite knowing that Agnes's children are her own grandchildren. They would not exist without her own now-thwarted womb.

Margaret has heard rumours of the spell Mary ordered to be cast during her first pregnancy, to ease her birthing pains while delivering Prince James. Only three years earlier, Mary had allowed the Witchcraft Act to pass in Scottish Parliament, making any witchcraft a capital offence – although this did not stop Mary and her helpful countess. Margaret finds this ironic, although the greater irony is yet to come. Years into the future, James – the royal child born with the aid of a spell – will grow up to hate magic. Over a thousand witches will die during his reign. He will be fuelled by a vicious hatred of women, and by paranoia. The seed of this paranoia will take root during a great storm, when a fleet of Scottish boats sets sail to Denmark to fetch James's new bride. The storm will spare James's boat, but there will be other casualties, including a ferry boat crossing the River

Forth, carrying Scottish women ready to welcome their new Danish queen. The stormy weather will later be blamed on witchcraft – on witches who confess after torture. Many of these witches will be women who are older and widowed, like Margaret Erskine.

And so, the great witch hunt will begin.

Returning to that ferry boat due to set sail years in the future. Almost all its passengers will die in the water; only two will survive.

Jane will be on that boat.

Four years ago, the new French king – younger brother of Mary's sickly first husband – issued an edict declaring that the New Year, *Anno Domini, the year from Christ's birth*, will be measured from the first day of January, rather than Lady Day in March. Scotland has not yet adopted this ruling, meaning that for the next three months, the country is technically a year behind, stuck in the past – a fact Cuckoo delights in (as she always does in mocking the Scots) because there is little else for her to delight in during Scotland's winters.

In late January the rains come, and the water rises, muddying the ground, lapping at the exposed parts of the castle, and Jane thanks God they are no longer in their previous rooms, but high up in a tower, away from the threat of flooding. Out of their windows, the women watch servants carrying damp furniture across the courtyard below, sodden velvet cushions tossed into the dirt. They can see the shores of Kincross, the faint lights in the early evenings before utter darkness. The nights are bitter. Mary is used to palaces, where there is always someone awake, always a lit fire, a candle, an extra pile of blankets and furs. Cuckoo catches a cold and spends days snuffling into her handkerchief and coughing up phlegm at night, snorting like a horse.

Snow follows rain, swathing the courtyard and kitchen garden and the thin stretch of land circling the ramparts in white folds like a swaddling sheet, and it has the curious effect of making the dark water look more solid than the ground.

The women have not been outside for days, perhaps weeks. A walk to the water's edge is proposed and then embarked on, the women flanked by surly guards and accompanied by Agnes and her scowling maid. The air is sharp and clean and cold. Jane shuts her eyes, breathing deeply. She had not realised until this moment how much she has missed fresh air within the confines of the tower. When she opens her eyes, she sees Seton has been watching her. Above them, snow is thick on the branches. Spider webs are strung with beads of ice. Parts of the loch have frozen over, around the edge. Mary puts a foot onto the ice, her face like a naughty child's, and the other women scream and laugh and drag her back before the men have time to shout out.

They hear the boat before they see it: the sound of oars cracking through floating wedges of ice. Cuckoo is the first to lift her head; later, Jane will wonder if some part of her already knew, or suspected, who was aboard. When the boat and its passenger become visible to the others, they see there is a young man sitting huddled in the hull, his legs so long his knees almost touch his chin. He is tall, then, and with dark red hair. He has a handsome, bearded face, *a nose you could be proud of,* Jane thinks. He is the image of the man Cuckoo describes when drunk: her imagined future husband.

The man's name is Andrew Melville. He is a courtier, but a minor one: in reality, he is little more than the errand boy of his older, influential brothers, including Robert, the diplomat who gave Mary the scrap of paper hidden in his scabbard. Andrew Melville is here on his brother's orders now, at Lochleven Castle, delivering supplies to Mary, pieces from her palace wardrobe that she wrote and asked for months ago: most particularly, a gold necklace she commissioned before she fell at Carberry. He does not bring her the black pearls or diamonds, but still, it is something. He has a nervous smile, anxious to please. There are some single men who remain unfinished even when they are long past adulthood, like wet clay, easy to mould to the sculptor's desires and whims. Jane thinks, *He would be easy for a wife to shape.* He is courteous to all the women: not just to Mary and Seton, but to Jane and Cuckoo, too. His manners are gentle, the movements of his hands measured, even delicate, as he unwraps bundles and removes objects, dusting down skirts and laying out perukes, hair pieces, and ornaments for inspection.

'You've taken such care of them,' Mary tells him in Scots.

'So much so, you would think he was Mistress of the Robes,' Jane quips, in French; but Melville glances up at her, in surprise and amusement, and she realises he understands the language. Of course he does. She has grown complacent, too used to cracking private jokes around Agnes.

Mary frowns at her. 'Forgive her, sir; Jane has a dry wit.'

'No indeed, it's a relief to hear a jest in these times,' Andrew Melville says in French, before adding, with a courteous bow to Mary, 'they have grown dark since your absence, my lady.' He looks at Jane again, and she recognises in him a man who likes to be teased and mocked; here is a boy in man's clothing, a boy who perhaps grew up in a house without laughter, or with a mother or nursemaid who scolded him, and now he wants a woman who names his faults with a smile on her face. *I will have to tell Cuckoo,*

Jane thinks. Out of the corner of her eye, she can see the French-woman ducking her head and smiling with the new knowledge: he speaks her language.

At night, beside Cuckoo once more, Jane listens as her bedfellow lists Melville's many qualities, just as she did with the handsome George Douglas: *his eyes, his smile, his great height*, almost as tall as Mary's brother. 'Surely that's a good sign,' Cuckoo says, and Jane does not have to look over to know she is gesturing crudely with her hands, widening the space between her two palms.

'You never saw him at court?' Jane whispers.

'No, I'm sure I didn't. I couldn't have done, as I would have remembered him. But perhaps, if I did, I saw him only fleetingly, and thought nothing of it, but in my imagination, I began to fashion an ideal based on his image.'

Even in the dark, Jane can hear Cuckoo's smile. 'If I were you, I would be cool with him, when you are in the same room,' Jane says. 'I would not smile or flirt too much. I believe he is the type of man who prefers to like a woman more than she likes him.'

Cuckoo scoffs. 'You have learnt this how? He is only here a short while; I must make an impression.'

'It is just my advice.'

Cuckoo considers this. She is approaching her late twenties, an age where she is wondering where her husband has been hiding. She thinks of the lute player, who she has not seen since Twelfth Night. She is not sure why men never return her love; why they always seem to shy away like skittish ponies the moment they have touched her. *Is there nothing in me for them to love except that?* She is beginning to worry that there is some naked eagerness in her that she cannot disguise, like a customer trying to haggle but unable to hide their desire. Cuckoo wonders what it would be like to be Jane, whose face is unreadable; Jane is surely one of those customers who can hear a price, and shrug, and walk away, no matter how badly she wants something, only for the shopkeeper to chase after her at the last moment and for her to turn slowly, cool and careless, as though it did not matter to her if they chased after her or not.

But Cuckoo has never been good at taking advice, especially not from a woman like Jane, who is younger than her, and shorter, and less conventionally attractive, a Scot who speaks French with an accent that makes her sound, to Cuckoo's ears, as though she is grimacing, her jaw tight, every *du pain* high and nasal like a Gascon at market.

There is a rustle of sheets. In bed, Jane feels the warm weight of Liz The Cat, padding across the mattress to curl up at the feet of Cuckoo, the only person who still treats her (or him, Jane cannot get close enough to tell) as a kitten, and not the hissing, spitting, feral beast she has become.

'Did you know that Seton has taken a vow of celibacy?' Cuckoo says, sleepily. *No*, Jane did not. She feels suddenly awake. 'It explains why you act strangely around her,' Cuckoo adds.

'Do I?'

'She is like a Mother Abbess; and your kind do not like nuns.'

There is silence. Cuckoo seems to reconsider the tone of her last comment; when she speaks next, it is half conspiratorial, half apologetic. 'Andrew's father was executed, you know. For supporting the Protestant cause. I asked Seton about him. She said the estates were all forfeited, for fifteen years; it was only a few years ago they were given back to his family.'

*No wonder Melville is so anxious*, Jane thinks; he knows what it is to lose both kin and wealth in an instant. He can only have been a boy at the time. She wonders if he was present at his father's execution. If he kept his eyes open. She wonders if he ever wakes up in the middle of the night and feels his own head wobble on his shoulders, and looks up to find silvery ghosts swimming among the rafters.

The next day. The musicians who played at Twelfth Night return to Mary's rooms, their lutes cradled loosely in practised arms, like a man bouncing his third or fourth child. Jane glances up, and sees they do not recognise her without her red dress. Cuckoo glances up, too, before a deep flush seeps across her neck and she turns away, ignoring the lute player's presence. Andrew Melville plays cards with Mary and the two noblewomen, Seton and Agnes. He is paired with Mary, and he is flustered, eager to win for her, to compliment every lady's skill, and to disparage his own.

'I am a stupid player,' he says, slapping his forehead and turning to Mary. 'My lady, our score is no reflection on your skill, but mine alone. I am a poor partner.'

'At least he is not insincere,' Jane whispers in Cuckoo's ear, the two of them sat apart from the others. When he glances back at her, she keeps her eyes on her needlework.

'Nonsense, he is simply out of practice,' Cuckoo retorts, loud enough to ensure he hears. She is daydreaming about Andrew Melville leading her away from the group, into the shadows, and taking her up against the wall. In this fantasy, he rolls up her skirt and undoes his codpiece with deft hands and an urgency that tells her already how good it will be, that he will know how to please her. She fantasises about how he will feel inside her, and he will tell her that she is not just pretty, but beautiful, and after they fuck, he will press some token into her hand, something expensive, not a payment but a promise. He will take her away from this place. *He will be home.*

The four players switch to a different game, to Primero, where each individual plays for themselves with the aim of bluffing the others into betting against them. Of the group, Seton is by far the best, her face cool and impassive, her every move calculated, without the giggles and lip-biting of the other women. She has no kind word for Melville when he praises her playing; her mouth is pinched, as though annoyed with him, although Jane cannot see why she has taken against him. To the others, he is a welcome distraction; and besides, he will be gone in the morning. He shuffles through his hand and Seton fiddles with her earring, impatient. Only Jane notices. She looks at Seton's fingernails, and sees she has been gnawing at them in secret.

Mary struggles to concentrate on the card game; she is too preoccupied with what message she should give Andrew Melville to convey to his brother the diplomat. And she thinks, too, of what additional report he will deliver when men in Edinburgh ask him for news of Mary's health, of how she looks, and how she behaved in her prison at Lochleven.

Cuckoo pours Melville wine, leaning as far forward as she dares, and Jane knows he will be able to smell the orange-and-clove scent that follows Cuckoo throughout the day and lingers at night on her bed sheets. But he does not inhale the scent; he does not look up, he does not steal a glance at Cuckoo's cleavage. He is looking, instead, at Jane. He is looking into her eyes: the dark eyes of a selkie.

'Your turn, sir,' Seton says, her voice as pinched as her mouth.

Melville looks down at his hand, a crease at the bridge of his nose. He shuffles through the cards; he seems on the point of discarding one. Jane, who has just finished pouring wine into Agnes's cup, bobs down and mutters in his ear: '*Keep it*. You might find a use for it.' She steps back before any of the other women notice: all except Seton, who looks up at Jane with an unformed question in her eyes, one that Jane does not answer.

The musicians change their tune.

When Melville leaves for his own room that evening, he makes a show of doubling back, of forgetting his cup, which Jane hands to him. 'I hope I see you again,' he whispers.

'I will go where the queen goes. It may be a long wait for you.'

'I can wait,' he says, so low she can barely hear him.

'A safe journey, sir,' she says, cutting him off, her tone almost careless. But she touches his hand when she gives him the cup. A finger brushed across his wrist; she feels his pulse, the thrum of his blood. The backs of his hands are tanned from the sun.

Behind him, she sees Cuckoo staring at her, her eyes accusing, and Jane wants to tell her, *You did not listen to me; his wants were easy to read*. Like a spare playing card, a man like him – a man of clay – would be good to keep in hand. *I might find a use*.

Andrew Melville leaves Lochleven, and days later the frost sets in. Away from the fireside, the rooms are so cold the women can see their own breath, like pale puffs of incense. There is ice on the insides of the windows and within the stiff folds of the curtains. At night, the sheets are so cold they feel almost damp. Cuckoo does not look or speak to Jane in those first few days and nights after he leaves, and Jane dreads a return to that same awkwardness that lay between them before Mary's miscarriage and abdication, when they were drawn together through their – *what?* Through their suffering? But it was Mary who had suffered. Perhaps their uneasy friendship was born of sympathy for her, or their shared desire to protect her. Mary does that to people. She inspires a kind of religious devotion, something primal, a need to guard her against the world: the embroidered, grey-brown beasts Jane once imagined made flesh, as though for a brief time Jane and Cuckoo were two wild creatures, their differences put aside as they prowled the castle's edges, their teeth bared against the world. But Jane is not Cuckoo; neither can ever truly understand the other: one so eager to spill her thoughts, the other just as eager to conceal them. They lie close to each other at night, for warmth, but Cuckoo does so with a grim little mouth, stiff as a frozen corpse, her eyes averted. In the silence, they can hear the whisper of something scuttling across the rushes on the ground: a mouse, or a large brown spider.

Mary's twin babies would have been born this month, had she not miscarried. None of her women mention this, but they are too attuned to Mary's body not to have marked the months and remember. She would have begun her lying-in by now. Officially, she had been due in February, but the women all knew or could have guessed she had been further along than she claimed; that in all likelihood she was already pregnant when she married Bothwell. Mary herself remembers her due date and pictures two little boys: one redhead, one dark. She sees them in her mind's eye, sitting in her own mother's lap, content. Mary's babies were not baptised but she still imagines them in heaven alongside their grandmother. *Is it sinful to think such things?* She does not wait for an answer but asks her God for forgiveness all the same.

Agnes is due to give birth in early spring. She is barely able to move without aid, and she is so happily wretched in these final months of her pregnancy that Jane often hears Cuckoo grinding her teeth during the woman's long complaints, which are so threaded through with her too-familiar verbal tics – *Of course* – that they verge on self-parody; every speech seems designed to test Cuckoo's already limited patience.

Margaret Erskine also seems to find her daughter-in-law trying – perhaps this is why she prefers to keep to her own rooms – but at least her presence checks some of Agnes's worst behaviours, her otherwise-constant insinuations and questions. Margaret reclines now, heaped with furs, occasionally cracking her long, creased neck, and Mary leans forward to engage her, smiling politely, shaking back her sleeves again and again, speaking with her hands like an Italian. Margaret avoids looking at Mary directly, as though shielding herself from a bright light. She eats very little, Jane has noticed; she thinks that it must be out of vanity, and she wants to tell Margaret that she should eat, because women of a certain age cannot have a slim figure without a gaunt face. *Is it Mary's charm or her beauty that Margaret Erskine cannot bear?* The others have unconsciously grouped themselves to frame these two women, the queen-that-was and the almost-queen, still lovely at fifty, the woman who but for bad luck could have sat where Mary's mother once sat, and slept in the king's bed not because he deigned to ask her, but because she had the right.

Mary seems hardly to notice this framing about her – it is natural, she has been the centre of attention since she was made queen at six days old – but even if she does, she is too focused on Margaret Erskine, and on appearing engrossed by her conversation. Mary is smiling and speaking and listening to the older woman, but her thoughts are elsewhere, on something she would like to say to Margaret, and she is trying not to appear like those men at court, the men like her brother who would sit and nod as she spoke, their faces arranged to reflect the appearance of interest; but their hands were restless, their eyes unfocused and their mouths half-open: they had already formed their next sentence in their mind, their next witticism or rebuke, and they were impatient for Mary's lips to stop moving, so that they could speak their clever words aloud.

Mary wants to ask Margaret Erskine about her own mother as a young woman, but she knows she cannot. Instead, she looks at Margaret, at her huge eyes, as though by looking into them she might eventually see the faint reflection of Marie de Guise as she was when she first came to the Scottish court. A French noble-woman, when she was just twenty-one years old she was already a widow, a beauty lighter by two sons, and courted by two kings: James V of Scotland, and Henry VIII of England. Marie de Guise rejected Henry – the wife killer – on the grounds that although she was tall, she had only 'a little neck': a sly reference to the ill-fated Anne Boleyn. Marie chose James instead, and was forced to leave behind her old life and two children – one living, one buried – in exchange for a crown. Now, at Lochleven, Mary thinks often of her mother as a young woman, and of that same moment of decision, pulsing with opportunity and chance, the crossroad when her mother had both countries at her fingertips, weighing one in each hand, like apples, and chose Scotland over England. Had she chosen differently, chosen Henry over James, the lion over the unicorn, would it be Mary – red-headed, per-haps, but still her mother's child – who sat on the English throne, and the bastard Elizabeth shunted to one side? Mary has thought often of this, ever since Twelfth Night. Take back Scotland, and the English throne – with all its wealth and promise – is again in reach. It is her birthright, and her destiny: the missed opportunity, her mother's inheritance. She is still rising; her story has yet to be written. Mary is not the Golden Fleece, a motionless prize to be won; she is Jason of the Argonauts, and the fleece is England itself: at their wedding feast it was always she, Mary, and not her sickly limp-prick husband, who was the one fated to seize it.

A few hours of bright winter sunshine, a burst of reprieve. Outside the castle walls, the surface of the loch glitters with reflected light. A robin, its feathers puffed up against the cold, finds warm, temporary relief in a patch of sun on the ground. In the tower, dust motes are suspended in shafts of light. Mary stands by her window, apparently lost in thought, her face turned towards the view and hidden from the rest of the room. Her women know not to interrupt her reverie. But handsome George Douglas does not know Mary yet, does not understand her changing moods. She is no ordinary woman, and so it seems her emotions are never ordinary; there is only ever blinding light or utter darkness. He approaches her, leaning against the wall, daylight illuminating one side of his face, and it is only now he sees her expression.

Mary takes the handkerchief he offers to her; she is relieved to see there are no lions or dragons embroidered on it. Only a violet stitched into a corner. George Douglas is not so much younger than herself in years, but when she looks in his face she sees he is still more boy than man: green, untried, unburdened. He waits for her to speak first. She attempts a smile.

'You know how I lost my two sons here on this island,' she says, so quietly he must lean closer to hear. 'I am a mother, you see. I have many hours of idleness from waking until nightfall, and so I imagine them as they would be, had they lived. I shut my eyes, *like this*,' she says, and she closes them, and George can now stare at her face without embarrassment, 'and I see them as babies, then as boys, then as young men. I see them age in my mind's eye. I see my life beside them. I see myself as their mother. A mother they knew and loved. But these boys are not boys, only shadows.' Mary opens her eyes and finds George looking into them, as she knew he would be. 'I suppose you cannot understand,' she says. She looks away again, and George watches her as she absent-mindedly traces a finger over her lips and then down her neck, slipping beneath her collar to touch her bare skin. George is sure that she is unaware of the effect these touches have on him.

'I have not yet married or been blessed with children,' he says, haltingly, 'but I understand a little of your pain. My father died fighting the English. I have no clear memory of him. I did not know him as he was, as a man. I pray for his soul. I mourn him daily. But I mourn most those shadows you speak of, the shadows of father and son, of the bond that might have been between us, had he lived. I imagine him just as you imagine your children.'

Mary looks at him, at George Douglas, as though this is their first meeting. She has stopped tracing patterns on her skin. He has surprised her; he sees this in her face. His tenderness has proved unexpected. Mary is so tall in person that they stand eye-to-eye; or perhaps she is a little taller than him. George is used to women who bustle about below him; he is used to a view of their caps, or their bare-headed scalps. From that perspective they are partly hidden from him. Faceless. But here is Mary, who matches him, who does not need to stand on tiptoe, and he finds he prefers it this way.

George and Mary are not related by blood, but they are connected. They both share a bastard half-brother: Moray. Margaret

Erskine is both George and Moray's mother, and the late king fathered both Mary and, before her, Moray. But within the Scottish nobility, everyone is in some way connected to one another: the criss-crossing threads in the Minotaur's maze. The only thought Mary spares in regard to their family link is this: she imagines Moray's face when he realises she has seduced his half-brother.

Night sets in before the day even begins, dull skies dimming from midday onwards. The women are idle. Agnes is not yet there, meaning they are more at ease, but less diverted: her presence, which both infuriates and amuses, also unites them against her. They play cards, or sew, and when their eyes are tired they ask each other questions—the types of questions that are meaningless, and yet have all the meaning in the world.

*Who would you be, if you could be a man for a day?*

'A man of leisure,' Cuckoo says at once. 'A rich gentleman. I would gamble and dance and learn all the court gossip, all the things that men say when they are alone among themselves, away from women. I would learn all these things and then report back once I was a woman again.'

Mary claps her hands. 'Very good,' she says. 'And I think I know what type of man my girl, *Saint Seton*, would be. A monk, surely?'

Seton shakes her head slowly, smiling, but she does not contradict her; Jane wonders if that truly would have been Seton's choice, or if she prefers to stay silent, to please Mary, and to make the others jealous of their long intimacy.

'Jane, what would you be?'

What wouldn't she be? What wouldn't she do? She would do

everything. She would invent. She would sleep naked in a field. Trade. Fight. Fuck who she pleased. Travel. 'A painter,' she says, finally. 'A court painter.' It is a profession she has long admired. At court, painters are not considered artists; they are merely crafts-men. But there is something about capturing a person's likeness – it is like witchcraft. They say the German, Hans Holbein the Younger, was the most gifted at this; that he did not paint you as you wanted, but as you were. In her mind's eye, Jane imagines a canvas and brushes spread out before her, her fingers outstretched.

'Who would you paint?' Seton asks.

'Women,' Jane replies, at once. After a moment, she shrugs. 'What's a man to do?'

Mary laughs. She is distracted, her thoughts still on her conver-sation with George Douglas, of what he might do for her in the months ahead. At the same time, she wants to encourage this more relaxed, smiling atmosphere among her women; it makes it easier for her to plot. 'But what about a sculptor instead of a painter?' she asks Jane. 'To work with your hands: is that not more manly?'

*Why not both*, Jane says. The painter Michaelangelo carved the *Pietà*, the Virgin Mary cradling the crucified Christ; they say she is so lifelike that you expect her to glance up, to exhale: that it is all a ruse, she is a real woman, her face and body painted white. But it is no ruse, no painted woman; it is flesh come alive in a cool slab of marble. Decay, too: the decay of Christ's flesh. They say Michelangelo studied corpses. Vagrants became models for Christ. But it is the Virgin Mary, her face younger than her adult son's, who is the true focus; Jane thinks she has never heard of any-thing so Catholic.

It is not entirely true that Jane would only paint women. There is at least one man she can think of. In addition to the *Pietà*,

Michelangelo also painted the fresco of the Last Judgement in the Sistine Chapel. Biagio da Cesena was a Papal Master of Ceremonies who famously criticised the fresco, calling the nude figures shameful. He sneered and said the fresco was better suited to the walls of a tavern. Michelangelo responded by painting Biagio's face onto the body of the donkey-eared Minos, a snake busily devouring his member.

Lord Lindsay is Jane's Biagio.

Cuckoo, who delights in any opportunity to mock the English, remembers hearing that during the reign of Henry VIII, courtiers commissioned portraits of the king to hang in their own houses, and every few years they would write to the artist and ask them to paint over their sovereign's face, to add lines or bulging cheeks to better match its real-life ageing counterpart. 'They didn't realise they should order a new painting,' Cuckoo laughs.

Cuckoo: a gentleman. Seton: a monk. Jane: a painter. But when it comes to Mary's turn, she looks surprised, as though she has forgotten she should be asked the same question. 'Who would I be?' she says, to herself, and she is silent for a time, her face lowered. When she looks up, she is smiling, enraptured. 'I would not be a man for a day,' she says. 'I would only be me. I am content with myself.' She says it with such wonderment, such shock at realising that she would rather be herself than any man in the world, that the others smile, too.

'Now,' she says, her voice changed, crisp and resolved. 'Let's drink to it.'

They drink young white wine fresh from the barrel and shipped from southern France. Seton swills it in her mouth: it tastes of citrus, of fragrant lemon and orange groves and dusty fields, the earth paled by the sun. She looks across the room at Jane; she is watching her face as Agnes arrives in all her state, hands on her belly like a grey seal floating on its back, flippers cupping the exposed freckled flesh. Seton sees Jane smirk, for the briefest moment, before smoothing her features, as swift as a practised courtier. Blank-faced, she nudges Cuckoo beside her, who turns and does not bother to hide her glee.

'Cuckoo, come show Lady Agnes the bookmark you made me,' Mary calls out. She does not want to be left alone with Agnes.

There are bright pink spots on Cuckoo's face; it is one thing to listen in to Agnes's speeches, but another to stand next to her and nod with gritted teeth. She hesitates, though only for a moment. Seton watches as, at the same time, Jane ducks her head, and seems to melt into the background, escaping to the bedroom.

Seton follows.

'Is he the type of man you like? Andrew Melville.'

Jane turns, in the process of laying out Mary's nightdress on the bed behind her. Seton is stooping beneath the doorway; like Mary, she is too tall for them, genuflecting at every entrance. She straightens up. They are alone. Both Mary and Cuckoo are in the other room, entertaining Agnes.

'I don't usually like any men,' Jane replies.

'But he is different?'

There is a pause. *Where is this going?* Jane thinks.

'When I asked you who you would paint, I thought you would say him. Melville.' Seton's face seems very angular, all jaw and cheekbones and hard edges. She does not have the same sensuality as Mary does, but there is a strange and quiet beauty in her features, one that Jane is still trying to understand.

Seton hesitates. 'He is wrong for – he isn't equal to you.'

'He is my better,' Jane says.

'Don't marry him.'

'What?'

'Don't,' Seton says. She has walked forward; Jane wants to step back, but she feels the wooden bedframe press into the backs of her legs.

'I met him only a handful of times. We barely spoke,' Jane says.

'He saw you and wanted you. He said he'd wait.'

'You listened?' Jane says. There is an anger in her voice that she knows should not be there. Seton is a noblewoman, and she, Jane, is a chambermaid, barely a step above the serving girl who throws out the piss. But it is more than that. *What did she expect?* From the cradle, women are taught to listen to men. Of course Seton would pay attention to Andrew Melville's words.

She says, 'His words – they meant nothing. Men usually say these things. He wanted a fuck, that's all.'

'Usually. But he is different.'

'You said that, before. Not me.'

Seton is standing in front of her. They are so close now that they can see their own reflections in each other's eyes. Seton seems calm; only the rise and fall of her chest betrays her hurried breathing, quick-quick, her breaths scattered, jagged, almost like a panting child seconds from giving way to a tide of tears. 'Don't marry him,' she says again.

They will not be sure, later that night, lying in separate beds, who reached for the other's face first: whether it was Jane who arched herself up, or Seton who bent her head. But there they are: the softness of their mouths, bodies pushing together, the scent of dried lavender, a kiss they feel in their bellies, the shock of teeth, cracked bitten lips, the salt-tang of blood on their tongues and neither is certain in the moment, whose blood it is. Seton can taste the colour of Jane's eyes: rich honey wine. The weight of the kiss pushes Jane backwards onto the bed; she is lying on Mary's crumpled nightdress, a white shadow beneath her, caught between the bliss pooling inside her, and the thought that this isn't right, that women do not kiss like this. *Is this what these jewelled ladies do, in their idleness? Practise with each other for their husbands?* But then she remembers that Seton took a vow of celibacy, and yet here she is, above her, eyes bruised with desire, her hands on Jane's waist, and beneath it all, beneath their bodies, is the ghostly fragrance of Mary's skin.

'Jane?'

A voice is calling for her; the moment it does, she cannot tell whose voice it is. It does not matter. The women break apart at once: Seton steps to the side, her expression hidden as she begins to smooth out the nightdress on the bed, and Jane is running to the doorway – there is no pause to duck beneath it, there is no need for her – and she is gone, she does not see Seton press her fingers to her lips, or a second later when she covers her face.

Neither of them knows that, one day, Jane will marry Andrew Melville.

By that time, Mary will already be dead.

The day after Carberry Hill. The night-time ride to Lochleven Castle, Lindsay and Ruthven urging the horses on. They took a short ferry to Fife before riding on towards the loch. The brightness of the moon, the dim outline of the land barely visible through the gloom, as though it were made of smoke. The smell of the summer night and of the damp grass churned under hooves.

They rode through the night. One of Lindsay's men went ahead with a lantern lighting their path. As they left Edinburgh behind the night seemed to contract, the dark closing in, before their eyes adjusted and the world expanded into vastness. The wild landscape seemed to shift and sigh as though it were alive. They could make out the outlines of giant hills and rocky outcrops, of sleeping livestock, and the millions of stars above them. There were no lights from villages except the odd distant flicker of a bonfire. All the modern markers of their world were stripped away by night, as though they were living in any time, or that Time did not matter. It did not exist for those hours. This might have been any night from any century, and Scotland's shadowy outlines would not have changed since, not really; only shrank or expanded, or moved slightly to one side, as things have a habit of doing at nighttime, always just at the edge of your vision, seen out of the corner of one eye. And Lindsay was a character from a nightmare.

'Do you think we should just do it here, Lord Ruthven?' he called. 'Under cover of darkness?' He swung about to look at Mary. Only a slice of his face was illuminated by the lantern, giving him an eerie, half-formed quality. For a second he resembled a rotting head on a pike, half his face pecked away. He smiled his yellow smile.

Lindsay stopped the group so the men could take a piss, and as Mary's horse slowed to a trot she leaned out of the saddle and vomited on the ground. One of her chamberers called out to her, loud and in French, but the other men hushed her. Mary wiped her mouth and kept her eyes down. *Who might hear them here? Who are they evading in this night-time flight?* Only then did it occur to her that some of her own supporters might be following in pursuit, hoping to rescue her.

Behind Mary, Lindsay was laughing at her, and Ruthven, too, and when she turned in the saddle she saw Ruthven had not yet done up his codpiece, that he was standing naked and careless, exposed to the elements, angling himself into the lantern's pool of light. He wanted her to look, she realised. And so, she did. She gave him this small, senseless victory in the hope it would make him complacent.

The starry sky seemed brighter than the ground below. At every opportunity, Mary halted her horse, claiming she needed to vomit again, or to piss. She called out loudly to her women. She stalled and she made noise, and it was the thought of rescue that burned in her belly, a flame keeping her unborn child warm, and throughout the night she carried this double pregnancy of hope.

Months later, despite sickness and despair and the loss of her babies and her crown, Mary still carries this flame.

The sky is white with a narrow slash of blue. It is too cold for their daily walk in the gardens. The women embroider; Jane is working on a purse to hold Mary's comb. George Douglas is here – handsome George; spoilt, romantic George – and he sits close to his mother, Margaret Erskine, amusing her with jokes, those casual asides that courtly men labour over in the quiet hours, but at each punchline he looks not to her, but to Mary, to see if she laughs. This is noth-ing new. Everyone looks at Mary, man or woman. Margaret Erskine, who misses little, does not seem to see any harm in this. Jane also notices George's furtive, hopeful glances at Mary. *How different he is from his older brother*, Jane thinks. William Douglas, bent-backed from wheezing and, perhaps, from the sheer weight of his family, hobbling after his bastard brother Moray – *regent* now, *his grace 'Regent Moray'* – as though it were he, William, who was born illegitimate and second-best. He carries the burden of comparison that his father shouldered before him, when Margaret

Erskine looked at him sideways and sneered, seeing only a Douglas, and not a King of Scotland.

Seton is not thinking about George or William Douglas. She is remembering the kiss with Jane; all morning her chest has felt tight, her throat closed, waiting for something to be said, for Mary to catch her wrist and hold her back and say, *Jane has told me what you did to her.* She is ambitious, Jane; Seton cannot rule out this possibility, that she may blackmail her, or expose her to curry favour. Since they were children, Mary has nicknamed her 'Saint Seton'. *If she finds out, she will not call me by that name anymore*, Seton thinks. No one will.

A bird darts past the window, a flurry of dun, too quick for anyone to distinguish what it is. Cuckoo looks up at Jane, hopeful. She is remembering the voices she put on for the chickens; she is like a child, eager for another game. *More, more.* They all hear the bird, trilling somewhere outside.

Mary goes to stand by the window. 'You see, they are calling me, like sirens,' she says, her voice low so that Margaret Erskine will not hear her; but George, young handsome George Douglas, hears her, and he stands, joining her at the window, his head bent; Jane hears a whispered inquiry, and Mary's hesitation, perfectly timed, like music, before responding in that same low voice. *She is a mother missing her child. She is a queen stolen away from her people.* The birds call her like the sirens: those half-bird, half-women creatures who called to Odysseus. They sing of her country. They tempt her. *Seduce her.* Jane watches Mary, still turned towards the window. She watches as she lifts a finger and presses it to the corner of her eye. She watches George's face: transfixed. He fumbles, searching for a handkerchief, breathless, almost dropping it in his haste to hand it to her. Jane senses, rather than sees, that Seton has edged forward like herself, the better to watch and to listen.

For a fleeting moment, Jane imagines the mole at Seton's throat. *Do not think of that now.*

'What do you think the siren sings of?' George is asking.

'Perhaps it is different for every listener,' Mary says.

'You know, everyone always says that the sirens set out to seduce,' he says, and there is a schoolboy's eagerness in his tone, 'but they didn't sing about flesh. They sang about fame. About legacy. *Come with me, and they will tell stories of you, they will sing songs about you, they will remember you.* They promised these things in exchange for love, and if the sailors didn't follow them, the sirens would throw themselves into the sea and drown.'

'They died? The sirens died?' Mary says. She shakes back her sleeve – a quick movement, only visible to her women – and puts her white hand on George's arm, as though to steady herself.

He stares down at her fingers, at the exposed wrist. 'Without love, they died,' he says.

'Perhaps the Greek poets were mistaken,' she says. 'Perhaps these sirens truly wanted those things for the sailors – fame, tributes – and their price was devotion.'

'Devotion,' he repeats, slurring, intoxicated.

Mary turns her head, looking back into the room; and Jane finally sees her, perhaps for the first time. She sees and she understands. There are no sirens calling for Mary to follow. *She* is the siren. She sings her song of seduction, her very presence promising those around her a place in history, in the songs their countrymen will sing in the years to come. A life beyond the ordinary. *You will not be erased.* But she exacts a price: she demands love. Adoration. Devotion. Without it, without the love of others, she will die. For the first time, Jane sees the power she and the other women hold over their captive queen. Mary needs them. *Did the sailors know this, too?* Jane wonders. *When they jumped from their ships, did they follow the sirens with eyes open, knowing what they were risking? Was it a sacrifice? Did they follow for the promise of fame and glory, or because they loved, and could not bear to watch a siren die?* Jane had once imagined sirens to be ugly, monstrous creatures, harbingers of death, neither of one realm nor the other: the ghosts that swam across the ceiling, weaving between the rafters with their silver fishtails and corpse faces. But now she pictures Mary – as tall as a man, a demigod of two worlds – with huge feathered wings, dark and glittering like a swallow, flashes of jewel-bright greens and blues and the dark red slit at her throat. She sings her promises of glory – what was it that Seton told Jane? *You nurse her only to return her to power, to raise yourself up; you think nothing of the woman.* But this is not wholly true. Jane sees Mary's amber eyes, half proud and half pleading. Jane pictures this, and she knows in her heart that she would follow her beneath the waves. *You cannot choose who you love.*

'Perhaps the sailors wanted to hear the sirens,' she says, loudly. She is looking directly at Mary, her chin up, as it was on Twelfth Night; she ignores George standing to the side. 'Perhaps they heard their songs and their promises and chose to go to them. Or perhaps they knew the sirens would die if their songs did not work on them, and chose to save them.'

'But the sailors knew they'd be doomed,' Mary says, not yet understanding.

'They didn't see it that way.'

In the corner of the room, no one notices Agnes, round and full like an olive, her narrowed eyes fixed on George. He is staring at

Mary, his face slack, mouth open. It is Agnes, and not the clever
Margaret Erskine, who first thinks: *This will be a problem.*

And it is Agnes, not Margaret, who begins to plot.

Before Lochleven, Jane had not felt desire – true desire – for many
years. Sexual acts were not pleasure but punishment, battery, no
different from a beating that left you unable to sit down for days,
your mouth bile-dry and your insides pulped.

She was very young when it first happened. She knew of other
girls who had been younger still. But she bled for a long time
afterwards, too long, and so the man – an older man, a man of
high standing, her parents' neighbour and her father's friend – left
her alone for a while. During that time, Jane learnt to hold her face
still throughout the day, to mask any emotion: fear, anger. Rage.
When he tried to touch her again, she turned to him blank-faced
and broke his nose.

She did not bleed that day. But he did.

The women have fallen asleep by the fireside, surrounded by the
night's debris. Mary demanded they stay up late into the night,
gambling with money they did not have, calling for supplies from
their jailers' cellars. The wine has dried the roofs of their mouths:
they can smell it on their own skin, in their sweat. The alcohol
and the taste of last night's dinner, pork fat, on their breath. They
are woken by the sun – the curtains were not drawn, no servant
dared step over the sleeping forms of the women – and as they
stir, they see that Mary is not among them; her place is empty.
The women – Jane, Cuckoo, Seton – all look up, only to see she
is dancing, though there is no music, no sound; her eyes are half-
shut as though in ecstasy.

'*Dear*,' Seton whispers, before she stops herself, and Jane realises she is talking to Mary; Jane feels a heat in her abdomen, a clenching sensation as though in anger. Or lust.

Mary is dancing with the night, with the sunrise: she takes the dark between her hands and turns it to gold. The women are gathered about her now; they step forward, drawn as though she is a pulsing source of heat; as though she has attached strings to their wrists and now tugs them to her. It is not dancing as the others have seen – following steps, a choreographed touching of palm and waist – no, she is dancing for the pleasure of moving her body, stretching her limbs, flexing her hands and feet. She takes her mantle in her hands and flings it back, to free her body, and Time is suspended as the folds of cloth billow out from her shoulder blades, like a great pair of wings. She is feathered, a bird twisting and turning, like a swallow dancing in the sky, exultant in the knowledge that, finally, it is returning home.

*Spring*

It is just after dawn. Jane looks out across the water and the hills that surround Lochleven Castle. They are almost like mountains, casting the loch in their shadow. Like a weaver sorting through threads, she groups the colours: moss green, pale lichen green, the flash of yellow flowers high up on the hills, the inky waters and silver reflections, the blue of the sky – bright blue. A painter's blue. The colour of spring. She remembers the pink sky the morning they arrived at Lochleven, the castle a dark silhouette reflected on the loch's surface, like an underwater fortress.

Today is the day she will jump from its walls.

Except for their daily walks into the kitchen garden or by the shore of the island, surrounded by silent escorts, the women have been confined to the same rooms every day, week after week, month after month. At dusk they are locked in by the laird,

William Douglas, jangling his keys. Their horizon has shrunk. The atmosphere in the rooms is fretful, oppressive. The constant indoor scents of the piss pot, of each other's breath and stiff unwashed hair. From the tower window, they learn to track the daily rhythms played out in the courtyard cobbles: the arrivals of messengers, the herding of fowl with their circular movements around the yard, like the shadows on a sundial. Visitors to Mary's rooms – in particular the men – feel to Jane as Ruthven did when he staggered, drunk, into their midst; they are exotic animals, both danger and distraction.

The women all cope with imprisonment in different ways. The worst is Cuckoo, who complains more and more. She becomes obsessed with the idea of returning to France, to the French court where Mary has relatives, and protection, and a clear place amongst the royal family. Cuckoo's habit of disparaging other countries, other courts, of incessant moaning about the Scottish skies, becomes unbearable. The others begin to roll their eyes whenever she speaks in this way, and Mary, who wants quiet when she is plotting, finally snaps.

'You forget, Cuckoo; Scotland is my country,' Mary says. She thinks, but does not say, *You think I don't mourn the French summer skies, too? This wilderness is my inheritance. Mine.*

Jane does not trust herself to look up at Cuckoo's face. It takes Jane effort to maintain this blank mask of hers, and months of captivity have depleted her inner resources. She can't always hide a smirk.

But even Mary's rebuke does not stop Cuckoo's words, at least not for long. When Mary is distracted, Cuckoo lowers her voice and mutters her usual insults. Nowhere is safe, it seems: not Scotland, and not England either, where there is plague and the *sudor anglicus*, the English sweat. The others say, *The sweating sickness has not been reported for ten years*, but Cuckoo is determined. 'Even if that is true, why is it the *English* sweat?' she says. 'It follows Englishmen even across borders, across seas; it's a judgement from God. Who would go to a country with its own sickness?'

She will not say the real reason why she wants to return to France: that she thinks – and hopes, and fears – that her brother Toussaint has sailed home.

Sometimes, when Cuckoo stands still long enough, she remembers the sunshine and promise of her adolescence, the French palaces filled with light, and she cannot understand how she came to be here, how the years have slipped past. *I should be with Toussaint, we should be eating honey cake or laughing in the gardens*, she thinks. *Where is he?* He would not have left the country without her, surely. No, he would not abandon her unless he was in danger. Her brother always loved her best, always knew how to calm her or make her laugh. In Edinburgh, when Cuckoo's quick temper sometimes offended the other servants, Toussaint would run to and fro like an emissary, pleading her case, tending hurts, smoothing out disagreements. Unlike his sister, he learnt to speak Scots, and she became complacent, believing he would always be nearby to translate, to tell those she'd insulted that it was all a misunderstanding. He, the blond, smiling valet, would flatter and soothe and finally return to Cuckoo. He would clap his hands and say to her, *All sorted, ma chérie.* But here at Lochleven, she is isolated. The women in the tower need no translation to understand her words. And there is no Touissant to defend her.

Mary's thoughts have also turned to a reunion: of her and her son. Of reclaiming her rights and freedoms as a prince. She knows herself cheated of her birthright, and she has begun to plot her escape – starting with the seduction of George Douglas. In the long months of illness and captivity, Mary's women had begun to forget what it is to see her flirt. They had forgotten the way she can entrance a man. Like a tailor repurposing fabric, transforming an altar cloth into a gown, Mary can pick apart a man's very being. His ties to kin, his pride, his love for another woman: all are snipped free. He is remade, he is untethered from himself, lost without Mary, a man whose will is hers to bend. The women have watched on as George Douglas becomes such a creature, stitch by stitch, from head to hem. He lies awake at night, planning Mary's escape. When he learns she has been deprived of ink, he teaches her the schoolboy trick of mixing water with chimney soot. At dawn, he bribes the boatman and smuggles Mary's letters – pleas to foreign courts – out across the loch and waits for the replies, for the offers of help that will never come. All this he does for Mary, enthralled by her as so many others have been, and will be.

Such privilege also makes Mary vulnerable: to jealousy, to those determined to possess her, and to the tangled mess of contrary expectations the lords heaped upon her when she arrived on Scottish soil. An interloper, out of place: a woman in a man's realm, a Catholic in a Protestant country, neither quite Scottish nor quite French. The lords wanted a powerful leader who was also a dutiful wife. A woman who took advice, but only the right advice. Sexless yet fertile, a broodmare who was also impermeable, a mother who was untouched; in short, they were ex-Catholics who demanded their queen embody all the impossibilities of the Virgin Mary. The lords will hate her all over again for seducing George Douglas right under their noses, right from behind the very bars of the jail they condemned her to.

But Mary does not care. She has a plan. And the next step is for Jane to jump from the tower walls.

The moment Agnes began her lying-in, safely cloistered away in a dark room for her final weeks of pregnancy, Mary started to speak of escape options, to lay down plans, and Jane volunteered herself when Mary suggested, in an offhand way, that they should first test the dangers of jumping from the tower into the garden. Jane suspected even then that it had been Mary's desire all along, for one of her women to put herself forward. But Jane also knew that if she did volunteer, if she succeeded, then she would have a place beside Mary for years to come. *I will not be erased*, she thinks. It is a test of loyalty, too. Through one act of seeming self-sacrifice, she might fulfil Mary's wants while also serving her own ambitions. It is possible for someone to take something of you, even as you are slyly reaching into their own pockets.

Cuckoo sulked after Jane volunteered, wishing she had thought to do the same. And Seton, too, appeared agitated; Jane has noticed her thin mouth and the receding stubs of her fingernails.

Now, the women stand huddled in the walled kitchen garden, looking up at the tower. It is March, and the soft ground is filled with ripening vegetables: carrots, turnips, leeks, parsnips and, resting on the soil bed, the large doll-faces of white cauliflowers. Bursts of vibrant yellow: dandelions, grown for their medicinal properties. Seton glances down at them and tastes acid on her tongue. The morning had looked fine, a clear spring sky; but now the women feel a drizzle of rain, hear it tapping against frilly green leaves, and beyond the garden, on the surface of the loch.

'Scotland,' Cuckoo says, by way of explaining this sudden change in weather.

A stray midge buzzes before Mary; she claps her hands, trying to catch it between her palms, but it darts free. Seton is still staring up at the tower, at the windows that mark the location of their rooms. 'It's higher than I thought,' she says, almost to herself.

Mary turns to Jane; she takes her hands in her own. 'Jane, you don't have to do this thing for me. We can find other ways, make other plans.'

In response, Jane only smiles, and shakes her head, squeezing Mary's hands.

The rain continues, and Mary releases Jane, pulling her veil over her head to protect her hair. She rushes towards the courtyard entrance, and Cuckoo runs behind her, eager to return indoors. But both Jane and Seton are slow to react; they hold back, lingering amongst the vegetable patches and the damp trees that have not yet borne fruit. Neither woman has looked directly at the other since the kiss they shared, the night they drank pale citrus wine and Seton followed Jane into Mary's room and onto her bed, onto the crumpled shadow of her nightgown.

'You need not do this,' Seton says, her voice quiet. She is looking away, at anything and anyone but the short, dark-eyed, bareheaded woman standing beside her. If Jane would glance up at her, she would see the crease between her eyebrows, the anxiety in her face.

'You could break your neck,' Seton says. 'You can change your mind.'

'I won't,' Jane says, curt.

'But –'

For a moment, Jane believes Seton is jealous; jealous that it was Jane who volunteered for this task, and not her. That it will be Jane who gets credit for her daring, for her sacrifice.

'You don't need to do it,' Seton says again, after a pause.

'That is easy for you to say, her childhood friend,' Jane says, her tone sour. 'She likes you no matter what you do; you can be as dull as you please, and it won't matter. You are *Saint Seton*.' She realises a moment too late that Seton is not jealous at all – she is nervous. Perhaps even frightened.

Jane regrets her words almost at once; she says, 'I didn't mean –'

But Seton is already striding away, her long legs carrying her towards the courtyard, away from Jane, who stands still for a moment longer, her wet hair dripping down her neck.

The midday meal is subdued; the women all listen to the rain, half-afraid of it continuing, and half-afraid of what will happen when it stops. The plan is this: the other women will lower Jane from a window and onto the top of the high wall that wraps itself around the kitchen garden, separating it from the courtyard and tower. She will then jump. Much thought has been put into where she will jump; it is decided she should aim for a thick patch of bushes, rather than the fruit trees. She will then sneak back into the courtyard, under the pretext of fetching dandelions to brew in a tea for Mary. George Douglas will be watching from his rooms, ready to rush out and supplement her excuses to any guards who might be passing. He has been plotting Mary's escape for weeks, advising her, preparing for the day when she will flee her rooms and he will row her across the loch and to freedom.

Seton pulls Mary to one side. 'Can we trust him?'

'You think my judgement is flawed?'

'No. Only that you have been . . . too kind with your opinions in the past. Especially with men.'

'I know.'

'He is young.'

'He is idealistic. Chivalrous. He wants to play at being the white knight. I can use that.'

Earlier that week. Mary's head bent close towards George's. She wore a generous amount of perfume.

'Who would row?' she whispered.

George could smell her floral scent, could distinguish the rose water in her hair. 'I would row you,' he said, also whispering. 'Once you were in the gardens, I would meet you there.'

'And would we be alone?' she said, dropping her voice still lower so that he was forced to bend forwards, his cheek almost brushing her own.

George swallowed. He said, 'There are horses enough for you to bring an attendant. Perhaps one who would not attract attention.'

'Jane,' she said.

'Fine.' He was distracted. He wanted to tell Mary that she was the most beautiful woman he had ever seen. He wanted to tell her that her eyes were like amber, her skin pale and delicate as sea-foam. But he saw, too, beneath her flirtation. He saw that she had been left brittle by circumstance. He remembered the day she was forced to abdicate; how he had looked on like a coward as Lindsay raged and bullied. How Mary, days after her miscarriage, had tried to defy him. How strong she had seemed.

George watched as Mary shook back the cuffs of her sleeves – *had other men ever noticed this habit of hers? Was he the first?* – and selected one of the dried pears he had brought to her, picking it up between her forefinger and thumb.

'The jump from the wall into the garden,' she said. 'That is the only part of the plan that frightens me.'

'Perhaps,' he said, after a moment, 'you might ask one of your women to test it? Do you think they would?'

George watched as Mary raised the pear to her mouth and sunk her teeth in. She swallowed.

'Yes,' she said, smiling. 'Yes, I think they would.'

Just before dusk. The rest of the household disappears for their evening meal, the gardens empty of servants. The rain stops, and the women begin to prepare.

Seton watches Jane as she smooths back her hair, her face set. Since girlhood, Seton has always been clumsy; she spent so long trying to minimise her height, hunched into a servile pose, that she no longer knows how to move through the world with the body she has, rather than the one she wishes for. By contrast, Jane moves with deliberation, with purpose. She knows exactly her place within the air around her: her position to the people who stand about her, to the objects that crowd the room. There is a grim determination in the set of her mouth and jaw, which reminds Seton of the aged nuns at the priory in Poissy, their faces tanned and creased, deep lines around their lips as they bent over their tasks, refusing help. *Jane will outlive us all*, Seton thinks.

She is wrong.

Jane sits at the edge of the windowsill, her legs dangling out the side of the tower. Now she is here, she is not sure how best to attempt it – she worries she should have climbed out backwards. She turns awkwardly; she can feel the blood-beat in her neck. Seton and Cuckoo take hold of her wrists and begin to take her weight. Behind them, Mary stands with her hands clasped as though in prayer. Jane's whole body is now dangling and the women are holding her wrists and arms; they are trying to lower her down so that the drop will not be as far. The wind has picked up; Jane feels it moving her skirts, flicking loose strands of her hair across her face. She keeps her gaze trained down, at the garden wall; she tries to kick out, pointing her feet, but they meet only air. She feels the grip around her left wrist loosen, and suddenly it is not there at all, she is dangling from one arm – pain shoots through it, her whole weight, her wrist will snap – she hears grunts behind her, a frightened squeal like a pig. Jane's body slams against the side of the tower, and she gives a muffled cry of pain.

In the time it takes to breathe three ragged breaths, Jane registers fragments of her surroundings: the sight of her feet dangling, so close to the wall below; the view of the loch in the gloaming, and the uniform rows of vegetables in the kitchen garden; the smell of rain; the grain of the stone wall, patches of moss growing in the cracks. The sound of a bird calling from far away.

But there is also knowledge, a flash of certainty: the hands holding her, gripping her right wrist, are Seton's. It is Seton who is bearing Jane's weight, who will not let go until she is pulled head first from the window. *She will break her neck*, Jane thinks, and so she begins to twist and pull like a fish on a line; she wriggles her arm, she digs her nails into Seton's palm. There is a lurch, and now Jane is teetering on the edge of garden wall, the toes of her boots grazing stone; she looks up, and she sees she was right: Seton is leaning out of the window, the two other women clutching her waist and skirts, and Jane looks into her face fully, for the first time since they kissed over a month ago; their eyes meet just as Jane slips from Seton's grasp.

Jane is lying on the soft damp ground, her eyes shut. The last few seconds are blurred: she thinks she tumbled from the wall at an angle; her palms feel raw from where she clutched at tree branches, scrabbling for purchase, anything to slow her fall. She feels a dampness on her cheeks, and realises she is crying in pain. All at once she thinks, *My ankle, my ankle,* and it is the only thought, there can be space for no other.

Jane is conscious in only brief bursts. Seton is there, touching her head, cupping her face and blowing cool air onto her bleeding hands; Cuckoo is kneeling in the dirt to unlace Jane's boot, and Jane wants to chastise her – *You have the wrong shoe, Mary is over there* – but she is too tired, and now she is in George Douglas's arms; she knows this because he is speaking loudly, proclaiming he saw the whole thing, *the poor girl*, it's a miracle her brains aren't spattered across the ground. A moment later, she is lying on Mary's four-poster bed, and the bald surgeon is prodding her ankle – his hands are so cold – and she realises she has shouted in pain, because her mouth is open – air on her tongue, in her cheeks – and she can hear a horrible noise. Another moment later, she is in her shift. Somewhere close, Cuckoo is saying, 'Look at these bruises, they go all the way up one leg,' and Seton says, 'That's because you let go of her.'

Cuckoo – who can never take criticism – begins to excuse herself, to explain, and Jane turns her head away.

The bruises are plum purple. Seton looks at them and gags; in their colour she tastes elder vinegar and bile.

'Thank goodness she is so sallow – they won't show as much,' Cuckoo says, and she seems genuinely relieved for Jane. The bruises are so dark they look painted on. Jane's ankle is discoloured and swollen; she couldn't fit a boot on if she tried. Mary lends her the soft, overlarge velvet slippers she first borrowed on

Twelfth Night. They are embroidered with flowers – Jane herself stitched them, whiling away time by mending and adorning Mary's clothes. Now Jane looks down and sees her own craftsmanship—two gold marigolds—on her own feet. The pleasure, the temporary reversal of herself and Mary, is almost too much for Jane to bear. But still, all she can think is, *Mary cannot use a lame chambermaid; I have failed her, she will not take me with her now.*

*Without her, I will disappear.*

*Without me, the siren will crash beneath the waves.*

For the remainder of the week, the women revolve around their invalid as though performing the galliard. Mary and Seton assist Cuckoo in dressing and undressing Jane, in tending to her needs, in helping her to the piss pot or washbasin. They sit around the bed and read to her, or play card games to amuse her. At mealtimes, Mary holds her own cup to Jane's lips and wipes her mouth for her with her own handkerchief, embroidered by Cuckoo over the winter: the grey outline of a unicorn in the bottom corner.

When the surgeon returns, he demands to see the bruises extending up Jane's thigh and buttock. The other three women insist on staying with her, arranging Jane's skirts so that the least amount of flesh possible is exposed to his cool, probing fingers. They hold her hand as she winces with the pain and humiliation of it; Seton wipes away her tears, and Jane is too tired to feign distraction or indifference – she stares back at Seton with an open, frank gaze, and Seton does not look away.

The bedroom is dark and shrouded, tapestries blocking every window, every patch of sunlight. Agnes is sitting up in bed, wondering if this is how her unborn child feels, curled in the pitch-black of her womb. The midwife sits in one corner, her head bent over needle-work, squinting. In the other corner stands the sour-faced maid, the one Agnes sent chasing after Jane and Cuckoo the day they returned with Liz The Cat. The maid fiddles with her collar, loos-ening it, beads of sweat standing on her brow. The room is hot and cloudy with herb-smoke, the fireplace lit day and night. Only women are allowed within these four walls. A small amount of saf-fron has been sprinkled on the floor to ward off plague and contagion. Bright red threads among the carpet of rushes.

*Crack.*

Margaret Erskine sits at the foot of Agnes's bed, bending her neck from side to side until she hears the bones pop beneath papery skin. The gloom is kind to her; in the firelight, she looks younger than her years, cheeks flushed, the lines on her face softened. Whenever she moves, the other women catch the scent of her per-fume: the musky whiff of incense.

'You are sure?' Margaret says, addressing Agnes.

'She has him under her spell; George was there when one of her maidservants tried to jump from the wall. The Scottish one. He is part of their plan somehow.'

Margaret cracks her joints again. 'You must be mistaken. Your maid must have misinterpreted things.'

'I didn't, I swear, my lady,' says the sour-faced maid, stepping forward, eager, her words tumbling out. 'I have been watching them. He stares at her all the time, he'd do anything for her, I swear. He is helping plan her escape.'

Margaret Erskine holds up a finger, and the sour-faced maid shuts her mouth at once. The older woman looks around at the tap-estries: they are almost all pastoral scenes, chosen for their supposed calming effect on a woman with child. Margaret remembers her own lying-in, when she was pregnant with George. He is the child who most closely resembles her; it is a consolation, to look into his bright face and see the vestiges of her own faded beauty.

'I knew he liked her,' she says. 'What man does not? But this intimacy between them . . . I did not think it would rule him, as you say it does. That it would drive him away from his family.' Margaret sighs. 'We will send him away. We will cut off contact between them. I will speak with William, now. You did well,' she adds, looking at Agnes. 'You did well to bring this to me.'

When she has gone, Agnes sinks back against her pillows, hands on her belly. She congratulates herself. In the dark deprivation of her birthing chamber − sightless, soundless − she has still kept watch over the captive queen. A blind spider, she felt the vibrations at the edge of her web, and slowly, surely, she began to reel in.

There are damp curls at Jane's temples. She is asleep, her lips parted, her eyes moving beneath their lids. Her body smells clean, of fresh linen and sea air. Seton is sitting up in bed beside her. On her other side lies Mary. She, too, has fallen asleep, but Seton cannot. She is praying. *God forgive me, God forgive me. Forgive me my trespasses, lead me not into temptation.* She wants a Catholic priest to confess to, but she knows that William Douglas's religious tolerance will only extend so far.

Desire for another woman is not unheard of. It is common enough in nunneries for the church to take action, to put penalties in place for those women who act on their desires. In the priory where she grew up, Seton never heard a stifled moan of lust in the dead of night. But she wonders, now, about the shared looks, the lingering touches she is sure she witnessed.

Sex between two women is denounced as sodomy. In Toulouse, women have been arrested and tortured for their sins. Sex between women is a capital crime, according to the Constitution of the Holy Roman Empire. Seton knows of a woman who was burned alive in Foy, in the Ardennes.

Seton – *Saint Seton* – is a pious woman. A life in a nunnery was always a more appealing alternative to marriage, to a life spent in the bed of some sweaty, drunken lord, his beer belly pressing into the small of her back. Now she sees she has hidden behind her piety, and she has hidden behind Mary's skirts. She has been protected by her proximity to her.

Seton believes she is formed wrong somehow. She must be different from ordinary women. One hears of rare individuals whose four humours are imbalanced. Men are meant to be hot and dry, women cold and moist. One hears of women, however, who are too hot, too much like men in their humours – an excess of blood or choler perhaps – which makes them dry and undesirable. Too much like a man. Seton might cut her arm and drain herself of blood – she has contemplated it before. But she will not. She is frightened of God, she is frightened of pain. She is frightened of herself.

Seton wants to confess about the kiss she and Jane shared, but a part of her yearns for confession only so that she might relive that moment, touch by touch. She bites her nails and thinks of dressing as a man with Mary, of striding through the streets of Edinburgh, their hair hidden under caps. Seton remembers the women who looked up at her with kind eyes when they thought she was a man. She thinks of elsewhere in Europe, where women are pilloried in iron collars for the offence of cross-dressing. She thinks of that most famous cross-dresser, Joan of Arc, accused of acting against divine law, of forgetting female decency. They said that as she burned at the stake, she kept her eyes on a small cross held aloft by a priest. *I can never leave Mary*, Seton thinks. *I cannot*. Seton loves Mary, a woman who needs love the way common people need air. Mary needs Seton, and Seton needs her.

Jane opens her eyes and all she can see is blue, lapis-lazuli blue. She knows, as dreamers know, that she is lying at the feet of the Virgin, and her blue mantle is covering Jane's mouth and nose, and so she is choking, she cannot breathe.

At the same moment, while Jane drowns in lapis folds of holy cloth, Mary dreams of a peacock. She has not seen peacocks since she left France. Before feast days at the French court, the peacocks intended for roasting were allowed to roam the gardens, always with attendants. The birds sat on low branches, their long tails fanning out behind them like the spangled trains of fine gowns. They had jewel-bright bodies, but the feathers hidden beneath the tail were tawny brown, like those of a common hen. The peacocks called out in threes; a desperate, melancholy quality to those calls. There was a sadness to those birds: creatures symbolising immortality, and yet each marked out for slaughter. They would be plucked and roasted before they were served up, the feathers carefully reapplied to the carcasses, the quills piercing unfeeling flesh. A cook once handed Mary a peacock feather – the same man, though Mary did not know it, who would claim he invented marmalade while picturing her breasts. She thanked him for the feather, but was careless afterwards with it, eventually gifting it to another girl. Now, here in bed at Lochleven, she dreams there is a peacock standing at the end of a dusty road, its eyes on her. There is the faint hum of buzzing flies.

Mary knows, as people know in dreams, that this is the same peacock whose tail feather she gave away and later regretted.

*Why didn't you just fly away?* she asks the bird. *Why didn't you hide yourself?*

*How could I hide myself, with all my colours?* the bird says. *Besides, it does not matter. I am here, immortal, because you remembered me after all these years.*

Mary wakes, and beside her Jane is gasping for breath, thrashing from side to side as though she is trapped underwater, her legs tangled between the sheets. Mary takes her in her arms and rocks her, wiping her forehead. She feels no resentment or frustration towards Jane, despite her failure. Mary loves to be loved, and she sees Jane's twisted ankle as a badge of devotion. It is the middle of the night. There is a noise outside the bed curtains, and Mary knows, without looking up, that Seton is there; she has always been there. The two of them sit either side of Jane; they soothe her, they stroke her hair, they lightly run their fingers up and down the undersides of her arms. Over her head, they glance at each other. Somehow, it is more frightening to see Jane like this than it would be with another woman; Jane, who is so cool, so inscrutable.

'Do you remember when I nursed Darnley?' Mary whispers, and Seton nods: *Of course I do.* 'That was the last time I attended someone like this,' Mary says, gesturing down to Jane.

Seton remembers. She remembers how, in the early days of his courtship with Mary, Darnley fell ill with chickenpox. Mary nursed him; at his sickbed, she fell in love with him. Even then, Seton could see that Darnley's tall frame hid a smallness, a deficit in character, a certain pettiness: mean to his servants, jealous of the other lords, of their lands and titles. But the tender feelings between nurse and patient had already given way to desire.

★

The smell of clean linen: this is the first sensation Jane registers. Second: she opens one eye, and sees above her Seton's long neck, the sharp lines of her jaw. The third sensation she registers: the sound of a woman crying. Then, the low urgent tones of a man speaking.

'What's happened?'

Seton puts a finger to her lips; she is listening to the voices in the other room. The bed hangings have been opened; Cuckoo is kneeling on the floor, her face pressing against the crack in the door. Jane says nothing more. She is too tired from her fall, from her nightmare. She allows herself to be held. It has been so long since someone took care of her.

Outside the tower, the yowls of cats fighting, their screams so loud they sound like feral children.

The room is warm, the fire lit. Mary thinks she can hear the sound of cats fucking somewhere outside.

'You can't leave me here,' she whispers. 'If you go, that's my chance gone, my chance of escape.' She clasps George's hands. A part of Mary will always think she needs a man by her side. This is what she thinks when she looks at George and believes the plan will fail without him here in the castle. She opens her eyes wide and steps closer to him, knowing all the while that this seduction is pointless. He must leave whether or not she wills it.

'My mother must have guessed at our plan, but I came here to tell you there is still hope yet,' he says. He is once more an earnest school-boy in his expressions, desperate to console her. 'I have an hour before my departure, and I have already laid out the foundations of a new plan. I have bribed my brother's little bastard son, Will. I will send him instructions. He and I will find a way to liberate you.'

'How can you promise me this? How can I know you'll come back for me?' Mary feels herself close to tears and begins blinking, willing them to come, to flow down her cheeks so he will see.

George kneels before her and kisses her hands. It is the kind of adoring worship she likes. They are alone, Mary and George. She knows her women are listening at the door, that they would break it down if the need arose. But she has never felt at risk in George's company. Not once has he proposed marriage, or groped at her body, or even kissed her mouth. Mary has been married three times. The first was to a sickly child the common people called 'The Leper'. The next husband was a spoilt petulant man who only saw Mary as a means to her crown. The third was her rapist. She has never been in love, only in lust. She does not know what it is to be loved by a man for herself alone, and not for the power she wields – or that she did, before.

When George stands up, Mary pulls him to her. They kiss. His mouth is soft, his hands light and hesitant, fluttering like butterflies at her waist, unsure where to land. Afterwards, he looks light-headed, his eyes blinking and unfocused. She tucks a stray curl behind his ear and smiles catlike at him. *He will come back for me*, she thinks.

Cuckoo is irritable. For Catholics, it is now Lent. The residents of Lochleven tolerate Mary and her women fasting in private; if the captive wants to voluntarily reduce the cost of her upkeep, let her. Across Christendom, meals are meatless and purposefully bland, but still, Cuckoo finds fault with Scotland. *Why can't the Scots learn to thicken their sauces with flour, as the French do?* Instead of flour, they use an emulsion of beaten butter and water; but in Lent, no butter or eggs or cheese can be consumed, and so their meals at Lochleven are now dressed in little more than water and vinegar. Jane, who is not Catholic, is the only woman among Mary's retinue who does not fast. In normal times this might isolate her or lead to resentment among the others, but because of her fall she is forgiven. Mary sits and feeds her candied orange peel and sugared caraway seeds that stick in the teeth.

Cuckoo has been sulking for many days now. Ever since Jane's fall, Seton has been distant with Cuckoo – she seems to blame her for Jane's injuries. Mary, too, has been distant; George Douglas was sent away, days after he was seen carrying Jane from the castle garden. Cuckoo wants to shout, to say again, as she has said before: *She slipped from my grasp, it wasn't my fault, she was too heavy.* But at night, she remembers holding Jane's wrist and feeling the tug of her weight pulling her down. She felt the backs of her heels lift off the floor, and Cuckoo – paralysed with fear – let go. She comforts herself with the knowledge that Jane's ankle is only sprained; the damage is not permanent. Yet she is also jealous of her injury, watching in silence as Mary and Seton – a queen, a noblewoman – stroke Jane's hair, and dress her, and place cushions under her foot. Every time Cuckoo tends to Jane, she has an urge to press her finger into the large, wine-coloured bruise on her thigh. Would the flesh be hard, or softer, like a marked apple? Would her fingertip leave a mark, or a dip in the skin? The urge is more childish than malicious, as is her annoyance and guilt: a child caught in the act of slapping its sibling.

The air is sun-warmed and tastes of salt, as though the castle were situated not on a loch, but in the middle of the sea. Jane feels the prickle of grass blades between her fingers, feels the heat of the day on her back. The women sit on large cushions in the kitchen garden, under the partial shade of the blossoming apple trees. The ground is littered with their white and pink petals. Jane imagines herself looking down at the tableau: the four women sitting among the spring greens of the garden. The day is unseasonal, too sunny, too bright; it feels almost sinister to her, the heat and the heady, heavy perfume of the flowers. Sitting on the ground, her eyes are level with the plants and gnarled roots of the fruit trees. It is the viewpoint of a child, and it renders her vulnerable. Around her stand the ghosts of her former, frightened selves. In years, Jane is the youngest of the four women, and yet she often feels that she is the eldest – the most weary – among them: the Crone to Mary's Mother and Seton's Maiden. A cynical older sibling to Cuckoo.

Mary is weaving a daisy garland with practised hands, as though she is a kitchen maid or shepherdess and not a prince. She slices into the end of each green stalk with her thumbnail, piercing a hole through that fleshy part before threading the next stalk through. The white flowers on the ground look like scattered pearls. Mary's face is flushed, her fingers busy, her lips pursed with concentration as she shakes back her sleeves. A fly is crawling over her hair, but she has not noticed yet, and Jane does not want to spoil this rare moment of tranquillity. Around Mary's neck, the gold chain Andrew Melville brought to her. Ever since George Douglas was sent away, she has become more serious. She is more guarded, paranoid of being overheard. The night George came to her rooms, he spoke to Mary in hushed, urgent tones. She has not yet told the other women what passed between them.

In the walled garden, the women cannot see the loch – but they can hear it, smell it, feel the close presence of that large body of water, seeping into the ground and their skin, in the water they bathe in. Last summer, they would have delighted in these hours spent in the garden. Now they see it for what it is: a prison within a prison. Swans and geese take flight beyond the walls, their wings clapping as they rise up into the air. The quiet that follows is hushed and expectant, like the silence in church.

'Jane,' Cuckoo says, and when Jane looks up at her she nods towards the edge of the garden. There, the supple, slinking form of a black cat is visible – only for a moment – pacing the top of the wall, before it leaps down and out of sight. It is the black cat Jane rescued from drowning. Jane remembers releasing it into the castle grounds, before carrying its ginger sibling up to the tower and delivering Liz The Cat to Mary, her thoughts still with the thin shadowy creature she left behind. Jane turns to look at Cuckoo again and the pair share a smile, both remembering the sack of kittens by the water's edge, and Jane understands that this is Cuckoo's way of making amends.

'How is your ankle?' Seton says to Jane. She speaks in Scots; among the four of them, they rarely speak it, always preferring French. Jane wonders if she means to put her at ease.

'Better,' Jane says, in French. She is avoiding Seton's gaze – she feels Cuckoo's eyes on her – when she first notices the map. Spread out on the ground before her, Mary has arranged the chains of flowers into the lines and shapes of Lochleven; turning her head, Jane can see the outline of the island, the circular tower, the walls of the very garden they now sit in. She can't understand how she didn't see it before. She wants to laugh; the extraordinary incongruity of the daisy chains – innocent ornaments of children, of young women – and their use here in the gardens by a prisoner plotting her escape.

Mary glances up; her smile, as intimate as prayer.

'You cannot ask this of me.'

Seton is shaking her head, her hands pressed to her chest. Mary is sitting on a stool, the sun shining through the tower window behind her; the light spins her hair to gold and bronze. They are alone.

Mary is frowning. 'I don't understand,' she says. 'It is not such a great task.'

'It is to me.'

'But you know I would not ask you to do this, if there was another person who could play the role. Our whole life, people have pointed to the similarities between us. Neither Cuckoo nor Jane could pass as me, neither one of them could convince a guard. You are the only one who can do this.'

The new plan is this: there will be no more talk of jumping from walls. Mary will escape disguised as a laundress. She will be rowed across the loch to Kinross, where she will be met by the handsome George Douglas. On Easter Monday, the day after Christ emerged from his tomb, escaping death. Seton understands the symbolism, and the hidden message; Easter celebrations are banned in Protestant Scotland, just like Lent and Christmas.

Seton also understands the last key component of the plan: that she will be required as a decoy. That she must become Mary – wear her clothes, her hairstyle, mimic her way of standing and moving – so that Mary can escape undetected. Seton understands all this. But the idea is repellent to her, a feeling as strong and non-sensical as the fear she experiences when a spider scuttles before her. It is the same panic she has felt at every Twelfth Night feast when the cake is served. Seton remembers the taunts of her adolescence. *Hunchback. A poor copy of the queen.* Before Mary she kneels, her hands gripping her friend's knees. She does not realise that she has taken up the position of a supplicant, the same pose the ancient Greeks and Trojans used, to plead before kings and warriors. The idea is to degrade yourself in exchange for protection.

'I can't,' she says.

Mary looks down at her and sighs. She does not understand Seton's fear, and so she does not take it seriously.

'You have always been so loyal. The Seton family has always supported my cause. George tells me that your brother hopes to meet me at Kinross. Lord Seton is coming with troops to escort me to his castle, and then on towards Glasgow. He risks much.'

Mary pauses, allowing her last sentence to hang in air between them before she puts a hand to Seton's cheek.

'All I am asking of you is to put on my dress and stand in this very window, here, for everyone to see. Please. *Saint Seton. Ma chère amie.* My sweet friend. It is only a dress.'

Seton buries her face in Mary's lap, and Mary – whose own hair is teased and combed and arranged by Seton daily – begins carefully to stroke her friend's hair, her fingers tracing the pale length of her parting. Mary is not heartless or emotionless: no one could accuse her of that. But she expects adoration from her people, wants their compliance, their unquestioning loyalty; like the siren of Jane's imagination, Mary needs it to survive. She needs it to escape. *Does Seton not love me as she once did?* Mary has spent nine months imprisoned, and she is past impatience. Her son is waiting.

'Think of this as your Easter gift to me,' she says. 'To your queen.'

All other concerns are laid aside. The women speak and think only of escape. With Agnes hidden away elsewhere for her lying-in, the women in the tower talk freely. They recite the details of the plan, testing each other's memories. All the women except for Jane are fasting, and in their hunger tempers fray more quickly; they are all in a constant state of expectation, the anticipation building with no release, like hot air in a closed pot. Food cannot provide comfort. Their allotted daily walks no longer give them the same sense of relief. Now the women have something to hide; they are more nervous, always aware of those watching them, of the guards who follow them. Each woman is terrified that she will be the one to slip up; the dread of spoiling everything even seeps into the women's dreams.

Cuckoo, who has shouldered extra work since Jane's injury, is more irritable than ever. She takes this out on Jane, imitating her nasal French and miming limping when no one else is watching. But she is careful to be more considerate of Jane in front of Mary, and now Seton, too. She is aware of a shift in the group dynamic, of some unspoken push and pull between Seton and Jane. She sees that Seton often watches Jane, and Cuckoo mistakes this for protectiveness following Jane's fall. But the bond she perceives between them still annoys her. Why should Seton prefer Jane's company, when she has never even set foot on French soil? And why should Jane prefer Seton over Cuckoo, after all that she and Jane went through together during their first months of captivity?

In an attempt to mollify Cuckoo, Mary declares that she, Cuckoo, will be the one to dress her in her disguise on Easter Monday. Cuckoo shoots Jane a triumphant look behind Mary's back, as though she and Jane are two squabbling children.

As they draw closer to Easter, Seton must try Mary's hairstyle on herself to ensure she will resemble her. She sits stiffly in the centre of the room, waiting for either Jane or Cuckoo to arrange her hair. Jane is relieved when Cuckoo steps forward. Mary sews by the fire and Jane lolls on a cushion by her feet, stretching out her injured leg before her. Cuckoo is midway through her task when she looks over and sees Mary lean down to whisper something to Jane. Cuckoo's stomach growls; she feels light-headed. Resentment bubbles up inside her.

'A little help?' Cuckoo says, speaking through a mouth full of hairpins.

'Fix that part by her ears,' Mary instructs, motioning for Jane to stand. Cuckoo is behind the chair, fiddling with a beaded hairnet, as Jane shuffles to Seton's side and begins to brush through loose strands, backcombing them ready to shape around her face. The loops of hair feel silky and light in Jane's hands. She can feel Seton's eyes looking up at her. *Don't look at her, don't look down, don't look down.* A heat spreads across Jane's face, in her ears and down her neck and chest. She is burning.

'You're red, Jane, are you too warm?' Mary looks up at her, concerned. 'Are you feverish?'

'It is the heat,' Jane says, confused. 'The fire – I am . . . Excuse me, my lady.' She hobbles out of the room, wincing in pain. She hears Cuckoo call after her – *That's right, leave it all for me to do* – and Mary, tired of moderating, snaps at her in rebuke.

Jane shuts the door behind her and slumps against it. She holds her face in her cold hands; she digs her fingers into her cheeks and drags them down, as though hoping to draw out the heat. She is trembling.

Jane is used to being in control: of her body, her speech, her facial expressions. But now she blushes. Now she cannot help glancing at Seton. Every day is a fight to contain herself, to suppress the urge to look over too often, to tamper her overwhelming desire, at all times, to touch her. It leaves Jane tense; she feels raw, exposed, childlike in the little allowances she grants herself (*You can look at her three times today, two tomorrow*). Her longing is a bruise she keeps pressing. At first Jane blamed the kiss for this shift inside her, but now she realises it began the moment Seton arrived, disrupting the rhythm of Jane's days, usurping her position in the dance of Mary's morning toilette, upending the careful choreography Jane and Cuckoo had perfected. Jane is still jealous of Seton's friendship with Mary. But she is also jealous of Seton's affections. She wants Seton's gaze for herself. And where Jane once felt anger towards Seton, she now feels lust. Real, adult lust, and not the girlish crush she has tried to convince herself she feels in its place.

The tower itself has changed in Jane's eyes. It is now haunted. Certain buildings hold memories: of trauma, of tears shed, of long-ago births and deaths. And of kisses. Jane is convinced that the room where Mary sleeps remembers the kiss between herself and Seton. The space seems to hum whenever she re-enters, the lines of the bedposts shuddering and dissolving, the untouched sheets rustling in anticipation. The very walls have absorbed the women's desire. Jane's body also remembers the kiss, and in that remembrance her body betrays her. She is like a damp hearth where a fire has been recently lit and the flame sputters and smokes, revealing the long absence of warmth. Jane cannot put out the fire, and it terrifies her. She thinks not only of the kiss, but also about the possibilities it invited, what might have happened if they had not been interrupted. The thought of it makes her ache. At night, Jane's fantasies often begin with herself undressing as Seton watches. But to actually do so would be to surrender control, to trust another with everything she has. She cannot allow herself that.

Jane waits until she has mastered herself, her cheeks cooled, her body no longer trembling. As she rejoins the other women, Cuckoo is subdued, repentant. When Jane is faced with limping back to the other side of the room to fetch more pins, Cuckoo stands instead, and hands them to her in silence.

★

Since she was a child Mary has loved Easter. It is the high point of the church calendar, the yearly reminder of Christ's miracle. Christ was on the cross at Calvary, *the place of the skull*, his Virgin Mother in the crowd of onlookers under a baking sun. Now, today, on Easter Sunday, he is risen. *Christ is risen, hallelujah*. In France, Mary loved the triumphant prayers, the packed cathedrals, the pomp and display and the rituals. But in Scotland, this grey country she inherited, there is no longer a place for Easter. It is seen as a papist festival. They say, *Where in the Bible does it proclaim Easter a feast day?*

The women gather and eat their evening meal in their rooms. It is their first since Lent, and marks the end of their fasting. They are dizzy with anticipation, drunk on the smell of the feast before them. There is beef pie in a hot-water crust, the edges crimped. Meat juices trickle down Cuckoo's chin and she is too hungry to wipe them away, leaving the red dribble to dry and scab on her skin. She gorges on buttery cakes and washes them down with Bordeaux wines shipped from Leith. Long after the other women stop eating, she is still crunching and scooping with her fingers, the mashing and grinding of her teeth the only sound. The other three women chase crumbs around their plates, lost in their own private anxieties.

Tomorrow Mary will put on her disguise: a ragged bundle of grey clothes, the attire of a laundress. The clothes were secreted into Mary's rooms by a boy – the same boy the women once saw snapping a chicken's neck in the courtyard. The boy's name is Will. All the household knows him to be the illegitimate son of the laird, William Douglas. But Will is unacknowledged; he has finer clothes than most of the servants, but that is the only indication of his parentage.

The dress was provided by Will on the orders of George

Douglas, but it is Jane and Cuckoo who made the modifications needed: the hem brought down, the sleeves lengthened, the full cuffs to hide Mary's white hands. And each stitch was threaded with Jane's disappointment. When Mary escapes tomorrow, she will be travelling alone. Seton will be the decoy. Cuckoo cannot speak Scots, and so she is too much of a risk. But Jane — wren-like Jane, with her unaccented Scots — would have been the perfect companion, were it not for her ankle. It has not yet healed; she still walks with a limp, unable to put weight on it. And so she stays. She will dress Mary in the lumpen grey linen, and Seton in one of Mary's velvets, and she will stay. Seton will be called to Mary's side, Jane is sure of it. And what if she, Jane, is forgotten? What if Mary does not summon her, and she never sees Mary — or Seton — again? Jane quickly dismisses this thought. She has proved herself. Mary will surely send for her.

Night comes, but the quiet stillness that usually settles over the island does not. Lights are lit, torches are burning, and somewhere in the castle, the disembodied screams of a woman in labour. In the courtyard below, two women carry water between them. They begin to run, and the water slops over the sides of the pail.

'Agnes,' Seton says, although there is no need. The other three women stare down at their hands, or into the fire, and remember another night, the night Mary miscarried. None of these women hold any affection for Agnes, but they offer silent, winged prayers that dart off into the darkness like summer swallows.

The women do not go to bed. They listen to the distant grunts and moans of birth and keep vigil. They lay out cushions by the fire; they think, *This is our last night here, together.* It seems right that just as one soul arrives at Lochleven — God willing — another should leave by boat.

The moans grow louder, more frequent.

'Someone sing – or recite – or pray – someone say something,' Mary gasps. Seton reaches over impulsively and pulls Mary to her side, their faces pressed together. Neither Jane nor Cuckoo would ever dare make such a gesture; they watch as Mary turns to kiss Seton's cheek. Jane catches Seton's eye.

After a moment, Seton pulls away.

'I remember a few verses by La Belle Cordière,' she says. She sees a look of confusion on Jane's face, and when Jane does not say anything, Seton adds, to no one in particular, 'The poet, Louise Labé. The ropemaker's daughter.'

In her shift and nightgown, Seton draws her knees up to her chin. Silhouetted in front of the fire, there is something impressive about her, Jane thinks: the boyish pose, the long frame, the sharp jutting lines of her jaw and nose. Like the hunter goddess Artemis, or grey-eyed Athena. Seton looks away from the others as she recites.

> Ô beaux yeux bruns, ô regards détournés,
> Ô chauds soupirs, ô larmes épandues,
> Ô noires nuits vainement attendues,
> Ô jours luisants vainement retournée.

Jane, listening to Seton, finds she cannot easily translate the poem in her mind; she is too distracted. She hears only the first words: *Oh beautiful brown eyes.*

Agnes's labour lasts almost throughout the night. Her room stinks of Margaret Erskine's incense-scent, and of blood and faeces. The windows are all barred shut. After the baby's head finally crowns, the rest of its body slithers out onto the bed sheets; *it cannot wait to be free*, Agnes thinks. She can feel her cheeks burning from her efforts, and from the room's oppressive heat.

The baby is a girl. She is late to the world and larger than her siblings were. Agnes looks into her child's face, the eyes scrunched up, the mouth red and open and toothless like a baby bird's. Agnes is disappointed; the baby is not as she'd imagined it, all those evenings crouched over and whispering to her pregnant belly. The babies are never as she imagines them. They never emerge as friends; they emerge as strangers.

Easter Monday. For weeks Mary and her women have schemed and planned for this day and, now that it is here, they are impatient for it to be over, to have done, for there to be no more waiting. In the morning, it is decided that Mary and Seton should be dressed at the same time separately, so there will be no delay between Mary's departure and Seton taking up her position at the tower window. The castle is already bustling with activity as the servants prepare for the feast to mark the child's safe delivery. There will be beef, goose, fish, shredded pork, and freshly plucked chickens stuffed with herbs, all baked or fried or minced into pies, or served up whole on engraved silver platters. The servants will not pay attention to a grubby laundress striding amongst them, or to the bastard boy Will. At least, that is the hope.

Jane is the one to dress Seton. They stand in Mary's room, by the same bed where they kissed in the winter. They have not discussed the kiss; their conversation in the garden before Jane's fall was the first time they had been alone since that night. Now they are alone again. Jane is all briskness, careful to control every gesture, every expression, as she lays out Mary's black dress on the bed, bringing forward the petticoat and stockings, the black and white satin doublet. She kneels to guide the woollen stockings up over Seton's ankles, over her calves. The skin is soft, the hairs pale and downy. Seton's legs are trembling. Jane looks up at her, and sees she is gasping in panic, her hands on her heart, eyes bulging.

'Lady Seton,' Jane says, standing up (too quickly; bright spots of light in her vision, a pain in her ankle) and clutching at the other woman's arms. Seton sits down on the bed, shaking, breathless; she grabs hold of Jane's wrist and slips her hand beneath her own shift, to her own chest. For a moment, Jane thinks it is some bizarre form of seduction – but then she feels through her palm Seton's rapid, jumping heartbeat.

'I feel it, I feel it,' she says. 'You must breathe. Lady Seton, please. Lady Seton. *Mary.*'

It is the first time Jane has called Seton by her Christian name; the first time that name has been used for anyone but Mary Stuart since Seton arrived. The shock of it – the sound of her name, the use of it in Jane's mouth – makes Seton turn her face towards her. Jane mimes slow, exaggerated breaths; her hand is still pressed to Seton's chest, to her heart. The two women inhale and exhale. Seton fills her lungs and tastes again the dark honey wine of Jane's eyes. The heat of her touch. She feels her breathing slow. Jane pulls her hand away; for a moment there is resistance, her hot palm sticking to Seton's bare skin.

'Was it a fit of some kind?' Jane says at last.

'No. I don't know.'

Seton stands abruptly, and Jane takes this as a signal their discussion is over, that Seton wants to resume dressing, to forget what has just happened. Jane turns her back, bending over the items of clothing laid out on the bed. But when she turns, holding out the sleeves, Seton does not raise her arms. She looks down at them as if they are two black snakes.

'*Mary*,' Jane says, and again Seton seems shocked at the sound of her given name; obediently, she raises her arms, and submits to being dressed. But she shuts her eyes.

Cuckoo runs into the room without knocking. She is on the verge of tears. 'She's gone,' she says. 'He came and they were in such a rush; she left without saying goodbye.'

Jane gestures to Cuckoo from across the room; pushing aside her own despair, she does not want to upset Seton, standing there with her eyes still shut. But Seton says, 'Well. She never liked goodbyes.'

The women hurry to finish dressing her.

'You are lovely,' Jane says to Seton, when they have finished.

Seton shakes her head. 'Please, don't.'

Jane looks at Seton, in much the same way Cuckoo once looked at her: as though she were a painting Jane had only ever seen upside down. 'A veil,' Jane says at last. 'You must wear a veil, the thickest we can find.'

When Seton is veiled and stood by the window, she finally opens her eyes fully. She sees her reflection in the glass panes, but somehow it is not her own reflection. It is Mary's. Somehow – perhaps it is the clothes, perhaps the thick veil, or perhaps the unwashed glass itself – Seton is standing and moving as Mary does, shaking back her sleeves, arranging her hands just so, as Seton has watched countless times. She finds she has been studying for the role of *Mary* – Mary Stuart – her whole life. She moves to the side, so that she can be seen from the courtyard below – and she cries out.

The other two women rush to her and then step back at once,

gagging and retching at the unmistakable stink of decaying flesh.
It is Jane who pulls back the heavy curtain, because Cuckoo
refuses. Behind it they find a massacre. A nest of stiff grey mice,
some decapitated, some with their bellies sliced open, their hind
legs frozen in the air.

'The cat,' Jane says. She resists the urge to turn to Cuckoo, to
say, *Your cat*.

'But what can we do?' Cuckoo says, panicked. 'We can't call for
someone to clear it away – they'll see Mary is missing. And we
can't leave them here, Lady Seton couldn't bear the smell.'

'We do it ourselves. We put them in the fireplace,' Jane says.

'I'm not touching them.'

'Yes, you will.'

'I can't. Please, Jane.'

There is a pause, during which the two women stare at each
other, holding their

breath. 'Fine,' Jane says.

'I can help,' Seton begins, but the others tell her not to move
from the window.

One by one the mice are carried in scraps of cloth and tossed
into the fireplace. Jane limps as she paces back and forth. By the
time she is done, her hands are covered in blood and a strange, foul
green liquid. The water jugs are empty, used up this morning, and
so Cuckoo stands beside Jane over a basin and pours ale on her
hands.

Throughout this, Seton stands by the window in Mary's clothes,
her mouth set. Watching her over her shoulder, Jane reflects that
Seton – *Saint Seton* – perhaps loves in the same way that the Irish
saint Kevin loved, when he lifted his hand to heaven and a blackbird
happened to land on it and decided to build a nest there, and he,

Kevin, was too compassionate to move. He stood through sun and wind and rain, his tendons fraying, the blood draining from uplifted arm, never shifting, never sighing, until the last chick had hatched.

There is no view of the jetty from the castle window, or of the route the boats take from Lochleven to the shores of Kinross. And so the women wait.

Mary stands on the jetty and stares at the open water, at the short crossing that separates her from the town of Kinross, where George Douglas will be waiting. In the sky, the dark shape of a wild bird of prey, circling above the trees in the distance. She watches it dive towards the ground with the old, savage thrill she once felt watching her own pet merlins make a kill. Soon she will be free once more. She breathes in the cool, clean air; she tastes liberation on her tongue. Her heart is thudding with excitement and nerves, but at this moment she feels almost total confidence in the plan; she can visualise herself stepping onto the opposite shore. She is elated, radiant with certainty, the urge to grin almost overpowering.

Behind her, she hears the boy Will and the boatman chatting in broad Scots, so broad she can barely catch what they're saying. She keeps her head down, pulling the scarf tight around her neck and lower portion of her face. Her borrowed grey clothes smell of damp, but she does not mind.

'Come on, girl, down you get,' a voice says, and Mary realises that the boatman is speaking to her. He is thin and hollow-cheeked, skin weathered, his arms lean and muscled. She avoids his gaze.

'Let me help you there,' Will says, stepping forward to help her into the boat, so that the boatman won't feel Mary's soft, tender palms, untouched by any labour.

The boat pushes off, and they are away; they are in the open water. Mary has been picturing this moment for weeks, dreaming of this exact sight. She has imagined the disguise, the boat bobbing in the water, the steady rhythm of the oars. What she did not imagine was the boatman himself.

'Show me your face, girl,' he says, almost at once. 'Come on, show me. No need to

be such a prude.' He begins a steady stream of crude coaxing, cajoling. 'Give me a smile, girl, don't be a tease.'

The oars splash and slice through the water's surface. The air is clouded with tiny flies.

'You must be a virgin, so demure-like,' the boatman says. 'But I can always tell.' He says, 'Open your legs, let me see your snatch-blade. Let me see your cunt.'

Still Mary does not speak, does not look up or meet his eyes. When she does not, he begins to curse. She is *a cock-pit, a loose-lipped whore*. Mary stares at her feet, at the borrowed, mud-splattered boots, a size too small for her. There's no whalebone in her disguise, no hooped farthingale to protect her body. Grey rags over her linen shift. Cool air on her crotch. She tries to adjust her scarf, to pull the ends over her breasts without exposing her face. She feels a fly or insect nip her ankle.

'Whore,' the boatman says again – and because she is frightened, because she is fumbling and bent-backed and desperate to hide her body, Mary forgets. For a moment she forgets herself, and makes the same gesture she has always made to comfort herself, ever since she was a girl.

She shakes back her sleeves.

The boatman stares. They are white, ringless hands, the nails clean and pink and unbitten. There are no calluses, and there are no cooking scars. There are no dye-stains that mark a laundress's chapped fingers. There are no sun spots. No animal bites, no pock-marks, no silvery marks from a childhood beating. These hands are whole and unspoiled. The colour of fresh snow, blue-shadowed and smooth. The hands of a water nymph. The hands of a queen. The boatman's first, desperate thought is: *She's a well-kept whore.*

'Show me that face,' he says again, and he lunges with one hand, jerking her scarf down past her chin.

Mary Stuart is sitting in the boat opposite him. He remembers her from her first crossing – of course he does. There are tears in her eyes – from the shock, from the humiliation, *she has always cried easily* – as she stares back at him. Here she is. The mother of the king. The queen-that-was. Wife to the King of France. And now the boatman doesn't know what to do. He cannot take her to free-dom, to Kinross; William Douglas, Laird of Lochleven, might have him flogged. He would lose his job, his livelihood. They might take him to the woods and hang him, without prayers. But he cannot return her to the castle, because of everything he has said to her, when he thought she was a poor laundress. She might write to her supporters and have him killed, a knife in his ribs. She might regain power and have him boiled alive before a crowd of spectators; he has heard of such things happening.

The boatman lays the oars down in the wooden hull and, still more awkwardly, the boat rocking side to side, he kneels before her. She recoils; she does not know what he will do, whether he will turn her in. She is struggling to breathe. He stares down at her size-too-small boots. He begs forgiveness, and Mary looks down at his scalp, at the balding patches, the skin red and spotted. She listens to the distant, triumphant cries of a bird of prey. A pere-grine, perhaps. A kestrel.

'I cannot take you where you want to go, my queen,' the boatman says, addressing her boots. 'But I can return you to the castle and say nothing of this. None of the household needs know. I will tell no one. I swear on my dead mother's bones.'

And Mary can only stare out to the shoreline, the taste of her own tears in her mouth. Finally, she nods.

April. The loch swells unexpectedly, and animals are drowned. In the air, the damp smell of stone and the whiff of the water's edge, of life and decay, the brown sludge scent of sediment and rotted leaves and floating water voles and rats.

The boatman kept his word. The boy Will managed to smuggle Mary back to her castle rooms, into the arms of her women. They held each other and wept, united in their grief and exhaustion. The household still does not know how close they might have come to failure, to possible ruin. In the days after the failed escape, Mary was inconsolable. She had seen the shoreline, she had felt the spray from the oars. She did not leave her bed, and Jane was reminded of that first, terrible fortnight, when Mary refused food and drink, the flesh between her ribs hollowed out even as her still-pregnant belly expanded. Now, however, Mary is up, striding about the rooms every day. She is like a caged lion that has known freedom and gnaws its shackles. It is somehow even worse for her women, to see her like this. She is more like her old self – it is a terrible thing to see this passionate woman confined. The space seems smaller around her, her head almost brushing the ceiling. When she was bedridden, at least they could fuss and care for her. Now they are helpless. Powerless. And her pacing also reminds them of their own confinement. It reminds them how long the days are.

Mary thinks of her former confidence standing on the jetty, picturing her first steps onshore, and she rages at herself, at the boatman, at every Scot who has played a part in her downfall. She feels emboldened in her anger. Reckless.

What cheers Mary the most, more than anything, are letters. Letters from her supporters, from handsome George Douglas, and from Seton's brother, who has joined George near Kincross and brought his soldiers with him. Through the boy Will – his pockets now lined with coins – they post secret messages of hope. They hide in the woods and they wait for the moment they can take their queen to safety. It is George's idea that, when the time comes, they will steal the horses from the Lochleven stables, situated so conveniently on the mainland.

A letter comes, passed from Lord Seton to Will and now to Mary's hand. It is from the red-headed Andrew Melville. Cuckoo's ideal man. The man who only had eyes for Jane.

'He greets me and all my attendants,' Mary says, looking up at Jane and smiling.

Beside her, Seton excuses herself, and leaves the room. She is back a moment later, however, because Mary gasps – *she is always theatrical* – tears brimming – *she is always so close to tears*.

'Cuckoo,' she says, looking from the page to her attendant and back again. 'I did not know . . .'

Cuckoo sits very still, her hands full of embroidery threads, frozen in motion. Her mouth is open; Jane has the urge to reach over and shut it for her.

'Cuckoo, your brother – I didn't know – he sent a message to you. He found Melville at court, before. He has left. He has sailed for France.'

Colour spills across the floor – greens, yellows, brick reds – as Cuckoo drops the threads she has been holding. 'Where? Where in France?' she says.

Mary scans the letter. 'He hopes to find a place at court again. Under the new king – and Catherine de' Medici.'

'And if not?'

'He does not say. Or perhaps he did, but Melville has forgotten.'

'Perhaps.'

Looking at her, Jane does not know if Cuckoo is in a mood to celebrate or despair. She touches Cuckoo's hand, expecting she will snatch hers away. She does not. Together they pick up the spilled colours, scattered across the rushes like crisp autumn leaves.

In the evening, Mary pulls Jane to one side. 'The letter said something else,' she whispers. 'The letter from Melville. At the end, after he spoke of Cuckoo's brother, he also spoke of you.'

Jane knows better than to ask what he wrote; it would seem immodest for a chamberer to expect what she knows he will have written.

'He does not say it outright, but I think he means to marry you, if he can,' Mary says. There is a pause after she speaks. She does not offer to show the letter. For a moment, Jane considers the position she would gain, in marrying Andrew Melville. If Mary were to ever abandon her, Jane cannot be certain she would find employment at court again. She may be tainted by her association with the fallen Catholic queen. With Andrew, she knows how her life would unfold. A husband, and a family. A small household of her own. A rise in station.

A rise into obscurity. Into invisibility.

'I don't know what he means by saying that, my lady,' she says, her voice low. This is her chance: her chance to prove to Mary how much she means to her. How much she, Jane, deserves to remain by her side. How much she is willing to sacrifice to stay there.

'I told him not to entertain those ideas when he was here,' she says slowly. 'I told him it was foolish. I told him I would not leave you now. I could not.'

Another pause.

'My dear Jane,' Mary says, apparently relieved. She kisses Jane's cheek, the same way she often kisses Seton. Jane feels the soft press of her lips, the slight wetness of her saliva when she pulls away.

They say nothing more of the letter.

The first swallows return to Lochleven, bringing hope to those who see them. They swoop down over the castle walls, over the grey stone buildings and courtyard and kitchen garden and the tower where the queen-that-was is imprisoned. The swallows dance, flirting their long tails, racing the air currents that toss them higher, high over the larch trees and the loch itself, a long stretch of grey and silver ripples. A cormorant dives for fish among the water plants: stonewort, the rushes and reeds that line the loch shore and provide shelter for ducklings hiding from foxes. Jane secretly admires foxes; they adapt and endure, eating everything from ducklings and unhatched eggs to pink worms and fallen fruit. They are survivors, like herself. In the damp of the long grass, a slow worm – the *deaf adder* – slithers in search of prey. After the living death of winter, the earth has woken up.

The four women – Mary, Seton, Cuckoo and Jane – walk along the narrow bank of the island, flanked by both guards and by Agnes and Margaret Erskine. Agnes moves slowly, placing one foot after the other with careful deliberation; this is her first walk since her laying-in. Beneath her clothes, she can feel her nipples begin to leak. Her baby is with the wet nurse. Margaret Erskine cracks her joints – her neck and shoulders, *crack*, her knuckles, *crack* – as though she, too, is only now waking with the spring, like a bear rousing itself after hibernation. The other women resent their intrusion, and what it entails for the future. Agnes will soon re-join them, trailing them from morning to night, and there will be no opportunity for them to discuss an escape, no way of leaving the castle without her seeing.

Mary and Seton walk arm in arm ahead of the others. Once, Jane might have felt perturbed at the sight of them, their backs to her, each woman striding in time, engrossed in shared conversation. But for Jane, each still-painful step is a reminder of her sacrifice. If it weren't for her, it could have been Mary who fell from the tower, Mary who almost died. Jane thinks, *She will surely reward me for my love, for my obedience. She will* see *me.* Cuckoo is also watching the two women ahead. She remembers how all four women embraced and wept together when Mary returned to them. She thinks, *Why can't it always be that way?* At court, Cuckoo never pictured herself as one of Mary's *jewelled ladies* ; she lacked both Jane's ambition and the imagination for that. Cuckoo, who is predisposed to envy, was jealous of those women, of their wealth and clothes and friendships, but she did not imagine herself as one of them, among them, until Lochleven. The months in captivity have blurred the distinctions between the four women, making it more painful whenever Cuckoo is reminded of the reality: that she and Jane are not noblewomen, and even if they were, they might still be outsiders. In any group of people, there is always one person whom everyone gravitates towards. Mary is such a person – and in this group, Seton has the prior claim to her.

To comfort herself, Mary is remembering the countless feasts and banquets held in her honour, in France and in Scotland. When it felt like all the world was in thrall to her. She recalls aloud the opulence laid out before her over the years; how she was always guest of honour, with every attention paid to her. The life-size papier mâché elephants built in Rouen to celebrate her betrothal to Francis. The sound of the gunfire at Edinburgh Castle, announcing her return to Scottish soil. Whole cities screaming her name. The delicious pleasure of it: the attention, the admiration. The *love*.

'Do you remember the silver ewer shaped like a mermaid?' she says, and Seton smiles and replies that of course she does. After one supper, the host for the evening brought out a luxurious ewer and basin for guests to wash their hands. The basin was made to look like a huge silver scallop shell, and the ewer was a mermaid, her breasts bared, a mirror held aloft in one plump hand. Her tail unscrewed and she was filled with rose water, and when she was tipped forwards the water poured out from her nipples. The host took it upon himself to pour for Mary, but when he picked up the ewer he suddenly faltered, unsure whether the mermaid was in poor taste. He fumbled, and slopped rose water down his own front, and Mary laughed. This took place years before the battle at Carberry Hill, when banners were made showing Mary as a topless mermaid, and onlookers screamed that she was a whore.

Cuckoo, who is eavesdropping, says loudly that she remembers the mermaid, too. The host had expensive, eccentric taste in silverware, or so his servants told Cuckoo. Among his cutlery were steel blades made in France and engraved with a Latin blessing and musical notes, each knife showing a different part of the sung harmony. The host had hidden these away after Scotland became Protestant and prayers were said in the native Scots tongue.

At the back of the group, behind even the slow-moving Agnes, Jane is standing by the edge of the loch, her boots sinking into the soft silt ground. Somewhere above her, a blue tit is trilling, *tsee-tsee*, the blue cap on its head as soft and delicate as if it were made of tissue. But Jane is not looking up. She is looking out near the water's edge, among the reeds. Something dark and wet is bobbing there. At first, she thought it was an otter, and waited for it to rise for air before diving back beneath the surface. But now she sees that the animal is unmoving. A shiver runs through her. She glances ahead, to where the other women and the guards are walking. None look back at her; their eyes are all on Mary.

Jane steps into the water, biting back a yell. The weak Scottish sun has done nothing to warm the loch. Jane wades in, her skirts ballooning around her. No one has noticed her yet. When the water reaches her waist she leans forward, stretching her arms out as far as she can. She catches hold of a paw and turns, towing the bobbing creature behind her until she reaches the shore, where she drops it on the ground. A sodden mass of slick wet fur. She turns it over with the toe of her boot.

The black cat lies on the ground. Death has robbed the animal of its slinking suppleness; its body is now rigid, the stiff jaws open, the eyes eaten away by flies or a passing pike. The black cat. Jane's black cat. The thin and scrawny creature she once rescued from the woman with a sackful of kittens to drown. She did not know until this moment how much it had meant to her to see that slipping shadow in the castle gardens, its body strong and glossy and alive. How often she had thought of it the previous winter, not knowing if it survived the snow. Whenever she looked at Liz The Cat — that feral ginger beast — she thought of the black cat and wondered if it had lived. Then, to see it alive and beautiful, even in that brief glance before it disappeared from view — it had seemed a miracle to her. Despite everything, it had survived this place.

And now here it is, drowned after all that. As though Death and Fate felt cheated by Jane and conspired against her.

She does not know that a similar fate waits for her, years into the future. By that time, a part of her will have already died. It will die on the same day Mary kneels before the block, dressed in the scarlet red of a Catholic martyr, as Jane ties a white blindfold over her eyes.

Jane stands over the small wet corpse for a long time, her dress dripping. When she finally turns away from the water, and back towards the castle, she finds Seton, and Cuckoo, and Mary, all standing a little way behind her. Seton walks forward to meet her at the shoreline. Jane can see from her face that Cuckoo has told the others about the black kitten. Seton does not say anything, only takes Jane's hand in her own and guides her back to the others, where they embrace her.

The days are longer. In the early twilight, bats emerge, black cut-out shapes in the amber-streaked sky. The bats are pink-faced and swoop low over the water, catching insects with their brown feet. At night, Jane dreams of the black cat, of its missing eyes and its bared teeth locked in a snarl. She dreams of the moment it drowned, when the waters of Lochleven swelled unexpectedly, and the air smelt of decay.

In the daytime, in the hours of embroidery and tired conversation in the tower rooms, Jane retreats — as she has always done — into her imagination, the way Mary retreats into the past. Jane imagines Seton kneeling on Mary's bed; she pushes this thought away as though it were a dog that continues to follow her and put its nose in her lap, nuzzling and begging her for scraps. She imagines instead the Muses, and Elizabeth Tudor, and now she imagines

Catherine de' Medici lying on the floorboards, looking through a hole and spying on her husband and his mistress as they make love. Jane wonders if Catherine found it instructive. She wonders if the mistress, Diane de Poitiers, ever knew she was being watched, and looked up at the ceiling to the place where Catherine lay. Jane wonders if she liked it. This thought leads her to think again of Seton, and again Jane pushes away the thought.

Jane imagines herself wearing the same red velvet dress from Twelfth Night. She imagines Mary looking at her with lamp-eyes, her huge, feathered wings folded behind her. She imagines Seton styled as the female saints in Catholic art, her mouth open and her hands clasped and her eyes rolling back into her head. Jane presses the tip of her needle into her thumb, and Saint Seton vanishes. Jane sucks away the blood.

Today, Mary is content. She is reading a new letter from George Douglas, smuggled in by Will. The letter is filled with plans and hopes. It is also filled with compliments: he praises her face, her compassion, her bravery, her beauty, *her beauty*. Some portions Mary smiles over privately. Other parts she reads aloud, always looking to Cuckoo, who gives the biggest reactions, almost jumping up and down in her seat. Mary plans to read the letter twice, before dropping it in the fire. She reads until the end of the page and then flips it over. She flips it again, re-reading the final, unfinished sentence before rifling through the pages. She looks up.

'What's wrong?' Seton says.

'The letter. The letter from George,' Mary says. 'The last page is missing.'

Agnes is staring at her new baby, watching it suckle at another woman's breast. She watches the wet nurse rocking the child, and she watches as the baby – her baby – puts a hand on the woman's bare breast with a kind of easy ownership, the tiny fingers kneading flesh. Its mouth on her chapped nipple.

'Lost in thought, Agnes?'

Margaret Erskine is looking at her daughter-in-law with an expression of distaste. She has never liked Agnes – few do – and she likes her even less when she stares, eyes bulging out of that slack face, or when she speaks in that sly, simpering voice. But Agnes is a broodmare. A woman who breeds every year always earns her place at the supper table, even if she is a strange and distant mother. Sitting on the floor, close to Margaret's feet, a little girl plays with a hound belonging to her father. She is one of Agnes's children, and Margaret has forgotten her name. She thinks Agnes has, too. The girl is about seven or eight years old, with a pinched look about her. She is using a scrunched-up bit of paper to tease the dog, throwing it between her hands and tossing it in the air.

'Agnes?' Margaret says again. *'Agnes?'*

Agnes finally looks away from the wet nurse's naked breast. 'Oh dear, I was in a little dream, Mother,' she simpers. She feigns putting a hand to her chest, but a beat too late. *It's like she's play-acting,* Margaret thinks. *As though she has watched other women and memorised their movements.* Margaret tries not to wrinkle her nose when Agnes calls her 'Mother'.

The dog is panting, slobber running down his jaws, but Margaret has the feeling that the little girl will never give the dog the scrap of paper. *How like her mother she is,* Margaret thinks.

'My girl,' she says, addressing her granddaughter. 'Give that dog the paper before he tears this room apart.'

'I can't,' the girl says, and there is a gleam in her eye when she turns to look at Margaret.

'Why not?'

'Because I want to show it to you.'

Margaret has the impression the girl has been waiting for someone – herself, or Agnes – to mention the piece of paper. She holds out a hand.

'Hand it over, child, and let's see what's so important about it.'

Mary remembers watching Darnley as he slept. His face was soft and beardless and boyish, pink lips parted, his tongue pointing out like a cat's and his hand closed in a loose fist. His tall, six-foot-long body curled under the sheets. Her *long lad*, she had called him. She remembers how they argued often, and afterwards she could not bear to be touched for a while, not by anyone. Not even a hand brushing her own. But Darnley was like a child, he always wanted to touch her after an argument, to reassure himself. He would reach for her even when she told him not to, when she swerved away from his arms.

Darnley was smothered. That is how he died. Mary usually tries not to think of it.

It was February last year, before Mary married Bothwell. She had persuaded Darnley to return to Edinburgh, to stay at Kirk o'Field, a house belonging to one of her connections. Mary slept in the room below his. His bed had beautiful velvet hangings, Mary remembers. Violet-coloured velvet.

On the morning of the explosion, Mary was not at the house. Two of her favourite servants were married that day, and she attended their wedding breakfast, laughing and handing out gifts. The sky was still blush pink when Mary heard what sounded like a volley of cannons. Later, she learnt that Darnley – the *long lad* who had proved so cruel, so unfit for his place beside her – was found outside the house in the orchard, his body partially clothed and laid next to the corpse of his servant. They escaped the explosion only to be smothered instead.

The people of Edinburgh still say Mary conspired to murder him. That she and Bothwell conspired together, so that they could marry. *Three months*, they say. *She married him three months after Darnley's murder.*

None of Mary's women have ever asked her if these rumours are true – although Cuckoo has wanted to, many times. Seton prefers not to ask. She prefers not to know. As for Jane, she finds it does not matter to her if Mary plotted to kill her husband or not. Mary is still Mary.

The sky this morning is the same blush pink as it was over a year ago, on the day Darnley was murdered. The missing page from George Douglas's letter cannot be found. Mary is frantic. The women search the rooms, and after that Jane finds and threatens Will. She corners him in the courtyard and grabs his jacket and whispers to him, and the other women in the tower watch them through the window as Will's lip trembles and he looks less and less like a young man and more like a boy.

'Is that what Andrew Melville likes?' Cuckoo turns to Seton, incredulous.

'What – that she is brave? That she is loyal?' Seton says.

Cuckoo is not listening. She is remembering those first few weeks at the castle, when Jane twisted the stockings between her hands and stood guard behind the door like the short, scarred terriers you see in the bear-baiting pits. *Mary's attack dog.* Often, when Jane is staring into the distance and half smiling to herself, or else playing games and providing voices for imagined characters, Cuckoo is conscious that beneath Jane's curt, discreet exterior there is a person with a rich inner world. But when she sees Jane like this, as she is now in the courtyard below, Cuckoo begins to wonder about the smile. She wonders, if only for a fleeting moment, if Jane spends her time imagining how best to murder them all in their beds.

'He does not know about the missing page,' Jane says when she returns. 'But he admits he may have been careless. He may have dropped it. Apparently, it has happened before.'

Mary covers her face with her hands.

'Could it be there in the courtyard? Did you check?' Cuckoo says loudly, desperately.

'There was nothing. And if there was, it's either been stamped into the ground – or it's been taken,' Jane says.

The answer comes a day later.

There are three dogs racing down the pathways in the kitchen garden. Dust rises into the air behind them. The dogs are lean and tall and grey, and belong to the master of the house, William Douglas. Mary has seen them before, but has never held out her hand to one, or reached out to pet them. She prefers squat little dogs with short legs and round black eyes, their soft bellies low to the ground, like the Skye terriers she kept at Holyrood Palace.

Today, however, she bends and holds out her arms, calling softly. She wants to feel a dog in her arms, feel its warm body, the rough tongue on her hand and wet nose at her neck and the silk of its ears between her fingers. The other women sit under the shade of the apple tree, watching her as she rubs one of the dogs under the chin. They watch as the little girl who was minding the dogs runs forward, and tugs at Mary's skirts and curtsies. They cannot hear what she says.

'How sweet,' Seton says.

Mary looks down at the girl. She is about seven, and small for her age. She is dressed finely – too finely to be chasing after dogs in the dust – and carries a little beaded purse embroidered with a lion and a dragon.

'I am Euphemia,' the little girl says. 'Euphemia Douglas, after my aunt. I am Lady Agnes's daughter.'

'Euphemia,' Mary says. 'It means "well-spoken" in Greek, do you know that? I was taught a little ancient Greek in my childhood.'

'You're lucky,' Euphemia says.

Mary, who is not often around children, thinks the girl is insolent and overfamiliar; but with a mother like Agnes, the child can hardly help herself.

'You're very beautiful,' Euphemia says suddenly, and despite herself, Mary smiles at this. She has always been susceptible to compliments. The girl continues, 'My own face is too thin.'

'Maybe now,' Mary says. 'But I think you will find in time that you have inherited your grandmother's looks.'

Euphemia does not seem pleased at this, and Mary supposes a child cannot perceive beauty among the old.

'I have something for you,' the girl says.

She reaches inside the beaded purse, fiddling with the strings. She produces a crumpled page and smooths it out. The white space at the bottom is crossed out so that no one can forge any additional lines. At the very top of the page, Mary sees George Douglas's handwriting. The conclusion to his letter.

> . . . *my dearest wish, and I think best if we were to journey across the river.*
> *Your faithful servant, G.D.*

'I found it in the courtyard,' Euphemia says, holding out the letter. 'I thought it might be meant for you.'

Out of the corner of her eye, Mary sees both Jane and Seton sit up straighter underneath the trees, watching her. They have seen the piece of paper and they are ashen, not knowing what to do, unable to shout out a warning to Mary for fear of exposing her.

'Are you leaving us, my lady?' the girl says. 'Because if you are, I would like to go with you. I can assist your escape, and be a lady-in-waiting to a queen. I will prove useful, I promise.'

Mary's fingers are already outstretched when she looks into Euphemia's eyes and sees Margaret Erskine looking back at her. It is like an invisible hand has seized her from behind and yanked her backwards.

Mary drops her hand. Her heart hammers. She tries not to blink. 'The letter is not for me, child. Perhaps it is meant for your mother or grandmother. And as for an escape, I cannot know what you mean. I am content here, in your father's house,' she says. She sees the flush of disappointment in the girl's face.

Euphemia watches the four women process past her and out of the garden, their skirts swishing behind them. She can smell the scent of rose water on their skin. The last woman to walk past her – short, dark, clever-looking – turns and catches Euphemia's eye.

'Did I ever tell you, Lady Seton,' the woman says, still staring at Euphemia, 'that I once broke a man's nose?'

Night-time. The sky outside is clear, every star visible and bright. Mary burst into angry tears the moment she returned to the safety of the tower, throwing herself onto the bed – *she is always theatrical* – and pounding her fists. How could she have been so stupid, to be almost outwitted by a child? Now she has asked to sleep alone. She wants the room to herself. Seton drags a pallet bed into the other room, and she and the other women take shifts outside Mary's door, listening to her breathing. Listening, even now, for an assassin in the night. Cuckoo, slumped against the door frame, can hear Mary pacing about the room, so panicked by the trap she almost walked into.

'It has to be now. By the end of the month,' Mary mutters.

Outside the room, Cuckoo begins to doze.

Jane lies on her back, listening to the sound of Seton breathing. There is a certain tension in the room, like a suspended chord in a piece of music. Both of the women sense that the other is awake.

Seton sighs aloud, rolling over to one side to stare at the dim outline where she knows Jane is. Jane has kicked one leg out from under her sheet; Seton can just make out the contours, the luminous shapes of her calf and ankle.

'Mary told me about Andrew Melville,' Seton whispers. 'His letter, I mean. And what you told her in response.'

In the darkness, Jane makes a small noise, either of assent or frustration.

'Are you sure this is what you want?' Seton continues. 'We don't know what will happen. We don't know if the escape will fail again. If Mary does escape, we don't know how the lords will react, or what they'll do. If she loses against them, she'll go elsewhere. Probably France.'

'Why? Because it is Catholic?' Jane whispers.

'Because she has family there. Her mother's family. And because she is the former queen consort.'

'Well,' Jane says. 'France, England; I do not care where we go.'

'*We?* You mean, you and Mary? Because it will not be you who decides where you go. Your life won't be your own. It will be Mary's.'

*It already is*, Jane thinks. Aloud, she says, 'I did not mean 'Mary and I'. When I said 'we', I meant all of us. Mary, Cuckoo. Me, you.' She feels her face redden in the dark. She says, quickly, 'You're going to stay with her, aren't you? You won't marry.'

'No,' Seton says.

'Neither will I.'

'You can't promise that.'

'And you can?' Jane says. 'What, because I am poor and you are not?'

'No, that's not –'

'I will stay as long as Mary needs me.'

Seton does not speak at first. She feels strangely numb and dull, as she always does when she cannot see colour. There is nothing to taste in the air. Finally, she says, 'I think you would like France, if we did travel there.'

'I would?' Jane says.

'Yes. I think you would. It is very different from Scotland. It might take you time to adjust.'

'What is different?' Jane says.

Seton thinks. 'The light. The colour of French sunlight is yellow.'

Jane says she likes yellow – yellow, the colour of a sweaty slab of butter, pale beneath the knife. The colour of childhood and courage. Seton wants to say, *That is my favourite colour, too. Yellow.* But she stays quiet, not wanting to sound trite. Or foolish.

'Tell me more about France,' Jane says, closing her eyes.

Seton smiles to herself. She speaks of walls mounted with exquisite tapestries, scenes of nymphs in green gardens: nature through artifice. Gardens you think must be more lovely than anything real until you step outside the palace doors, to the manicured lawns. Exotic fruit trees growing in neat lines. Seton once dreamed with Mary of a move to the English court, when Mary – God willing – would inherit the throne from Elizabeth Tudor. Seton imagined it much like the French court, a dazzle of colour and sweet scents and beauty. But now she begins to suspect that England would prove more similar to Scotland, where everything is green and grey. *I would like to die there, in France*, Seton thinks to herself. On the pallet bed beside her, Jane steps into colour. She imagines the bright blues and pinks of exotic plants and birds, many she has never seen before: bright orange, lime green, fuchsia, violet, vibrant yellow. Everything glitters with gold leaf, or cloth of gold. The only person in the room not wearing colour is Mary – younger, childless – who is dressed in white. Yet somehow she is brightest of all, as though she is made of silver.

Jane and Seton both hear the creak of floorboards at the same moment. They can both hear the sound of someone crying.

'Mary?' Seton whispers.

It is Cuckoo. She had returned to the room, ready for one of the other women to take over her shift at Mary's door. But when she heard Seton's voice and her memories of France, Cuckoo instead held her breath, listening. Today is her birthday; or at least, the date her parents gave her to remember as a child. Cuckoo misses her brother. She misses her country. She misses home. Now she wipes her eyes, and pretends to the other women that all is well.

A couple of days later, Margaret Erskine and Agnes are walking in the gardens. They are midway through a conversation.

'I was blind to his infatuation for her before,' Margaret says, referring to her son George. 'I will not be made a fool,' she says. 'I will not have us become notorious as the family who let her slip through our fingers. We will continue to watch.'

'Of course,' Agnes simpers beside her. 'But you know – of course, I have said before – but if only you had given *me* the task of presenting the page to her, instead of little Euphemia – but I will hold my tongue, of course I will. But I must say, I thought it was unlike you to place such responsibility on the child. Why, she is only six.'

'I thought she was eight.'

'Is she?' Agnes says.

Margaret gives her daughter-in-law an appraising look out of the corner of her eye. Agnes is walking with her feet turned out, as though she is trying to straddle the pathway. She has her hands – a flat square ring glinting in the light – folded at her waist. *She is already pregnant again.* Margaret's first thought is not of William Douglas, her legitimate son and the father of this unborn child, but of her bastard son the Earl of Moray. At last count, he has only one living child – a feeble girl – and both he and his elegant wife, Anna, have struggled to conceive in the past. Margaret will die a happy woman if only she knows her bloodline with the former king will continue.

'I understand the boy Will has been speaking with his father,' Margaret says. She says this to watch Agnes bristle. They both know whose son Will is. The clue is in the name.

'Yes,' Agnes says stiffly. 'He has always managed to charm my lord. He has convinced him that we should hold a Feast of Unreason over the May Day weekend. We have only a few days to prepare.'

*By 'we', you mean the servants,* Margaret thinks. *You'll be sat about for the next year.*

'I don't know how the boy convinced him of it,' Agnes says. 'Perhaps some story about raising the spirits of the household.'

'And I suppose Will has cast himself as the Abbot of Misrule?'

Agnes nods. Like the Twelfth Night feast but on a grander, greater scale, a Feast of Unreason sees chaos reign. A peasant or servant – usually a young boy – is appointed abbot and takes charge of revelries, disrupting the normal running of the household, insisting on dancing and drunkenness. It is a popish feast but one that has endured despite all, perhaps because of its informality. It is a day when every maid, cook, lady and lord will be preoccupied with merriment and drink. A day when, among the chaos, a queen might finally have a chance to escape.

The first day of May. Tomorrow is the Feast of Unreason. Until today Mary has kept from her women the plans for the escape. She has not shared the details with any of them, not even Seton, and the three women can only speculate as to why this is. Does she not trust them, after all this time? They do not know Mary has stepped back to conceal from them her own desperation, her own fears. After the missing page and the child Euphemia, Mary doubts herself. She is no longer certain of her own abilities. Next month it will be a year since she arrived at the castle. She keeps the date fixed in her mind as a deadline. No matter the danger, she must have left this place by then. George does not know that a part of his letter was discovered; Mary has not told him. She does not want to alarm him, because then he might delay their plan. She will not allow another year of her life to pass in this way, entombed by water, her throne cold and her child motherless.

Mary gathers her women about her early, before the doors are unlocked. They stare at her, knowing their future depends on her next words. Who will go with her, and who will be left behind?

'Tomorrow, Seton will be my decoy once more.' Mary is bouncing on the soles of her feet. 'It's a role for which no one else is so fit.'

Seton looks down at the floorboards.

'And Cuckoo,' Mary says. 'You will stay here to attend to her.'

'I will not go with you?' The words spill out from Cuckoo's mouth before she can stop herself.

'You are too conspicuous, dear.' Mary reaches out and touches a lock of Cuckoo's long blonde hair; in a burst of recollection Cuckoo is reminded of the lute player, who stroked her hair in the dark. 'Too memorable,' Mary says. 'I need someone –'

'Someone like Jane?' Cuckoo says. She is trying not to sound bitter; she and Jane have recently been on good terms. She remembers again the lute player of Twelfth Night, and Mary's face when she found Cuckoo in his arms. *Is she punishing me?*

'We will only be separated for a short while,' Mary says now, her voice soothing. 'Then I will call for you both – you and Lady Seton. Wherever I am, you will be by my side. I swear to you.' There are no questions in her speech; these are orders framed by gentle words.

Seton and Cuckoo will stay behind at Lochleven Castle. They will reunite wherever Mary goes. They do not discuss the possibility that she could die on another battlefield, or be killed by men acting on the pretence that they are defending her own infant son from her. The women will reunite. Seton and Cuckoo will come when Mary calls for them. She will call for them. She will.

Mary draws Jane to her, the two of them standing alone by the window. 'I would have brought you the first time, but for your ankle,' Mary tells her in a whisper. 'I feel certain that if you had been there, we might still have escaped. I have not forgotten,' she adds, smiling almost flirtatiously. 'I have not forgotten how you have served me these past eleven months.'

Jane wonders what exactly she is referring to. How she, Jane, held her stretched stockings between closed fists, ready to strangle an assassin for her? How she buried Mary's twins for her? Or was it the conversation in the dark, when Jane indulged her and spoke with Elizabeth Tudor's voice? But it does not matter. All that matters is that when Mary leaves this island, Jane will go with her. For a long time Jane has had the strange sensation that the moment she leaves Mary's side, she will disappear; she, Jane, will disappear, as though she were a shadow cast by the sun and living in fear of night-time. She is also certain that, in a similar way, Mary cannot exist without adoration, without obedience. If she is captured again with no one there to love her, she will be like the sirens whose songs are unheard and unheeded. For Jane, following Mary has always been a contradiction: it is as much about self-preservation as it is self-sacrifice.

There is one other reason Jane has decided to follow Mary. It is this: to stay with Mary also means staying with another person. The person who kissed Jane in the winter, bending her over a bed and crumpled silk nightgown, down, down, into the scent of Mary's skin.

Dusk. Cuckoo hurries across the courtyard, shoulders hunched, trying to ignore the men's stares and the comments made in their foreign tongue. She walks quickly, and glances up at the tower window. She can see a tall figure, veiled and dressed in red. She cannot make out much more than that. The windowpane is grubby and the figure half in shadow.

Cuckoo returns to the rooms, fresh fine linens in her hands – her excuse for leaving in the first place. 'It works fine,' she says to the three women, who turn immediately to look at her. 'I could see the red, but not your face; only a dark figure.'

'You see?' Mary says. 'I was sure it was a distinct enough red. And with the long black veil . . .'

The figure in the window was Seton. She is dressed in the same red velvet dress of Mary's that Jane wore on Twelfth Night. The hem does not trail on the floor as it did for Jane – it barely comes to Seton's ankles. Jane likes looking at the other places where the fit of the dress differs for Seton. The sleeves that seem shorter, the looser cut around the bust. The long narrow waist. Seton looks uncomfortable in the red dress, but not as much as she did in the black. When Cuckoo returned from the courtyard, Seton looked up, expectant, as though a part of her hoped the disguise would not work after all.

The mood is subdued rather than excited. They do not know how long it will be until they see each other again. Jane is remembering her fall. Or rather, she is thinking of the breathless moment before, when Seton was grasping her hand, leaning out of the tower, bearing her whole weight. Jane remembers believing she might die and meeting Seton's gaze, knowing the sight of her face might be the last thing she ever saw. She recalls the relief she felt in seeing her.

The regret.

Mary is quiet – she seems to be conserving her energy for the efforts of tomorrow. She must be at her brightest, her most charming, and then later, her most brave. She retires to her room early, and asks again to sleep unattended. Cuckoo will undress her and take the first shift at her door.

★

Alone, Seton and Jane cannot look at each other. The air seems to crackle. Years later, Seton will remember every detail of how the room looked that night. The long moving shadows cast by the firelight look like dancers. The smell of woodsmoke permeates the room, and the cushions and wooden stools used by the women during the day have been left out, grouped haphazardly, as though at any moment someone might take up their seat again. On one of the stools, Seton can see a half-finished piece of embroidery, a needle pierced through its centre.

'I'll undress you,' Jane says. Her voice is quiet. 'Turn around.'

Obedient, Seton turns on the spot. She expects Jane to undress her as she does Mary: as a chamberer, not as a lover. She waits for Jane's fingers to begin unlacing. She waits for Jane's breath on her neck, for Jane to kneel before her and begin rolling down Seton's stockings, her hands creeping up beneath the shift. Seton waits. The fire in the hearth is burning itself out. So is the stub of a nearby candle. She watches it, the single flame flickering from a stray breeze. Is it her own breath?

Finally, when Seton cannot wait any longer, she turns. She finds Jane standing behind her in her shift, her own outer clothes in a heap on the floor. Her dark hair is loose, the very ends an auburn colour. The shift is slipping off Jane's shoulders; Seton can see stray freckles. She looks at Jane, at the way the curves of her body slip in and out of the pale linen. Seton realises she is holding her breath. She remembers Jane in the bathtub all those months ago, and the way she opened her eyes and looked back at her.

Jane moves forward to touch the fabric of Seton's dress, to run her hands over the soft red velvet, stepping closer, closer. '*Mary*,' she says.

At the sound of that name – her own name, her shared name – Seton trembles. Jane presses her body against her, and when Seton moans, Jane claps a hand to her mouth. She pushes Seton onto the pallet bed behind them and lies down next to her. For a moment, neither is sure what they should do. They lie facing each other in that first arrangement of limbs, legs tangled, calves and ankles criss-crossed, and neither can breathe, neither can move. Slowly, Jane rolls up the hem of the dress Seton wears until it is scrunched at her belly. They are tentative, cautious, touching each other's bodies with soft, shy caresses. Jane slips a hand between Seton's legs, to where Jane herself likes to be touched when she is alone. She works her fingers over that part, watches Seton's face and neck flushing, her eyes screwed shut, her ragged breaths, sees her throw an arm over her face and bite at the sleeve of the red dress. Jane feels Seton's body begin to shudder beneath her hands and Jane turns her head and looks down the bed at their entwined bodies, at the dress she herself has worn.

*Mary's dress.*

Seton opens her eyes and realises she is crying. She feels full, almost bruised where Jane has touched her. 'I'm sorry,' she whispers, reaching to wipe the tears away with the cuff of her dress.

Jane shakes her head. She holds Seton's face between her hands, kissing the tears and tasting their salt.

Later –

'You must promise me something,' Seton whispers. 'You must promise me – if Mary . . . If you ever find yourself alone, without me, and without Mary, you will marry him. Marry Andrew Melville. Or someone like him.'

'Why would you leave me?' Jane says, and at the catch in her voice Seton pulls her into her arms.

★

Later still –

Separate beds, waiting for Cuckoo to return from her post by Mary's door. The fire has burned down to embers.

'Will you recite another poem for me?' Jane asks. 'By that poet. The ropemaker's daughter.'

Seton recites the sonnet in the original French, and Jane allows the words to wash over her. *Baise m'encor, rebaise-moi et baise.* Kiss me. Kiss me again.

Towards the end of the poem:

> *Then a double life to each shall ensure.*
> *Each shall live: you in me, and me in you.*

At these words, Jane wonders if Seton – biting down on the red velvet of her sleeve –remembered Twelfth Night, when Jane wore this dress, too. You in me, and me in you. *Chacun en soy et son ami vivra.* Each in themselves and their lover will live. *Because isn't that the highest form of love?* Jane thinks. *To become your beloved?*

In her own bed, the sound of Cuckoo's snores outside her door, Mary lies awake, staring up at the bed canopy, and opens her mind to Elizabeth Tudor. Ever since Twelfth Night, when Jane spoke to her in the English queen's voice, Mary has conversed with her cousin at night. She kneels to say her prayers to God before climbing into bed and speaking to another figure who is just as invisible and mysterious and just as omnipresent in Mary's life. At night, her familiar prison seems foreign, the empty space expanding and moving around her, the darkness looming, as though Elizabeth herself might at any moment step out from between the shadows.

Earlier today, Mary wrote again to the real Elizabeth, reminding her of a long-ago promise of assistance. *The head should not be subject to the foot.* They are fellow princes.

*Have pity on your good sister and cousin*, Mary wrote. *Be assured that you will never have a more near and loving kinswoman in this world*. It does not matter that they differ in attitudes to faith and marriage. Mary has always wanted that 'fortification' of a man by her side; not because she truly needed her husbands, but because she believed she did. Elizabeth never has such fears. Elizabeth does not bend to the will of men. She waits, and she watches, and she keeps her courtiers and advisors and foreign princes all dangling on strings. Her closest friends cannot predict her moods, cannot see into her mind. It is like staring down into a well. Even the clever Catherine de' Medici cannot play against her; no matter how Catherine coaxes, no matter how sharply she prods and pokes, she will never winkle out of Elizabeth what she desires: her promise to wed one of Catherine's (many) sons. Likewise, Mary could never convince Elizabeth to name her England's heir. This angered Mary, all those months ago, but now she sees it was only Elizabeth's fear of death that stayed her hand. *How can I love my own winding sheet?*

*If we could only meet face-to-face*, Mary thinks, *I might win her to my side*.

Mary does not know that even as Elizabeth promised vengeance on the Scottish lords, she was bidding on her cousin's famous string of black pearls. Mary does not realise that Elizabeth is far too shrewd to ever meet and stand beside a younger, taller, prettier queen, and invite public comparison.

Mary thinks of the letters she once exchanged with Elizabeth, when they joked how much easier it would be if they themselves could marry and unite their two kingdoms. To be loved is to be known, and who could ever truly know Mary except another female prince?

'If all fails . . . If I lose again . . . Would you welcome me?' she asks the empty gloom. 'Would you help me raise an army?'

In Mary's head, the red-headed Elizabeth Tudor smiles her answer.

The Feast of Unreason. First thing in the morning, Mary is dressed in the red velvet. Her women move about her as though in a trance, their fingers awkward and stiff, dropping things, at first guiding her arm through the wrong sleeve. In their clumsiness, the women betray the unspoken sense of unease in the room. Of dread. When Mary is finally laced into the red dress, she realises the fabric is curiously warm. She does not remark on this to the others; she thinks it is some kind of divine signal, sent from God to his anointed queen. Mary remembers too late that red is traditionally the colour of the Catholic martyr. A wet hand seems to grasp at her insides and twist, but a moment later she has reconciled this realisation: God means for her to take courage from those who risked all. Mary does not know that the dress is still warm from Seton's skin; that Seton wore the dress late into the night. The plan is to exchange clothes with Seton later in the day. Seton will dress in the red velvet and stand in the window, as she did yesterday, while Mary escapes wearing Seton's plainer dress.

'Seton, your hand is trembling.' Mary catches her friend's wrist. She looks around, motioning for the other two women to hold out their hands for her to see. 'Yours too, Cuckoo. Only Jane has steady hands.' She touches their hands, one by one: Seton, then Cuckoo, and then Jane. They will each later remember this touch, a brief brush of her fingers over their own, as though she were offering a blessing.

Mary is right that red is the colour of the Catholic martyr. On the day she is executed, she will wear a crimson petticoat and sleeves hidden under her outer garments. When Mary is on the scaffold, it will be Jane who deftly removes her outer clothes, revealing to the watching crowd the queen's dark red interior. It is Jane, chosen for her steady hands, who will tie the blindfold over Mary's eyes. Mary's last utterance will be in Latin. *In manus tuas, Domine, commendo spiritum meum.* Jane will not know what she has said.

There is one last, crucial aspect to the plan. Mary and Jane must leave before sunset. This way they will have just enough visibility in the twilight to get away, to get a head start before nightfall. If all goes well, by the time Mary's captors realise she's missing it will already be too dark for them to give chase. But if Mary crosses the loch too late in the day, then riding will be slow, and their pursuers may catch them. If her absence is betrayed too early, then the Laird of Lochleven may capture her before she has even reached the shore. He might decide to fire cannons across the water. Better a drowned queen than one restored to power.

The boy Will rises early. He wears bright colours: a scarlet-coloured jerkin and bells tied to his wrists and ankles. He jumps and sings and shouts out, loud enough for the whole island to hear, tossing his handkerchief in the air. The day is clear and sunny – sunny for Scotland – and food is brought outside on long tables, meat and bread and cheese and drink, great barrels of wine. Flowers are arranged between the great platters, and some of the young unmarried women have wildflowers threaded in their hair. Musicians strike up a tune; fiddlers and bagpipes. Will shouts his orders, disrupting every man and woman's routine, and beside him at all times, laughing and smiling at his antics, is Mary. He insists she accompany him wherever he goes. 'She will be my own queen for the day,' he shouts, and his orders are followed because this is his day to command, a day of misrule, a day of chaos and the social order upended. All the while Mary's eyes flick continually up towards the sky, tracking the movement of the sun. Today feels like their best chance at an escape; Mary does not think such an opportunity will come again. But if they are caught in the attempt, Mary will never leave this place. Margaret Erskine will never let her out of her sight.

The courtyard is bustling. All the servants and members of the household drink and eat and dance, and Agnes is shocked at how attentive Mary is to her, filling her cup as though she, Mary, were a serving girl. Agnes does not know that even now, across the loch, there are soldiers and horses moving among the trees, close to the water's edge. They are preparing for when Mary joins them, ready to whisk her away before the cannons begin to fire. Mary's plan is a simple one: ensure that everyone is too drunk to notice the soldiers on the opposite shore, too drunk to notice later when Will carefully pegs chains to all the island boats bar one. It is Jane, following Mary about the island like a shadow, who notices the hunched William Douglas peering towards the loch, briefly diverted by the sight of his bastard son kneeling beside one of the boats. And it is Jane who rushes to his side, who fills his cup and pretends to drop the cloth she carries for men to wipe their hands on; she bends down, feeling his eyes on her cleavage, and then later brings Mary to his side, so that she can distract him with conversation.

'Are you one of the queen's women?' a voice says, and Jane, standing apart, turns to see the boatman who first rowed herself and Mary and Cuckoo across the loch, his frame so tall and

haggard and gaunt he reminded her of Charon, the skeletal boatman who ferries souls to the underworld. She nods to him. Keeps
her face smooth, with no trace of her anxieties.

'Here,' he says, slipping something small and round and cool
into her palm. 'A gift from our friend, to give to the lady.'

The boatman strides away. Does Jane hear the clink of coins as
he walks? She is alone. Cupping her hands together, she glances
down to the dark hollow between her thumbs. There, she sees the
whiteness of a single loose pearl. It is the signal from George
Douglas. All is ready.

Jane's mouth is very dry. She staggers to the nearest wall and
heaves, vomit splattering onto the dust below.


Supper. It is around six in the evening, and the sky is already
darker, the landscape outside tinged blue. The sun will set fully in
perhaps an hour's time. Mary, her women, and Agnes are gathered
in the tower rooms. William Douglas himself serves his wife and
the queen-that-was their evening meal. Outside, the dancing and
drinking continue. Some of the young men have proposed a game
of handball.

'Drysdale will stay here and keep watch,' William Douglas says
to Mary, moving to leave, and Jane is not sure if he means to
threaten or to reassure. He points to the open doorway, and the
women turn to see the guard who served up the jug of piss, all
those months ago. *Drysdale.* Jane did not know his name until now.
She can still taste vomit; it burns at the back of her throat. Under
the table, Cuckoo's leg is shaking, her foot tapping the air until
Jane reaches out and puts her hand on her knee. If she could, Jane
would absorb Cuckoo's nerves and bear them for her, but she is
already brimming over with her own fears. It would take just one

person – a guard, a servant, Agnes – to notice something out of the ordinary, to raise the alarm.

Cuckoo wants the plan to succeed. She wants Mary to reclaim her crown. But there is a part of Cuckoo – a sharp, greedy little voice deep inside her – that is almost daring herself to slip up, to say something that will spoil everything and get them caught, because perhaps then the French will finally come to rescue their dowager queen; they will bring her and her women to France and Cuckoo can find her own way back to her brother. There is little evidence for this argument, but love does not bend to reason. The voice prods and claws at her, trying to clamber up into her mouth, and she is panicking, begging it to quiet, to leave her alone. *Shut up*, she thinks, *shut up shut up shut up*. She concentrates instead on the warmth of Jane's hand on her knee, anchoring her to her seat, and she realises how she will miss her. How much she would like to see her again, if only for the pleasure of their bickering. If the plan succeeds, Mary will send for Seton and also for her, Cuckoo. The four women will reunite.

*Say something*, crows the voice inside her, *or you will never see Toussaint again*.

Mary keeps the conversations as dull as possible; nothing for the guard to find interest in. She and her women feign fatigue. They are as quiet as possible without raising Agnes's suspicions, allowing the sounds of revelry outside the walls to fill the room instead.

Jane watches Drysdale shift from foot to foot like a fisherman watches the slow approach of a trout to his bait. She nudges Seton, who turns to Drysdale and says, 'You are very good, to keep watch over us women during such celebrations.'

Drysdale grunts.

'A man such as yourself,' Mary says, taking up the tune, 'would surely be missed during the games they're playing outside.' The guard looks up at this, his eyes darting towards Agnes. Mary continues, 'Perhaps just a game of handball? Surely we cannot deprive him of that, my dear Agnes?'

And Agnes, who is dear to no one, who is still thinking of Mary pouring wine for her, does not realise she is being played. She says, slurring her words, 'Of course, of course, Drysdale.'

When Drysdale has left, the women turn their attention to Agnes. They yawn and stretch, and Cuckoo pretends to doze off, her elbow slipping off the table edge. They complain of the heat and the effects of the wine. They complain that their feet are sore. Finally, Mary begins to express a desire to pray in her oratory, and Agnes – who finds herself feeling tired in truth now, and who does not want to watch a Catholic pray at an altar – leaves, too.

The moment she is gone, the women begin to undress Mary, converging around her, knocking each other's hands in their haste. They remove the red velvet and dress her instead in Seton's darker clothes and borrowed breeches beneath her skirts, ready for the escape on horseback. Her women add a hood to hide her face. Jane is also given a hood. It is Seton who pins it to her hair, looking down into her dark selkie eyes that taste, to Seton, of honey wine. Jane tries to memorise the feel of Seton's fingers in her hair, the simple childish pleasure of it mingled with her desire. Mary stares out of the window at the sun and tells her women to hurry, *hurry*. Her thoughts are not on the two women she is about to leave behind; instead, she is already picturing the shore on the other side of the loch, imagining the supporters gathered there with their horses, all waiting for her.

Outside, the Abbot of Misrule pours a drink for his father, the hunched William Douglas, and as he does so he tosses a napkin onto the table, over a large brass key. The key to the courtyard gate. When Will straightens up and moves away from the table, the key is gone.

The sun is beginning its descent towards the earth, the orange sky blazing an angry warning. There is barely time to exchange goodbyes. Mary is kneeling to pray, her eyes shut, her lips mouthing Latin words, when the boy Will arrives at the rooms, the key in his pocket. Cuckoo helps him untie the bells at his ankles and wrists, and Jane tosses him a cloak to throw over his scarlet jerkin. The women embrace and kiss each other's faces, clumsy, as Will looks on at them with childlike impatience, whispering for Mary to make haste, *the time is now, hurry.*

And they are gone. Jane and Mary are gone.

Seton does not hold the same fears she did when she first put on Mary's clothes and found she could not breathe, the day Jane put her hand to her chest. Now, laced into the red dress, Seton is still anxious, still feels as she does when a spider scuttles across the ground, but it is easier to bear in the same dress Jane once wore; the same dress she herself was wearing as Jane touched her last night.

Cuckoo kneels at Seton's feet, fiddling with the hem of the dress. 'When you and Jane spoke of France – of your returning to France,' Cuckoo says, her eyes on the floor. 'It is my own wish to return one day, too. I would like to die in my own country.'

Seton smiles down at her. 'As would I,' she says. She does not know – neither of the women can know – that they will eventually get their wish.


Agnes and Margaret Erskine are the first to realise Mary is missing. Agnes returns to the tower rooms; during the party, she misplaced some favourite item, and she believes she may have left it in Mary's care. She is already feeling the after-effects of the alcohol, her head pounding. She finds the door unlocked, and within the room she sees Seton in Mary's dress.

'Where is she?' she says, breathless, and Cuckoo smiles at her, showing teeth, before pointing out of the window at the horizon.

'*Elle est partie*,' she replies, and it takes Agnes a moment to translate, to understand her. *She has gone.*

Agnes runs straight to Margaret Erskine, who hears the news and begins to shriek, imagining what Mary and her men will do to Margaret's family, to her son Moray. What vengeance she will take. Mary may banish him. She may execute him. Or perhaps he will die in battle, as Margaret's husband did. When finally she quietens, she straightens up and slaps Agnes – her pregnant daughter-in-law – across the mouth. Agnes sways, her eyes unfocused, the flushed imprints of fingers splayed across her cheek.

'You idiot,' Margaret says. 'You stupid, stupid girl. How could you leave her room unlocked? How could you let them out of your sight? Have you sent men after them? No?' *Crack.* Margaret twists her neck in agitation and feels the bones judder into place beneath her skull.

'So be it. I will send them myself.'

A few drunk servants spot the boy Will hurrying through the courtyard, accompanied by two hooded women – one short, one tall – and wonder if they are serving girls, or whores hired by the boy's father. They turn away, back to their games and their loud music, and do not notice the boy locking the courtyard gate behind him and breaking into a run.

The water's edge. The setting sun is reflected in the surface of the loch, washing it the colour red of martyrdom. The horizon is a flaming orange but above it the sky is already darkening. The women can see the tall figure of the boatman, standing next to the one vessel Will has left unchained. Both the old man and the boy will row, ensuring that by the time Mary's absence is noted, she will already be on the opposite shore. If all goes well, they will reach the other side before the sun fully sets. Mary stares at the boatman, remembering his coarse insults, his first refusal to ferry her to Kinross. George must have paid him a great deal of money, she thinks. Even now, she is half-afraid the boatman will betray them all. But it is too late to change their plans. Far too late. She will put up with the boatman if it ensures her own escape. She thinks again of the men waiting for her on the opposite shore. If her captors are quick to realise she is missing — if they give chase — then her men will need to fight. Some may be killed while defending their queen-that-was. *So be it*, she thinks.

Jane steps into a boat for the first time in eleven months; there is no time for her to enjoy the sensation. She turns and holds out her hands for Mary to hold on to as she climbs in beside her. There is no need for Mary to hide her white hands now. The boy Will no longer has the gate key; in years to come, there will be uncertainty over its location. Did Will toss it in the mouth of a cannon? Or did Mary herself drop it in the loch?

'There may be some gunfire,' the boatman tells the two women, adjusting himself at the boat's prow. 'You'd best lie down on the boards in case.'

Mary almost whimpers at this, but she bites the noise down. She takes one last look at Lochleven, at her prison, at the island where, somewhere, her babies are buried.

The women lie down in the hull of the boat, their heads close to the boatman's feet. Jane lies on her back, her legs bent awkwardly, but Mary curls up on her side, her face on Jane's shoulder. There is the click of the rosary beads at Mary's hips as she adjusts her body. They breathe in the smell of damp, of the wooden boards. The tang of the boatman's leather boots, and the floral fragrance of Mary's skin and hair. Above all, the smell of the loch itself, of the water, at once clean and filthy, smelling of both life and decay. Jane shivers as though someone has stepped over her grave. She listens to the whisper, the words just out of hearing. The voice in the maw of the loch. Hidden in Jane's pocket are dried flowers: the daisies woven by Mary and arranged in the shapes of walls and towers.

The boat lurches as Will pushes it out further into the water. He climbs in, clambering over the women's skirts. He and the boatman pick up their oars and begin to row. Still lying on her back, Jane looks straight up. All she can see is the sky. The sun is beyond her view. Instead, there is only the lilac-blue of early evening. Already the moon is out before the sun has fully set, taunting Mary, a thin gleaming sliver of a waning crescent. Soon there will be a new, full moon, and the cycle will begin again. Have the men onshore decided the hour is too late? Will the boat be turned away? Suddenly, a bird flies across Jane's field of vision, across the expanse of lilac sky – then another bird, and then another. It is a murmuration of starlings; together, they move in the distance like a single piece of cloth billowing out over the sky, and Jane is reminded of that early morning when she found Mary by the window, and she, Jane, rubbed her fingers together by Mary's ear, imitating the sound of wingbeats. Mary had said the starlings were dancing on the Devil's back. Jane wants to say to her, *Look up. Do you see them? Do you remember as I do?* But she doesn't dare speak, and the murmuration sweeps out of sight and is gone.

The two women listen to the splash of the oars, to the water moving just beneath their bodies. They clasp each other's hot hands and listen to the receding sounds of music, stray notes drifting over the loch. Then, Jane hears a disembodied shout. The music has stopped, she is sure of it. In the sudden absence of song, the women wait for the sounds of cannon and gunshots. No one in the boat speaks, not even to pray. There are only the grunts of Will and the boatman, their muscles straining, the old man and the boy keeping pace. Four hearts thumping.

*Bang.*

The burst of sound rumbles across the valley. Jane's heart stops. The noise repeats, again and again and again.

'Fuck.' Will is sweating. But a moment later he exhales, breath whistling through his teeth. He whispers to the women, 'It's not cannons. It's drums. Drumbeats. I think it's for the dancing.' He sounds uncertain.

The drumbeats continue, but neither Mary nor Jane hears the music in them. Only the pulse of battle. Jane times the irregular sputter of her heart to the steady deep booms. All at once, the drumming stops, and somehow this is worse, not knowing why it has ended so abruptly.

They begin to hear a chorus of whispers from the other side of the loch. Men's voices lapping over each other's words like waves. *Look, look. There it is. Where is she?* The hushed whinnies and snorts of horses. At the sound of the men, Mary cannot help it – she sits up, she calls out to them, *I'm here I'm here*, she is all excitement now, her fear gone, and Jane, lying in the hull of the boat, does not need to look up to see what the men onshore see: the torso of a beautiful woman floating towards them, her feathered wings folded just behind her. George Douglas will be there, his eyes feasting on her, his queen. Her voice is the only one that matters.

There is a thud. The boat judders as the prow meets land beneath it. They have reached the other side of the loch. At once, bearded faces converge, filling Jane's vision, blocking out the sky as they reach down to take her hands, to help her out of the boat – no, not her. Mary. Mary goes first; of course she does. Jane watches as Mary is lifted up, as she kneels to kiss the ground, and Jane, behind her and unassisted, braces herself.

She steps out of the boat.

'You are here – only just, your grace,' Lord Seton says to Mary, bowing his head, but she is not looking at him, she is looking at George Douglas – George, who did not fail her, who has kept his promise to help her all this while. Above them, a twilight sky. Mary breathes in the cool night air – the sharp scents of mould and stagnant water, of the long grass and the horsehair – and she cannot remember when she last stood outside after dark. She has been locked in every night for the past eleven months. From the other side of the loch they can still hear the stray sounds of laughter and music on the tiny island. The castle appears so small now from a distance, dwarfed by the looming hills that surround the loch, casting it in shadow. In the gathering darkness the party can see the faint light of Mary's old rooms, where Seton and Cuckoo must be standing even now. The light shines as a beacon to Jane but she turns away from it, towards the men and the horses and Mary standing among them, impatient, ready to be gone. Mary, the axis around which they all turn. Everything begins and ends with her.

'We must hurry,' Mary says. She strides over to one of the riderless horses; the stolen animal belongs to her former captors, to the residents of Lochleven Castle, who all stable their horses on the mainland. She reaches up to grasp the saddle and does not even bother to look down before she steps into the waiting hands of one of the men, crouched down to lift her up onto the mare's back. They are George's hands. On her right side, Mary sees Jane standing below, turning this way and that, looking about for the mount appointed for her, but none is led forward, and Mary sees two of the men whispering, their eyes wide: they have forgotten Jane. In their anticipation for her, Mary, they have forgotten to prepare for her companion; Jane's face, comprehending, as she continues to revolve slowly on the spot, still favouring her injured ankle.

'Jane,' Mary says, and she holds out a hand. Jane looks up at her, confused for just a moment, before relief breaks like a wave across her face and she holds Mary's gaze, in a way that any onlookers might think insolent. But all Mary sees is her tenderness. There is no time for words. She motions to George, who lifts Jane into the saddle behind her. Mary looks down at Jane's hands clasped around her waist, her tanned fingers interlaced. She can feel Jane's quickened breath on the back of her neck, feel her heart thudding as she presses her body close, her cheek against Mary's shoulder. The scent of the polished leather, the heat rising off the animal's back. The last time Mary sat on a horse, it was on the ride here to Lochleven. She was pregnant then, and despairing. No longer. She wheels the horse about, turning its head away from the loch, towards the lights of Kinross and the purple hills and fields, beyond which somewhere, just out of sight, her son and her crown wait for her, ready to be reclaimed. She is running towards them. She is flying.

# Epilogue

All night, Seton stands by the window in Mary's red dress. She does not move, despite the chaos behind her: shouts, screams, Agnes and Cuckoo arguing, and Margaret, who comes to see for herself the rooms, now empty of the Lochleven prisoner. The hunched William Douglas arrives and calls loudly for a knife, swearing he would rather die than betray the rebel lords. It's an empty threat and everyone knows it. The room fills with people and empties again, like a sea tide dragging back and then surging forward once more, over and over, and among it all Seton stands still, an immovable rock among the crash of waves. She watches the sky darken and the bright orange of the horizon as the sun sets, and in that colour she can taste the young white wine she and Jane drank in this very room, moments before their first kiss. Seton refuses to move from the window, even when the night sky becomes so dark she can no longer see anything but her own reflection in the glass. She stares at herself, at the red dress, and remembers when Jane wore it for Twelfth Night. She thinks, too, of Mary; if she squints, Seton can see her childhood friend standing before her. It is only when dawn begins to break that Seton, shivering with cold and fatigue, registers the gentle touch of Cuckoo's hand on her own.

'Come away, Lady Seton,' she says, and Seton allows herself to be led to bed, to the wooden pallet where she and Jane made love.

Both Seton and Cuckoo will reunite with Mary, but it will not be in Edinburgh, at the head of some triumphant return to the city. It will not be in Scotland. Mary will flee to England, and her women will follow. Mary will hope that her cousin and fellow prince, Elizabeth Tudor, will help her reclaim the Scottish throne. Instead she will be kept a prisoner for decades.

She will not see James or Scotland again.

After seventeen years of damp English castles at Mary's side, Seton's health will fail. She will be forced to return to the warmer climes of France, and Cuckoo will accompany her, returning home at last. Jane will not go with them. She will instead stay behind to care for Mary.

Seton will retire to a convent where Mary herself once visited, mourning the deaths of her first husband and her mother, Marie de Guise, who is buried in the church. Two years after Seton sets sail, Mary will be executed and Jane is the one to tie the white blindfold over her eyes. After Mary is buried, Jane will marry Andrew Melville. Later still, Seton will learn that Andrew has remarried; as a mark of respect he will name his first child Janet, after his first, late wife, who drowned in the River Forth.

Seton will never marry. She will survive into the next century and live her final days in poverty, silvery ghosts swimming above her bed. There will be no colours for her to taste. An appeal will be written on Seton's behalf to King James, to the son of the woman she served for so many years. The woman whose red dress Seton wore, standing before the tower window at Lochleven Castle.

James will never respond to the letter.